TOLAGON

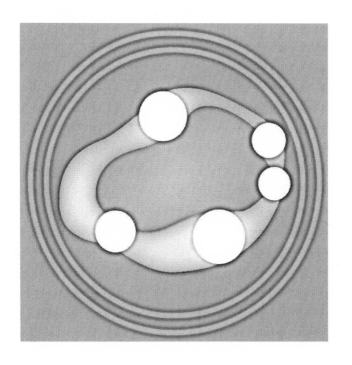

TOLAGON

Gregory Benson

Published by Blue Giant Publishing, LLC

First edition.

Print ISBN: 978-1-7340196-0-5

eBook ISBN: 978-1-7340196-1-2

gregorybensonbooks.com

tolagon.com

To my beautiful wife Dawn. Without her patience and support, this would have never been possible.

For we wrestle not against flesh and blood, but against principalities, against powers, against the rulers of the darkness of this world, against spiritual wickedness in high places.

– Ephesians 6:12

PROLOGUE
THRAXON WAR

As a Tolagon and bearer of the blue orb, Commander Corin Emberook drew a heaping breath and clenched his fist; he brought forth a blue aura around his body with a fluxing hum. Sweeping his gaze behind him, he observed the steadfast stare of his most trusted commandant, Creedith. The tall, long-maned, and muscular Andor stood closely behind Emberook with one leg propped up on a large stone. As an Andor, short, smooth fur covered his body, and his face was long and chiseled with pronounced cheekbones and large, flaring nostrils.

"It appears that Tolagon Tenier and the Solarans must have failed to take control of the outer gammac corridor, and thus allowed an auxiliary Thraxon force into the system," Creedith proclaimed in his thick, Andorian accent. The corridors used for travel between systems had proven to be a blessing and a curse for Nathasia.

Plasmatic fumes swelled over Corin with every rising gust of Nathasia's thin air.

"We'll stick with the attack plan," he said, keeping a focused stare upon his forthcoming adversaries. The tall leader's short, white hair matched the white stubble on his face. "Are Krath's troops in place?" he asked, referring to the secretly positioned Hybor shock force. The muscular, thick-hided warriors of Thale were the perfect heavy ground forces as long as their temperaments held steady.

"They are ready on your signal," answered Creedith.

As the Thraxon warships entered the planet's atmosphere, a heavy rumble filled the air and became a deafening thunder as they neared.

"Engage your battle armor and be ready!" Emberook announced through his comm unit. "Remember, as far as they are concerned, this is the whole of our force." A thousand multi-world soldiers stood directly behind him, slammed down their helmet visors, and mounted an assortment of embattled XA-type attack vehicles. The XAs were slender, wedged-shaped, single-unit attack vehicles that legions used for low-altitude strafing attacks.

A deep reverberation came from the Thraxon cruisers as they hovered about two kilometers from the planet's surface. In the distance, a luminescent red glow that emitted from their forward observation portals delivered the eerie sensation of eyes staring. The cruisers covered the ground beneath them with a crimson hue quickly engulfed by an enormous, living shadow and a spine-shivering screech.

This massive, black shadow swirled toward them like an ocean wave during a raging storm.

"Brace yourselves!" Emberook called to his soldiers as he pushed out a wall of blue energy from his power orb, covering his troops in a protective shield. The black wave engulfed them. His stomach tightened as his feet dug into the rocky surface. With a clenched jaw, he strained to keep the menacing force at bay. His blue shield receded and exposed his forward troops. The exposed troops frantically commenced firing into the darkness with their plasma rifles. Several near the edge of the barrier screamed in blistering agony as they fell, overtaken by the swarm.

These overwhelming, shadow-like assailants consisted of billions of nearly microscopic organisms known as entrocrows. This biological weapon recently adopted by the Thraxon forces became their first line of attack. The early encounters with these nasty organisms were disastrous as they burrowed through armor and devoured the host in seconds.

This time, Emberook's forces were ready for them. "Release the thermal grid now!" ordered Emberook. Timing his commands to allow the majority of the entrocrows to enter the battlefield, he initialized the counter-drone attack. A thunderous boom throbbed out as a half dozen forward-swept-winged TR300 class attack fighters roared down and dropped a rainstorm of drones. These drones hovered together and formed a cube-like grid directly around the entrocrow wave. Then, instantaneously, they stitched a bright-red beam between each drone and created the grid. This powerful new weapon generated a blinding light and an immense surge of heat, which pounded down upon everything and produced a shimmering appearance over the landscape.

The enormous shadow gave out a hawking shrill as it retracted, leaving behind billions of tiny black flakes that fell to the ground. The hundreds of drones, now depleted, dropped like rocks. Cheers from Emberook's Vico Legionnaires rang out over the briefly silenced attack. They did not let these small victories slide past uncelebrated for they understood, by this cunning feat of technology, their losses were greatly reduced.

"Commander Emberook," the eager communications officer had run forward and yelled, "Federation Command just informed us that the new Marck relief force is approaching with an ETA of sixty minutes. Our orders are to hold off the Thraxon attack force until they arrive, and then stand down our defensive position."

Emberook's brows wrinkled with rebuke. "These politicians have some audacity," he growled, angry over the new mechanized force, the Marcks, stealing away the glory of accomplishment from his legion at the last minute; they had lost so many to get here. "They obviously have no understanding of how to fight battles and certainly discern nothing of honor and sacrifice. Lieutenant, you tell them we will do as ordered, but not at the expense of my soldiers and the honor they leave on this—" Before he could finish, a large rock about twenty meters to his left struck the ground, ruptured. The explosions continued as the Thraxon cruisers opened fire on them with their pulsar cannons.

"Spector Five . . . Spector Five . . . Do you copy?" Emberook called to his orbital command ship.

"We copy you, Commander," a hurried voice answered.

"We require immediate suppressive bombardment on the Thraxon cruisers!"

"Copy that, Commander; hang on tight to whatever you can down there," the command ship replied.

TOLAGON

The sky blazed a deep green as a barrage of energy beams rained down upon the Thraxon cruisers, jolting them in a bouncing motion as their shields attempted to absorb the impact. At that same moment, an intense hiss emitted from the battlecruisers as Thraxon warriors swarmed out, gliding on their winged attack apparatuses from various access ports.

"Their ground forces are descending," a Federation soldier yelled over the comm. Thraxon heavy ground troops also poured down from the cruisers; their light propulsion packs slowed their descent.

Commander Corin Emberook stood with his hands cupped in the air and sent a vivid blue beam of pure light from the orb into the sky to signal his science officer Plexo, the Luminar. Plexo stood ready, well away from the field of battle.

As the inky-skinned Thraxons descended and took their place on the battlefield, iridescent waves of energy from Plexo's transporter filled the rock-strewn valley. The energy subsided and revealed Hybor shock troops that had weaved in and behind the unsuspecting Thraxons. The freshly transported infantry fired their rifles upon their foes, dropping them by the hundreds. The Hybor troops from the water-covered moon of Thale looked wild; their large eyes, thick necks, and immense, muscular forms were truly a fighting force to behold. The remaining ally forces, led by Creedith, engaged from the air in their XAs, taking down the flying Thraxon warriors, each with the grace of a dancer.

Commander Corin took flight, propelled by the orb's power, and started to grab and fling the Thraxons into the rocks below. Just as the Thraxon cruisers' energy shields began failing, the orbital barrage from the command ship inexplicably dissipated.

"Spector Five, why have you halted your attack!" Corin demanded an explanation.

A distorted and broken response came back. "Be advised— we are unable to—Thraxon hive ship—ent—" A flash of light pulsed in the sky. Moments later, flaming debris had begun to shower down from high above.

"Creedith! We just lost our command ship, and we now have a Thraxon hive ship to deal with," Corin yelled as he looked upward in horror at the emerging black silhouette of the hive ship high above them. "Have your XAs focus on the Thraxon cruisers' propulsion stabilizers and take them down while their shields are still weak."

Creedith was a bold and cunning pilot. He bore down on the nearest enemy cruiser from his XA assault fighter and called out, "On my mark, target the propulsion systems with your barbed atomics." He fired a single, spiked projectile that stuck into the skin of the cruiser near its stabilizer. The other XA pilots followed suit, and then as they pulled away, plumes of fire blasted from the aft section of the doomed Thraxon cruiser. Like a beast trying to throw its mount, the burning ship had begun to spin violently out of control. Its hull crashed into the front of the other Thraxon cruiser, and their fiery masses both plummeted toward the crowded battlefield below.

"Plexo!" Corin called.

"Parallaxing our ground forces now, Commander," a firm, whispering voice replied.

The strategically placed parallax projectors positioned around the valley glowed bright, and the Hybor forces phased out, leaving only the Thraxon's forces below to face devastation from their impacting cruisers.

A black object that had the appearance of a large umbrella shadowed the sky above. Its eerie manifestation made even the most hardened soldiers' hearts sink into their stomachs. The side profile of the umbrella slowly turned inward toward the planet as it, the hive ship, prepared to launch its attack force. Thin red beams showered down from the massive ship, each leaving a six-legged attack vehicle on the surface. Within just a few minutes, these scurrying, mechanical attackers littered the landscape.

Creedith swooped down on his XA and delivered precision blasts from his plasma cannons, bringing down two of the enemies' units immediately. Just as he was about to soar back up and assume another attack position, one of the Thraxon vehicles leaped up and latched on to the bottom of his XA. All six legs pierced into the armor and pulled the ship back down to the surface. As it was about to spew its amber substance—called "thax"—that dissolved metals on contact, Corin surprisingly dropped down on top of it and ripped open the canopy; he flung the Thraxon pilot out into a nearby rock. The damaged attack vehicle went limp and crumpled to the ground.

"What would you do if I wasn't around to save your hide, old friend?" Corin smirked.

"Behind you, Commander!" Creedith shouted as he jumped from his now-disabled XA that ruptured into fiery bits. Plasma blasts struck all around them, and they observed the sky above filled with an unending mass of Thraxon fighters; they were like incoming plumes of gigantic gnats.

The battle turned into a vicious struggle to survive. The UMO Federation desperately fought the onslaught to hold the valley. The Hybor ground troops once again returned to the battle from their hidden location, but this time, on foot. They charged onto the field ferociously with their shoulder-mounted plasma cannons and magnetic charges to repress the relentless spitors that the Thraxons had unleashed. The spitors scurried around and spewed their acidic dissolvent on wounded UMO troops to ensure their demise on the battlefield. The Hybors were motivated to destroy them all.

As death amassed on both sides, Corin observed a new wave of Thraxons that descended from the hive ship orbiting above. There appeared to be no end to the attack forces that the Thraxon hive ship could unleash.

Finally, seeing his forces depleted, Corin made the difficult call. "Plexo! Do you copy?"

"Yes, Commander, awaiting your order."

"I need you to parallax us out and scorch the valley."

"Commander, I feel it is my duty to remind you that obliterating the valley by use of sionic detonators will fail our mission." His Eesolan inflection sounded distant, as if from a dream.

"Plexo, just do it! It's my call, and I will take full ownership of it." The ground forces of the UMO Federation shimmered and faded out from the battlefield. Corin shot down like a missile and snatched up Creedith from the top of a Thraxon spitor. Before his saving lift upward, the dedicated Andor drove his tectonic blade into the fuselage, killing the six-armed pilot inside.

"XAs, pull back to the rear command!" Creedith called out to his units. His eyes sternly focused on the battlefield below. As they exited, a dozen shiny spheres sparkled into the valley, hovering about fifty meters from ground level.

"Engage blast visors!" Corin shouted. The valley behind them flashed an eye-blistering white. The ensuing shock jarred every bone in their bodies and launched debris past them at lethal speeds. The sheer blast of air escaping the valley slammed everyone not far enough from the epicenter to the ground with bone-crushing wrath. After a few minutes of sustained chaos, the land settled to a gentle vibration and, finally, stillness.

Grounded from the blast and covered in soot, Corin slowly pulled himself up and opened his visor. The protective blue energy field from the orb slowly dimmed away from around his body. The air swirled thick with dust, and their lungs burned with every new breath. A few minutes went by before Corin gave the order.

He rasped, "Sound off!"

"Forward ground force meridian online," the Hybor Krath answered.

"This is Battalion Master Fotan. XA Air Intercept Forces stand ready, but Captain Creedith is currently unaccounted for," another voice replied.

"No worries, I've got him right here with me." Corin pulled his Andor friend into an upright, seated position and unsnapped his helmet. Creedith's eyes drew upward and gave him a brotherly smile. Corin slapped him on the back with a friendly pat, happy to see that his friend was still in the living world.

Plexo followed up, "Science and Engineering standing by, sir."

"Plexo, give me a status of the valley and the Thraxon force," commanded Corin.

Linking up to the orbital observation platform, Plexo was able to use its advanced filters to get a clearer view of the valley.

"I'm just now getting a visual of what used to be the Meutor Valley. Visual coming in now . . . Yes, yes, as I anticipated, the valley has been flattened, as are all the deployed Thraxon forces."

The remaining units of the Vico Legion were scarcely combat effective. They amassed around the ruins of a large, stone-built home located on the outskirts of the Meutor Valley. The valley, in its zenith, was once a beautiful haven of wildlife, turquoise rivers, and emerald trees surrounded by rolling hills that were flamed with dark-orange flowers—before the war laid siege to it.

The wounded lay scattered. An Andor medical officer hurried about, attempting to stabilize the wounded. Corin sized up the remains of his force. He struggled to fight off thoughts of dismay.

Handing over military control to these Marcks is to be the worst decision the UMO has ever made. Our fighting forces are mostly depleted . . . I get it . . . still.

He watched as a Hybor gave sips from his canteen to a Solaran that struggled to maintain consciousness from his wounds. *These soldiers are the best of the best. We can and will fend the Thraxons off once more, but this Marck force is not the way.*

Generations of hate and war between these species meant nothing now. There was only the brotherly bond between soldiers fighting a common foe. Before this Thraxon War, none of the factions would have given a friendly glance to one another. The Mendacs ruled over their worlds as though they were all some sort of primitive, barbaric species. They sat back and casually watched the Hybors and Solarans destroy each other, once they were provided the technology to leave their respective worlds. Even though Thale, Solara, and Soorak were all neighboring moons of Oro, they didn't act very neighborly. That changed. Now there was hope—a perseverance that would not succumb to this current evil.

Just as Corin was beginning to feel surprised by the lack of a follow-up attack, a growing shriek from far above jolted his weary nerves. The shrieking multiplied and grew in intensity, but the sky was still not visible from the thick layer of ash and dust leftover from the sionic blast.

"Commander, the Thraxon hive ship has released a substantial number of Sarak attack fighters that are en route for an air-to-surface assault," a call from the science command station announced. The Sarak fighters were a highly agile, yet heavily armed, multi-purpose Thraxon attack force. The moment the distinctive roar from their Fathom drives poured into a system's atmosphere, they conjured fear in the UMO colonies. They had been the mainstay Thraxon attack vehicle for strafing assaults on supply frigates, outposts, and cities since the start of the Thraxon War. From almost every direction above, mass propulsion thrusters turned thunderous as they drew down upon the surface. Their relentless foes were not yet visible from the thick cloud of dust that still lingered in the sky.

"Form up for the next wave! Plexo, hit them with whatever you have left!" Corin struggled to stay optimistic and strong as the Vico Commander. Deep down, he knew that they were in no way prepared to repel this sort of attack in their present state, especially without a command ship. Still, he knew it was his duty, his responsibility, to give his legion every opportunity.

His exhausted force brushed themselves off and gathered whatever fight remained to repress the incoming Thraxons. Corin turned toward Creedith. "It's been a great pleasure serving with you, old friend. Casting every other honorable cause aside, for that reason alone, I have no regrets, no matter what the outcome is here today."

Creedith's focus changed from the sky above to Corin. "No, sir, the honor is mine; your strength and compassion have restored my faith in your people. There is no other place I would rather be right now than fighting at your side."

Plexo activated the remaining surface-to-air defenses. Beams of orange light swooshed over their heads and disappeared into layers of dust. The blasts were looking to quench the attacking fighters, but most were short of their elusive targets. The clouds flashed with cracks of explosions in the sky above them.

As his remaining force gathered around him, Corin drew a deep breath and held both hands toward the sky with his palms up. Snapping and crackling gave way to a transparent, blue dome positioned above the remains of his beloved UMO force. Just as the Saraks emerged from the dusty sky ready to unleash their deadly arsenal upon their targets below, they miraculously spun around in the opposite direction and back into the clouds. Their shrieking propulsion systems faded away into the sky above.

Corin pulled back his protective shell in bewilderment. "They could have wiped us out in one or two passes; why did they turn away?"

Creedith squinted his eyes toward the sky. "Marcks," he replied.

CHAPTER 1

C rix pulled a roll of sweet creams from his sleeve pocket and popped a small bit into his mouth then secured it back in his pocket for later. As he stood and observed the peaceful countryside, his mature, chiseled face revealed his transition from boyhood into a man. He stared up in tranquility, noticing several leaves drifting slowly through the air as they fell from the great breatic trees.

The scattering of light across his irises revealed his unique hazel eyes, which appeared enhanced with flecks of brown, light gold, and hints of green. His medium-brown hair tousled to the side as the occasional breeze glided through it.

His droona beast nudged him with its velvet-soft muzzle, and Crix gave the beast a warm smile. He pulled the roll out again and snapped off a small piece to share. The beast lapped it up instantly.

Sweet creams were the byproduct of the boiled skins from seacra pods. The bluish-green pods were considered a staple to sweetening food and used in Soorak cuisines among both Mendac and Andor cultures. Crix chuckled to himself, thinking of his droona's love for this creamy snack. The beast continued to nudge its rider for more, but a sudden echo of thunder quaked overhead, which pulled both of their curiosities skyward. He hadn't expected a storm this morning, and the war hadn't had any action close to the local system in many years. The rumbling rolled in and out again and sounded as though it was directly above. As he squinted and searched the clear, cobalt sky for the source, he thought he spotted a flicker of silvery light.

Crix leaped onto his droona beast—out of nowhere . . . boom! The sky directly above him flashed and exploded into a blazing white shockwave. His heart leaped from his chest, and his droona reared up, nearly throwing him to the grassy turf below. The sonic impact of the event was so powerful that he felt as if his clothes were nearly ripped from his body. His droona circled frantically, unable to regain its calm.

Droonas, a domesticated, four-legged creature used for transportation within the Andor communities, were not easily spooked.

Crix pulled back hard on the reins to stop it, and then quickly cupped his hand over his forehead, trying to get a view through the blinding light above. The receding white glow revealed a black oval inside. The oval was so black that it gave the appearance of looking into a hole.

Strange—he remained motionless while searching into the blackness for detail—*it's a ship.*

Enough features began seeping through the void to confirm his suspicions. The ship spun and shuddered in place for a few seconds before darting down into the horizon and disappearing past the cliffs that divided Troika and the wretched boglands of Drisal. All that remained in view was a white, glowing line that burnt away to a smoky trail. A distant thump let him know the ship had crashed into the boglands.

His droona snarled and flinched, still startled from the continued commotion. Crix patted his hand against the bare midsection of the beast in reassurance to the animal that all was okay.

The Drisal boglands were a vast stretch of low-lying land that provided a natural barrier between the outskirts of the Mendac and Andor territories. Commonly avoided by both species, Drisal had long been the source of folklore and ill fate. A dejected mix breed called Monoglades inhabited the boglands.

Crix felt an unnerving pull within to investigate the strange ship, but he knew it was a full day's ride on a droona. Besides, the danger of entering Drisal was real, as well as forbidden. Even the Marcks avoided that region as there was no political or strategic reason that would justify the use of resources in taming the lands. He wrestled with his emotions for a few minutes.

Tirix was going to be furious with him for ditching the annexis game. Annexis was his preferred pastime and an excellent way to get his adrenaline fix. He played the forward position in a five-member team named Gears, which he formed with his best friend, Tirix. They were to play against TZ Five, their archrival, led by his childhood nemesis, Akhal.

Akhal had hated Crix ever since they were children. He never accepted that a Mendac had the right to live amongst the

Andors, and he thought that Crix's presence there was polluting their culture. He always had this challenge growing up in Troika, but most of his neighbors and peers warmed up to him over the years. Yet, some Andors had never accepted Crix among them, and Akhal was one of the worst.

Still, he could not get the ship out of his mind; for some reason, his feelings would not give him rest. It was more than his feelings. It was the orb . . . calling him to duty . . . awakening inside. He was not going to be able to keep it concealed much longer. Over the course of twenty years, the orb inside him had never felt like this before. It was pulling him toward Drisal . . .

***

This unrelenting urge persisted, so he set forth. The great Breatic trees faded into the distance behind him. The narrow mountain wall that marked the edge of Troika was before him, and Drisal would be on the other side. He could see several small lines of smoke rising from the bogland.

As nightfall set in, his droona started to feel cold and clammy. This was a sign that the thick-skinned, brown beast had become fatigued and would need to stop for a rest soon. He wanted to enter the hostile region under cover of night, so he chose to leave his droona behind and continued on foot. The beast looked up at him one last time with its long snout as if it knew that he wasn't going to be back anytime soon. Fortunately, he packed himself a meal to eat before his annexis game; he was going to need it.

During the long hike, he began to think over his day. Haflinger, his keeper and the father figure who raised him, had him extracting minerals from the sabe field the day before, and observing the quiet Troika landscape was his favorite way to relax. His life growing up in Troika was more physically active than that of the normal, technologically pampered Mendac youth, and his physique prominently reflected this. Haflinger owned the rights to a section of the caina sabe fields.

The sabe minerals were a critical component for Soorak's orbital reactor stations. These minerals formed to a usable size annually, and the extractors, like Haflinger, were under pressure to make the outgoing shipment to Sectnine, a corporation that built and maintained the power grids, which supported the Mendac cities on Soorak.

Crix knew how important this time of the year was and that the harvesting of the minerals sustained them for the rest of the year. Yet his mind kept wandering away from the yield to Haflinger's comment the night before about "lifting the shroud." When he had asked what Haflinger meant, Haflinger flared his nostrils and glared at Crix from the top of his eyelids. He'd felt as though questioning this comment had been disrespectful. Deep inside, he knew what it meant, and that Haflinger was aware of this. He also knew that Haflinger was beginning to suffer from poor health, and he was going to have to assume a larger part in taking care of his keeper's affairs. Crix was uncomfortable with the future role that he must assume and where his place was going to be in this world moving forward. Throughout his life, he did as instructed since he was a child; he suppressed the power of the blue orb within him and kept it hidden from others.

As he walked, he thought about the past.

Twenty years had passed since the Marcks, a mechanized force, took over military control and eventually routed the Thraxon forces from the Oro System. Living among the predominantly rural lands of Troika, the Andors found themselves shielded from the war. The blue orb that merged with him shortly after his father's death, and had dwelled inside him ever since, had always been like a mysterious friend that he could never play with, though he felt a longing to do so. It would whisper in his ear, cool him during the warm months, and warm him in the cool months, but forbidden, Crix could not allow it to emerge. If discovered, the Marck forces would descend upon the Andor populace with merciless fury to retrieve the legendary blue orb. The surviving Andors would likely be imprisoned for slave labor on Dispor, the torturous prison moon of Vaapur-9.

Crix continued to hike toward the outer boundary of Drisal. He descended deeper into his memories of Haflinger. He had taught Crix the history of the Marcks, which had started during the devastating Thraxon War.

The Emergency Preservation Initiative of Oro required secret confinement areas that would place the orbs of Cyos in permanent stasis. The same power that once united the Oro System was to be hidden and forgotten. The last Tolagons were to facilitate that final act. All armed forces and security were to be under Marck control until the day of restored peace.

However, the system's leaders did not trust each other with control of this military force due to fear of subjugation by one of their fellow neighbors. Therefore, a final initiative called together a multi-world team of scientific minds that developed an independent, functioning, mechanized force based on the design of Joric Placater. The Marcks became self-governing and sovereign via their central control system. Then, the ultimate decision to hand over the orbs and allow the Marcks to oversee the system became law.

The blue orb of Soorak was *lost*, reportedly stolen, after the Marck handover. The yellow orb of Nathasia was destroyed during the Thraxon onslaught, and only the red and green orbs sat in their secret confinements as agreed. The Marcks had feverously combed the system in search of the lost blue orb but had never recovered it.

It was difficult for Crix to grasp that he was directly involved in this story, even though he had never known any of the characters. They were just a series of fireside tales he had grown up hearing about throughout his childhood. Haflinger was confident the Marcks monitored the entire planet of Soorak from orbit and could detect the energy signature from the blue orb, thus his stern instructions to Crix concerning the use of this now-illicit power.

Life was difficult for Crix as he could feel the orb urging him to take on the calling of the Tolagon. It was like a constant itch deep inside, which would only be satisfied through releasing its great power. Fortunately, his Andorian rearing gave him discipline and self-control, which had allowed him to ignore those nagging urges.

Crix thought of his droona. He had never left one behind before. With some luck, he would be back before the beast wandered off too far. He continued to tread faster toward the boglands and into Drisal.

Lost in his thoughts, he looked back at the peaceful landscape of Troika. He was wearing loose-fitted olive pants, and his top was a burgundy, padded undergarment from his annexis uniform. The padded top was his preference and was widely adopted by the Andor youth as a fashion statement. The traditionally reserved Andor populace recently saw its youngest generation take on more importance to the superficial, like sports and fashion. This had attributed to an inevitable bleed through from Mendac cultures that shared this world.

Crix had to bring himself back to the present. Pushing himself forward over the steep, rocky range, he struggled his way up the fanged summit.

The deceptive trek took a toll on his energy and time. He was aware that the dreaded, winged saber boars wandered the high, rocky regions. These vicious creatures used their leathery wings to swoop down upon their prey, slice them up with their razor-sharp tusks, and hungrily consume them. Crix would have to stay low and within the shadows to avoid their detection. He crouched down, hugging the shadow of a large boulder to remain unnoticed while he gained a panoramic view of Drisal.

It was a shadowy landscape littered with egg-shaped bushes and long, thorny spines that twisted and curled throughout any vacant space not filled with scrubby underbrush. The horizon was so thick with these unwelcoming flesh rippers that the view was nothing more than a blur. Screams and howls of beasts echoed throughout the region; this caused his nerves to flinch with hesitation. It was as though he was witnessing an awakening from the depths of some great fissure, and from that place, the release of all the dreadful monsters that haunted children's nightmares spilled out into the area below.

Trying to keep his fears in check, he focused on looking for the direction of the crash. With the smoke lines no longer visible, he lost its exact position. He decided to use the last place he could recall seeing the smoke as his reference point. The crimson glow from the massive parent world of Oro in the skyline gave the boglands a ghostly shimmer and the illusion of movement scattering across the landscape.

Crix rubbed his eyes to gain clarity. In the distance, he spotted a section of land that had the spiny brush pushed tightly together into a large mass with a plowed outstrip close by. A sudden feeling of anxiety clawed over him as he took a moment to think about what he was doing, though he felt a sense of relief when he observed that the crash site was not too far into the treacherous wild. He slowly emerged from the shadowy rocks and started to make his way down into the rugged terrain below.

The radiance from Oro was so bright that as soon as he stepped out of the shadows, his skin gave off a reflective glow. Startled by his blatant appearance, he dove into a tall patch of dried grass. Close by, he heard a subdued growl followed by an overlap of snorting. The snorts became more persistent as they neared. Crix poked his head slowly over the top of the tall grass to catch a glimpse.

Saber boars! At least five of them. Crix held his breath. The coarse-haired creatures had dark yellow tusks that stuck out almost a meter from their lower jaws. Realizing that the tenacious beasts had seen him, he jumped to his feet and sprinted down to the steep cliff nearby, hoping to find an overhang.

He reached the edge of the cliff and found a straight drop, at least a hundred meters, to the next ledge down. The boars spread out and surrounded him. They grunted and snorted faster in anticipation of their prey. Their eyes looked like cavities filled with blood and froth glopped from their jaws. They appeared focused, as though they were deciding on what part of him they would consume first before going in for the kill. Their skin-clad wings fluttered with anticipation, and the smallest of the group squatted down in a careful approach with his tusks pointed in a slightly downward angle.

Crix stepped back and stumbled over a heavy, citron green vine. He then saw the creeping vines from another bush located at the edge of the cliff, snaking down the overhang like long, crooked fingers. Without a second thought, he dropped down and grabbed a vine, allowing it to slide through his hands in an attempt to clear the ledge. His hands burned from the friction as he stopped near the end of the creeping plant's branches. He dangled wildly, unable to find a place to get a solid foothold. Loose rocks broke away under his feet and clacked all the way down the cliff's edge; soon, his hands and arms burned with fatigue.

Startled by fluttering noises above, he almost released the vine from his grasp. A terrible scream cried out from directly behind him, and he became aware that his perilous situation had somehow worsened. He looked back and saw a flying saber boar there to greet him. It was in an attack position and moving fast.

Crix quickly kicked away from a protruding rock and swung himself to the side. The boar tried to make a last-minute adjustment but smashed its tusks up against the side of the cliff. He took this precious second, while the boar was stunned from the impact, and jumped onto its back. The wild beast shrieked so loud that a deafening ring poured into Crix's ears. It continued the earsplitting shriek as it whipped its head around violently, trying to get a bite or tusk into him. He gripped tightly to its neck with his fingers, digging hard into its tough hide. He locked his legs around the boar's back as it soared downward out of control. Assuming that the creature was no longer able to keep flight with him on its back, he snuggled in as close as he could and braced for impact and hoped that the boar took the brunt of the crash.

Flying in with reckless abandon, they just narrowly missed several spines from the large bushes. The boar skidded to a frenzied landing; its clawed feet dug into the marshy ground. Crix remained clenched to its back. He was fearful that if he let go, it would come after him again. The creature hacked and grunted from exhaustion, still whipping its neck about, but a little less vigorously than before.

Crix took a moment and contemplated how he was going to get away from this highly agitated boar when he had a sudden recollection that he still had the sweet creams in his left sleeve pocket. He thought perhaps these saber boars would find them just as appealing as his droona beast and could be a perfect peace offering.

He took the treat from his pocket and snapped off a chunk then tossed it to the ground in front of the boar. The beast stopped its struggling, lowered its head, and snorted at the ground. It stretched its neck forward to reach the sweet cream without moving its feet, and then gobbled it up. As it chewed the delightful treat, the happy boar foamed and frothed at the mouth and gave out excessive grunts.

Crix snapped another piece and held it in his palm then attempted to lean forward to feed the boar. The animal startled and let out a squeal; Crix jerked his hand back and dropped the piece to the ground. The boar immediately lapped up the discarded treat without hesitation. Deciding to take a leap of faith, he dismounted the beast, and then stepped slowly forward and extended the stick in a peace offering to the boar. It cautiously leaned in and pulled the treat from his grasp. Then, surprisingly, the boar snorted around, looking for more. It approached him and began sniffing his clothes. It kept its head tilted so it would not lance him with the long saber tusks protruding from its face. The eager boar continued to nuzzle him, which caused him to chuckle from the tickling sensation. He placed his hand on its back to pat the five-hundred-pound boar like a pet as it continued to search for more sweet creams. After a while, the beast settled down, and he felt comfortable enough to head out in the direction of the crash, unconcerned about being this saber boar's next meal.

Crix nervously stared upward at the jagged cliffs behind him. At this point, now that he was deep in Drisal with no easy path back, he was much more concerned about running across a Monoglade. Monoglades were the descendants of a group of Andors that long ago immigrated into Mendac cities and eventually interbred. Once the xenophobic culture would no longer tolerate the crossbreeds, they banished them from their lands completely. When they attempted to return to Troika with their children, they were dishonored and unwelcomed. With no other options, they fled to the treacherous lands of Drisal.

It was an inhospitable region where their day-to-day existence focused on basic survival. They turned to savagery when the scarcity of resources caused them to abandon their morals. The Monoglade legend told of the beasts of the boglands feeding on them until only a handful of the most brutal and cruel remained. They lived by their claws and fangs as they adapted until the day when they finally ruled over the land through their own brutality.

Crix did not want to meet or tangle with any resident Monoglades. He heard a snap in the distance. His heart was pounding, and he leaned forward to examine the darkness. There was movement and another crack of a dead branch.

CHAPTER 2

The crash site was further away than he had thought; he slogged tirelessly through the marshy thicket. The menacing thorns that infested the landscape tore into his clothes and scratched his skin as he persistently fought through the undergrowth. Whatever had snapped the branch earlier had caught the attention of the boar, and it took chase, charging off into the thick brush. Crix hadn't seen or heard the boar since.

Pain and fatigue finally caught up with his steady drive, so he took a brief moment and caught his breath. As he stood there with his hands resting upon his knees, he felt a stinging pain as if hundreds of needles stabbed the lower parts of his legs.

What?

On the ground were thousands of tiny black insects scurrying up his lower extremities. He leaped in the air and dashed into another area not filled with the pests. He was exasperated. This place was teeming with life, and everything seemed hostile. Following close behind him, he could hear heavy thumps and grunts. It sounded like the saber boar; he hoped it was the same one from earlier.

It must still be following me. If the beast wants to follow, fine, but it needs to stay back and be a little quieter.

The noise that creature made was enough to get every Monoglade in the area bearing down upon him before he reached the crash. As he looked back, the boar's tusks poked through a dense patch of weeds. He tried to shoo the beast away, but that only made it want to come closer. Crix decided he would try to ignore it and press on and hoped it would lose interest and eventually go away.

He walked as lightly as he could in the marsh, and at times, he sank up to his thighs in the stinking muck. The humid, wretched air stunk of rot, and his wet clothes clung around his body; he felt restrained. This *wonderful* bouquet of aromas worsened the further he went on. Occasionally, a creature would tromp in front of him but always seemed to be more startled by him than he was of it.

Through the dampness and stink, he could catch the faint smell of charred metal, and he knew he must be getting close, but then he saw a sight that pressed fear deep into his bones. He had traipsed upon a monstrous, four-legged animal that had a long spear protruding out of its mouth. The jaws hung wide open with various-sized, pointed teeth, and its grey fur was stained with blood that slowly dripped to the ground. Crix could hear his heart beating as he stared at the creature's long, black claws, which had remained protracted as though it was still fighting against its slayers. The sight sent an uncontrollable shiver down his spine, even though the hulking beast was visibly dead.

His mind spilled over with the concern of what killed this beast and if it was still nearby. He then realized the crash site was right on the other side of a large brush pile, which unfortunately, was located directly behind the impaled behemoth. He carefully slid past the ill-fated beast and climbed over the brush pile to investigate. The uncertain boar would not approach the killed beast and kept a sizable distance from it.

At the top of the massive brush pile, he peered down with what should have been a good view of the crash site. However, the thick smell of burnt metal mixed with the pungent odor of the stagnate marshlands was almost more than Crix's uneasy stomach could handle. He squinted his eyes, but it still was not visibly clear through the darkness and mist, so he continued down the other side to get a closer look.

As he broke through the murky fog layer to see what was hiding beneath, he observed what appeared to be a strange fighter ship, and a large portion of that ship had sunk deep into the loose, marshy ground. It was small, and like nothing he had ever seen or even read about before, especially since he lived in Troika. Still, this ship was very different.

He noticed the ship's circular tail stuck out from the marsh, and it was translucent black, which he realized was why it had been so difficult to see before. All around the ship, he observed oddly shaped footprints; they were long and slender with short claws but appeared to come from creatures that walked upright. Most of them were quickly losing their shape in the soft marsh, which indicated that whoever they belonged to had only recently left the scene. *I really hope these weren't Monoglades.* He could hear the sporadic gurgling of the surrounding bog water as it bubbled up from around the crashed vessel. If there was something piloting this ship, it did not appear to have escaped; the cockpit seemed to be beneath the surface of the marsh. The ship must have belly slid for almost a mile before it finally dipped its nose and came to a stop there.

His thoughts raced; he had come this far and was not about to leave before investigating the wreckage. Again, he heard his heartbeat within his chest, but not because of fear but something else. The pure adrenaline that coursed through his blood triggered an intense focus. He found a flat rock nearby and used it to dig through the mud around the small ship. Working frantically, he realized that resting would only allow the waterlogged soil to seep back over his progress.

He followed along the ship's outer hull and continued to shovel while he fought the oncoming effects of exhaustion. He gasped for air and wiped the burning sweat from his eyes. Eventually, he located a small hole, possibly caused by an energy blast, on the side of the ship. He reached his hand into the hole, but it filled back in with the seeping mud and further obstructed his view.

He then cracked off a long stick from the brush pile and cautiously placed it into the hole. He attempted to clear the obstructing sludge while creating a view into the ship. All at once, the determination within him was reignited by what he saw next; slumped over, inside the cockpit, was a helmeted individual in a jet-black flight suit.

"Hey, can you hear me?" he shouted at the opening, but there was no reply or motion. He used the stick again, this time to nudge the hapless pilot. It was not in his upbringing to leave something or someone for dead, so he committed in his mind to retrieve the pilot from the doomed ship.

If the ship still had power, he might be able to open the forward hatch. He looked closer; there was a lever inside marked with the word *extraction*.

It almost sounds painful in a way.

He had an idea. The stick needed to be strong enough that he would be able to move the lever up, and if the ship had any power, he hoped the hatch would open.

Then, all of a sudden, in the scrublands off to his right, he caught a brief glimpse of a red, flashing light. Confused, he thought to himself, *No modern technology should be in Drisal,* so this struck him as unusual.

Though after a couple of minutes, he shrugged it off as his weariness and fatigue. Besides, he wanted to stay focused on rescuing the stranded pilot.

The ship must have some sort of auxiliary power system, but where would it be? His only view was from the far side of the cockpit to where the lever was located. As he leaned his hand against the ship's hull to regain his thoughts, the ground gave a steamy burp, and the ship began to slip further into the marsh.

He frantically dug next to the ship to keep the hole from filling back up with mud. There was a humming in the distance. It sounded as though it was approaching fast enough that it interrupted his efforts. As he looked forward, he noticed the red light again, this time with a much better view. A small, black and silver, oval object zipped forward and hesitated right in front of his face then flashed a bright red light. It backed up and flashed two more times at the ship before it zoomed off into the distance. Crix was bewildered.

The ship slowly slid further into the mud; he had little time left to save the person inside. He needed power to slide the hatch open, and there was none around except the orb.

Of course! The orb is pure energy, pure power; it could definitely power that ship!

The problem was that Haflinger warned him that the Marcks could possibly detect its energy signature from orbit and would come for it immediately. For this reason, he was never to bring forth its power, never to reveal the secret . . . until today. Besides, he was not in Troika; he was in Drisal.

His hands went numb and slowly gave off a subtle blue glow that crept up his arms. A bluish hue seeped into his vision.

What is happening? The orb has never done this before.

The light of day was upon him, and he could nearly see the sun break over the horizon. Now was the time! He always felt the energy deep inside of him, fluttering his heart, tickling the pit of his stomach. Nevertheless, the strict discipline from his Andorian rearing had provided him with the perseverance to subdue the urge to unleash this power. He was excited yet nervous. He placed the palms of his hands against the cold, wet surface of the doomed ship, let go of his clenched gut, his Andorian will, and allowed the surreptitious energy to flow.

A warm sensation whirled and tickled within his core, and then billowed throughout every nerve and muscle in his body. He felt each hair stand on end, and then he looked down at his arms and observed that they were ablaze with a blue aura. It felt good, almost like a drug that was going to be difficult to wean himself from now that he had tasted it.

The power of the orb caused the ship to start whistling and humming with a slight vibration that came from its hull. He looked inside and noticed the pilot's body was flinging and flailing around. The instrument panels illuminated and began blinking; he pushed the lever forward with the stick he had retrieved earlier. A small hatch just over the pilot seat slid open as the loose, wet soil poured into the cockpit; it left a small sinkhole above the ship.

He pushed his hands into the mud-filled cockpit and under the pilot's arms and pulled it to safety. He dragged the pilot to the side and located the helmet release latch so he could remove it. He was concerned that it might no longer provide life support. To his astonishment, as he pulled the helmet off, long, shiny, black hair fell out and revealed a fair-skinned young woman. Her skin was like smooth porcelain.

She slowly opened her deep green eyes, which made his heart skip a couple of beats as they made contact with his for the first time. She was beautiful, more than beautiful; she was unique and could be the only perfect thing he had ever seen. Until that moment, he had never seen a Mendac female in person, and now that he had, he never wanted to take his eyes off of her again.

She slowly regained her focus. "Who are you?" Her voice was subtle yet raspy, as though she had just awakened from a lengthy sleep.

Crix was at a loss for something eloquent to say. "Umm, I'm, uh . . ." He shook his head to force some sort of composure from himself. "Crix . . . my name is Crix. Are you okay?" He noticed that she was squinting and not looking at him but past his shoulder.

"Who's that?"

Shocked, he snapped his head around to witness, for a split second, a flash of a large face, a face of horror, one that you only saw in nightmares. It had grey flesh that was thick and cracked like dry mud. The rage-filled, bulging eyes of this monstrous being stared at Crix. Its enormous, black, flaring nostrils filled with wiry hair snorted out a pungent odor of rotting meat.

Crix was motionless; his unfortunate hesitation was just long enough for this repugnant creature's thick, bristly arm to wrap around his neck, and it lifted him from his feet. The weight of his body viciously smacked into the ground. The impact cost him his strength, and all went dark.

CHAPTER 3

High above Soorak, on Sinstar's zero-G weapons testing facility, a tall figure lurched over a young man huddled down on the floor of a dimly lit room. Zearic, the overlord of Sinstar Corporation, appeared acrimonious.

"If you're unable or unwilling to tell me where the Prototype X88T is located, then I have no more use for you, do I?" The man was painted red in his own blood, his face swollen, burned, and clothes shredded. Shivering, he said nothing but kept looking behind Zearic with terror in his eyes.

"Hmmm, how pathetic. You dare steal from me, you sightless coward!" He raised his left arm and spoke into an embedded device. "I'm finished with this worm. You have your next test subject, Pietal." His voice had an irritating pitch that tapped one's nerves when he spoke.

A broad, cloaked figure stood behind him. Its round eyes appeared red in the dimly lit room. He waved the shadowy figure back, and it hissed quietly then disappeared completely into a dark corner. Seconds later, Pietal, Sinstar's chief of weapons development, stepped in through the doorway as it slid open. A shiny, black cap covered his head with a slender pipe that had an emitting light blinking from its top. His large head lurched out from a floor-length coat, and a menacing scowl formed across his jawline.

Pietal glanced down at the bludgeoned man as if he was nothing more than a piece of lab equipment. He slapped his hands together, and two silver-clad guards wearing black helmets and visors marched into the room and hauled the man out by his arms. The man screamed, his terrified voice fading into the passageway.

"My lord," Pietal said as he snapped to attention and nodded in Zearic's direction; the eager scientist then quickly exited the room.

A rapid beep rang out from the device on Zearic's wrist. He tapped the device with his finger. "This had better be important."

"Please forgive me, Lord Zearic. There is a priority alpha encoded transmission coming in from orbital surveillance station 222."

"Allow it through then," he replied, annoyed, yet somewhat intrigued.

"Our searcher drones have detected and verified the X88T prototype in the Drisal region of Soorak."

Zearic's right eye illuminated, and his jaw tightened. "I want *that ship* back in our development station right now. Deploy ground forces to retrieve it immediately."

The voice continued. "Be advised, orb energy signature was detected at two short intervals in the matching proximity of the X88T."

Zearic clenched up, and the figure that remained lurking in the shadows of the room gave out a faint hiss. He smashed the bottom of his fist on the blood-soaked table next to him, and his appearance became grave as he spoke into his wrist unit.

"Now . . . turn up your audio receptors and listen to me. I want the X88T and the orb; the orb is of the highest priority. I do not care what the costs are; I want it brought to me, as well as the current carrier. Immediately! Put the Knactor Legion on the ground in Drisal now, and lock down the entire region! I do not care if you have to eradicate all of the life in Drisal to do so! Besides, no one will miss the sub-species waste there anyway."

"Affirmative, it will be done," the voice replied. The transmission ended with a fading whistle.

Zearic had spent two decades in search of both the missing and hidden orbs. This quest had driven him to the depths of madness. To him, the orbs' transcendent powers were the keys to his unquestioned rule over the system.

After just a few short minutes, the communication alert beeped again, disrupting his thoughts. "Lord Zearic, the queen has declined your request to send forces to Drisal for X88T retrieval," the voice said.

"What?" Zearic's eyes blazed with fire and hate. "What is her problem now?" he shouted.

"She says that she wants assurances that her forces are not getting wasted fighting off barbaric rabble for your own grandeur. She wants you to know that she is still queen over the Marck forces." Zearic secretly worked with the Queen for many years and owed much of his power and influence to her generous cooperation. He still hated her and viewed her as nothing more than *a necessary evil.*

"You tell her . . ." he started with a harsh rebuttal, and then settled on a tactical approach. "Tell her this is for the lost blue orb, and if she permits me to use her forces, we will assure her access to its power." Of course, Zearic thought quietly to himself, he would never share such power with anyone, especially the queen.

"Yes, Lord Zearic, right away." The communication faded out again.

Zearic gazed back at the dark figure. "She has her plans, and we have ours. We will follow her just a little longer to further our cause. Return to your forward command and await my signal. In light of these events, we must hasten our plans."

CHAPTER 4

Slowly recovering from being smacked onto the ground with raging force, the blackness began to subside. Crix found that he could not move his arms or legs and a sharp pain in his neck throbbed. He could hear breathless screams crying out. Crix's thoughts were still foggy; he felt as though he had awoken from a terrible nightmare. Yet, as his eyelids opened and adjusted to the light around him, he saw this was all too real.

The young woman pilot from the sinking ship was located a few meters in front of him buried up to her neck in soil and mud. She was unable to move, and it had become apparent that he was in the same situation. The cold ground felt like a heavy, wet blanket had wrapped around his skin and tightened with every move he made. She gasped and struggled while looking off to her right side.

From the corner of his eye, he observed an unnerving sight: a large number of partially flesh-covered and fully skeletonized heads were scattered on the surface; the area was crawling with extremely large, lively, translucent spiders.

This must be where the savages of this land cruelly dispose of trespassers.

He watched the spiders feeding off of the bits of flesh that remained on the skulls. The odor that emitted from this death hole was similar to the stink glands of a male droona beast. The domed cavern in which they found themselves buried and abandoned had an opening in the ceiling that allowed a single beam of light to illuminate the horrible scene. The cautious spiders appeared to avoid this direct light, which fortunately fell upon Crix and the frightened pilot, at least for the moment.

It is just a matter of time before the light moves away and the spiders make their way over to us.

He observed them quietly. The abnormally large spiders were mostly clear with tiny, black eyes; they gnashed and crunched as they picked away at the flesh and carried it down a nearby hole in the cavern wall. The young pilot, with a look of wild terror in her eyes, noticed that Crix was awake.

"You've got to get us out of this!" she shouted.

"I don't know how; I can't budge!" Crix replied, frustrated over his helplessness.

One of the hungry spiders started to approach the young woman, but it reared back and hissed when it came to the edge of the bright light. She struggled to free herself with desperate futility. Another spider, eager to acquire its besieged prey, leaped through the light and landed on her head. She thrashed her head around and knocked the spider on its back; it reared up aggressively for another attack. Several other spiders scurried in to assist. She had no hope to fight them all off in her current state. However, Crix noticed, she looked like she had the willingness and fight within her to give it a valiant effort.

The spiders pounced into the air to swarm her, but something quickly knocked them away before they could reach their target. The aggressive attackers flailed brutally against the walls. Crix heard a strong but familiar grunt, and then he saw their unlikely rescuer, the saber boar, as he heroically charged after their voracious aggressors. He must have sniffed out Crix's location and found him in the cavern.

Several spiders converged on the boar as he snapped his head wildly back and forth; he easily knocked and bashed them around like young Andor's play dolls.

From a small hole in the cavern wall, arachnids poured into the area. The boar smashed many of them into the ground and crunched their outer shells, sending bodily fluids spewing across the cavern floors and walls. The onslaught continued as even more highly agitated and massively large predators flushed out of the hole and swarmed the boar. It squealed in angst over its mounting adversaries.

Crix knew that, as vicious as this beast may be, he could not fend off this many. The relentless attackers had begun to pile up on the boar and bite chunks of flesh from his back and sides. Crix once more made the decision that he must use the orb's power.

He released himself to the orb's power, and once again, he felt it surge through every muscle within his body. It tingled like electrical energy across his skin. He looked up at the high ceiling and imagined himself there. The area started to shake, and his shoulders broke through the packed mud and dirt. He rose up slowly into the air surrounded by a vibrant blue glow. The saber boar belted out one last groan as it exhaled its last breath, and the spiders then started back to their original prey, the young Mendac woman.

Crix pounced down and began striking the spiders back from their intended meal. They jumped at him from every direction, but with his strength and speed hardened by the orb's energy, he was able to repel them easily and efficiently. Several of the spiders surged through his offense and gave him a nasty chomp, but the orb's energy shield minimized the damage to his body. During this short battle, he found them to be little match for his enhanced assault.

The quarrel soon ended. Dead and incapacitated spiders littered the cavern. Crix looked down toward the dark-haired, green-eyed stranger who, from her expression, was astonished over what she had just witnessed.

"You're a Tolagon?"

"A wha . . . are, uh . . . No, not really." He bashfully shrugged; he wanted her to be impressed but did not want to be deceitful.

"Well . . . get me out of here, quickly!" she demanded in a somewhat irritated tone.

Crix scanned the area and was unable to find anything that could easily help him free her from the soil. He thought of using the orb but was uncertain about his ability to control the power and was concerned that he might injure her in the process. Therefore, he attempted to allow the orb's energy to release into his arms and hands. He wedged his glowing blue hands into the compacted soil and easily pierced down underneath her arms and pulled her out.

Much of her flight suit ripped away due to the heavy weight of the mud sticking to the loose material. She peeled the rest of her torn flight suit off and tossed it on the ground. Beneath it, Crix noticed that she wore a black, tightly fitted outfit and was captivated; the fabric gradually transitioned to a nearly sheer material at her legs that she accessorized with a reflective grey belt around the waist and corresponding grey ankle boots with flat soles. She adorned herself in the fashion of the youthful female urbanites of Teinol, the epicenter of art and style of Soorak. Crix found it strange that she was piloting such a ship; pilots were not usually so fashionable, yet he was also pleasantly surprised.

Spellbound by her silhouette, he instantly snapped back from his thoughts as two hulking Monoglades crawled in through the entrance of the cavern. As they entered, they stood erect with long, grey, muscular legs, dressed in various beast hides, and wielding what appeared to be long, blunt objects that consisted of mammoth-sized bones infused with crude spikes. Their fanatical eyes were cloudy with little sign of color, which gave them an almost lifeless appearance, as well as little hope that they would be reasonable. They both took an offensive posture and carried their Mongolic weapons drawn behind their wiry-haired heads.

Crix and the woman stepped back, trying to keep their distance but quickly ran out of space behind them. Filled with bravado over the presence of his new companion, Crix charged up and lunged toward the closest one. The Monoglade lurched back and swung his weapon; he smacked Crix in the chest and launched his body into the wall. As he hit the wall, he felt everything inside him smack together. To his astonishment, he was physically unharmed due to the orb's shielding power but still had the wind knocked out of his lungs from the shock of the blow.

He remained down on a single knee, attempting to catch his breath. He felt the tightness and burning in his lungs. The other Monoglade charged after the young pilot, and she brazenly squeezed herself down a nearby spider hole and narrowly escaped. Crix labored back onto his feet again and, this time, carefully approached the Monoglade. Just as the creature swung his bone club, Crix ducked to evade, and then struck him between his legs, hoping that these creatures were vulnerable in the same places most were. The Monoglade let out a beast-like roar and fell to its knees.

Two more Monoglades entered the cavern, likely alerted by the commotion. Crix hastily slid face-first into the small spider hole after his new companion. One of the Monoglades smashed its club against the hole in an attempt to splatter Crix, just missing his legs. He squirmed with his elbows down the narrow tunnel with a feeling of temporary solace that the enlarging horde of Monoglades outside could not fit through the passageway. Space was tight and the ground somewhat spongy. His elbows sunk into the ground as he moved forward. It was cold and constricted his movement.

He continued to wiggle forward, and the growls of frustration from the Monoglades outside faded into the distance. Ahead of him was darkness to the point of pitch black with still no sign of the enigmatic and elusive young woman.

Who is she? Crix thought.

He kept going forward; space had become so tight that he had to suck in his chest in order to squeeze through the murky tunnel. A musky stench with a hint of decay permeated from the air ahead.

He questioned, *Did she go down this hole?* He had to know.

"Hey, are you there?" There was no reply. His mind started to race. *Where is she?*

All of a sudden, he came upon a drastic downward slant. He frantically gripped the walls to keep himself from sliding. The slant leveled off, and his face pushed into what felt like the bottom of someone's shoes. Unexpectedly and rudely, one of the shoes kicked him back. He then noticed that there was a trace amount of light bleeding through the tunnel ahead.

"Don't . . . move," she whispered back to him.

Crix was confused as to why she had stopped. "What are you doing?" A minute of silence went by, and he grew restless by her lack of reply.

"One of those spiders is in the tunnel . . . right in front of me. It is staring right at me. I'm hesitant to move," she said in a remarkably calm voice. Inside this tight space, she understood that she could do little to fend it off or flee.

The ground above them had begun to shake, and the tunnel vibrated. A heavy rumbling rolled in and out from the surface. Fearful that the tunnel might collapse, Crix loudly whispered out the first thing he could think. "Just . . . punch it in one of its eyes as hard as you can."

"Are you nuts?" she sarcastically questioned.

"Just do it!" The ground shuttered violently, and fragments of the tunnel showered down upon them and caused him to cover his eyes.

"Okay, fine!" she relented before thrusting her fist sharply into one of its eyes. Crix was happy and surprised she acted so quickly. The spider scurried back into the darkness. "It's gone!"

"Follow it!" Crix hurriedly pushed her forward. They both struggled through a small opening that led out into a large cave, which was barely illuminated. They saw shapes and movement but little detail. It was a relief that they could finally stand up.

Another shockwave hit the ground, and the tunnel behind them collapsed. She wrinkled her face over the pungent odor of decay. The air was stale and old. However, the walls danced with life, and they observed a strange movement. A column directly in front of them appeared to shift side to side, especially when the rumblings above intensified. They both pressed their backs up against a wall, uncertain of what laid ahead.

Crix noticed two other similar columns in the cave, possibly more. The lighting was poor. He saw a steep dropoff on the cave floor and carefully slid forward to have a look at how far the drop was to the bottom. As he peered over the edge, he observed thousands of those *delightful,* flesh-eating spiders they loved so much from their earlier situation and quickly noticed that the alerted spiders were scampering across the walls, heading in his direction. He slowly looked up, and then carefully backed away with a look of terror on his face. "We've got to get out of here!"

"What? What? What did you see?" she questioned.

"It's better if you don't know." He grabbed her soft hands and placed them around his neck. "Hop up and don't let go." His body gave off a brilliant blue glow, and with a couple of quick steps to the ledge, he leaped across the cavern to reach a small ledge on the far side. Just as he made the jump, a strong feeling of uncertainty flashed through his mind. His glow dimmed. He just missed the ledge and grasped the edge with the tips of his fingers.

Above them, a lurid hiss echoed throughout the cavern. The woman tightened her grip as she gazed up and let out a panicked breath. The hissing intensified; Crix struggled to keep hold of the ledge as his fingers slipped and burned against the gritty stone. Perched above them, a gigantic spider encompassed the area; its long legs curled down the walls and past the ledge he frantically clung to. It was now apparent that the swaying columns they observed earlier were massive spider legs. Its rubicund body was large with a round abdomen that swarmed with life as thousands of smaller spiders crawled about the giant mother. The smaller spiders clumsily climbed over each other due to the crowded space and spilled off the abdomen onto the ceiling and walls.

The "mother" spider gave another loud hiss and lowered its body down into the cavern. Crix's grip started to fail.

She whispered in his ear. "Just believe." Her breath tickled and made the hairs on his neck stand straight up. A chill chased down his spine.

Reenergized, he focused on the ledge above them. With a quick jolt, they sprung up and landed squarely upon the ledge. She hopped down, and both looked over the swarming cavern, and then, with one glance directly at the large red spider's jaws which hung wide open in front of them, it screeched and hissed as it chomped in their direction. Still charged from the orb, Crix's reflexes allowed him the ability to spin around, grab the Mendac woman, and dash into a narrow path that led away from the precarious ledge. The spider gnashed down again, crashing its mouth into the passage opening. Enraged, it crunched back and forth at the opening in an attempt to consume its prey. Dozens more of the smaller spiders jumped from the abdomen and poured into the passage after them.

Pushing her forward, they scraped and clawed their way through the uneven and tight passage as the spiders took chase. They frantically reached an incline and climbed a few jagged steps to the top, only to find a dead end.

"There's no way out of here!" She panicked and pounded her fists at the rocky end then turned around to face her fate. Crix positioned himself between her and the fast-moving, enthusiastic spiders. He charged up for a last stand. She braced herself for the battle.

An unexpected explosion jolted them to the ground, and a wide-open exit appeared behind the shocked woman. The light from the sky blinded their eyes. The world around them fell into absolute chaos. The jolting of blaster fire and detonations shattered their senses. Then, the screeching noises from the spiders subsided, the dust settled, and everything gave way to a sudden silence.

CHAPTER 5

The two slowly rose to their feet and pushed the fallen rocks and loose debris out of their way. The female pilot blocked her hands over her face and tried to adjust to the sudden blast of daylight. Together, they observed several Marck troopers blazoned in red.

The troopers glistened in the sunlight; their rifles pointed in a threatening manner. One of them dropped its rifle and cautiously approached Crix, clenching a circular apparatus in its hand; the Marck trooper pointed it at his chest. The device spun around and illuminated, as did the orb in Crix's chest.

"Orb located," it sounded off, its voice deep and refined, but it still had a mechanical undertone that would discern it from a living being.

Outside, the ground smoldered, and dead Monoglades were scattered across the area, their hapless bodies charred with anguished expressions frozen on their faces.

"Load them onto the transport," a nearby Marck ordered. Its armor appeared slender yet somehow still unwieldy.

Hovering just above the ground a little distance away was a heavily guarded ship that waited with its cargo elevator lowered. Troubled, Crix took notice of the fire and billowing smoke that sprinkled across the region. The ground still shook as the Marck legion carried out its campaign of subduing Drisal. Crix flexed as though he was about to charge the power of the orb within his chest, but his new friend quickly grabbed his arm.

"Don't, it's the Knactor Legion. They have a notorious reputation and will not hesitate to kill us both; besides, there are too many. We need to wait for a better opportunity." She recognized their legion colors and insignias. Crix noticed that she was highly perceptive as well as discerning for someone her age.

One of the Marcks shoved her forward and began to place an energy shackle around her body. Before he was able to finish, the ground quaked violently, and two giant, red legs burst up through the surface. The massive spider, still seeking its escaped prey, emerged from the ground. It was accompanied by hundreds of smaller spiders that spilled out like ocean waves cresting an empty beach. The Marcks fired wildly at the scurrying menaces, instantly filling the air with the stench of burned chlorine from the plasma gases.

The giant spider, now free of the cavern, instantly seized two Marcks and ripped them in half, and then it started after Crix, smashing any Marcks in its path with ease. Observing that their captors were otherwise disposed of, using the orb's power, Crix grabbed his companion around her waist and leaped on top of a huge nearby boulder. This gained them a few safe moments out of harm's way. A squad of Marcks blasting their weapons without pause had swooped down on hover disks and managed to slow the giant spider's pursuit.

Crix noticed the Marcks' feet and how they magnetically attached to the flight disks. These highly useful hover disks were the latest in individual troop assault and recon mobilization developed by Sectnine. The Marcks dashed back and forth, employing hit and run tactics on the mother spider. The mammoth beast jumped toward the airborne Marcks but always came up short in catching her swift opponents. Meanwhile, the ground Marcks subdued the swarms of smaller spiders after sustaining few losses of their own.

Crix capitalized on another provided opportunity, and he fearlessly pounced upon a Marck's back as it zipped by on a hover disk. He wrapped his arms around its lower torso and jerked his weight down and to the left, sending the disk and Marck spiraling toward the ground. Crix then positioned himself on the Marck's shoulders, allowing it to take the brunt of the resulting impact. The Marck became detached from the hover disk.

Crix then quickly and steadily squatted down upon it and leaned forward. The smooth, flat disk launched ahead, and he nearly lost his footing; he began rethinking his bravado. The slick surface made it difficult for him to stay on top of it. He took a deep breath and shifted his weight to turn the disk . . . *It worked!* Confidently, he then swung back around.

"Jump up!" He extended his hand, motioning her to jump onto his back. She happily accepted and swiftly secured herself around his waist. He leaned forward to activate the machine's forward propulsion and took extra care with the additional weight and added instability. Crix drove the hover disk away from the main Marck forces and in the direction of the rockface cliff, which would lead them out of the Drisal region.

He took a quick look back and noticed several Marcks had taken pursuit on hover disks, and they were closing in fast. Crix was hesitant to increase his speed as he continued to struggle to keep his footing. His stomach tightened. He knew, at this point, that he could not outrun or outmaneuver them. With the Marcks nearly on top of them, he quickly descended lower, hugging the ground. Since the Marcks never fired upon them thus far, he decided to take the gamble that their directive was to take them alive, and that might give him an upper hand. He had to make a quick decision.

At that moment, he energized both of them with the orb, twisted his hips hard, and jumped from the disk while still moving at a high rate of speed. The disk continued forward and haphazardly smashed into the cliffs ahead. As he landed, he was facing the oncoming Marcks with his fists clenched and his heels dug into the soil as he slid to a stop.

The woman lost her grip and flew backward; she tumbled and landed a few meters on the ground next to him. Several Marcks systematically flew by and circled back around. Crix waited in a defensive posture with his jawline tightened, and his eyes intensely focused on what was about to come, but before they reached him, unexpectedly, one of the oncoming attackers collapsed and slid off its disk. As the other two looked back to see what happened, each one violently arched backward as long metal bolts burst through their chests, sending sparks and sheared-off metal flying through the sky.

Crix scanned the area trying to locate the shots' origin. It was evident that someone or something was aiding them. *Who or what is it?*

From the cliffs, a low, gravelly voice called out, "Over here!" Crix noticed that the voice came from halfway up the cliff. "Get over here quickly! More are on the way!" the voice persisted.

Crix and the surprised woman sprinted toward the cliff with blind faith that the voice was someone they could trust, at least for the time. The distance to the cliff was far, and they could hear the alarming hum of the hover disks as they fast approached. They focused forward, not looking back, and ran until their breath escaped them and their lungs were on fire. The woman pilot, to Crix's surprise, easily outran him.

Two rapid flashes from an elevated position on the side of the cliff caught their peripheral vision. A pulsating screech approached from overhead and zipped past them as a hover disk and Marck twirled uncontrollably and exploded into the side of the cliff. They kept running without pause until they reached the base and looked straight up at the small overhang from which the voice originated. An unexpected cable dropped down.

"Grab onto it and be quick!" the voice shouted.

Crix stuck his foot through the loop and grabbed the cable with both hands. He looked over at his cohort. "Jump on!"

She placed her arms around his neck and wrapped her legs around his waist. The cable started to move up in short jolts, and as they neared the overhang, there were deep baritone grunts with each hard jerk of the cable. They reached the top and found a large, stout, dark-grey-skinned brute of a beast pulling the cable. He had hulking muscles and bulging veins that protruded from his neck and arms. Crix thought he was someone he would rather be friends with and not foe. His black pants frayed just below the knees, and he wore an old, sleeveless military jacket that was just as weather-beaten and dirty as he was.

"Are tya going to help me out here and get off the line, or do I have to just keep hangin' on to tya dead weight a while longer?" he snapped. He was scowling, his bare head and strained scalpline scrunched downward toward his solid black eyes. They both jumped away from the line like school kids in trouble.

"You're a Hybor?" the woman asked. Hybors, from the watery moon of Thale, had a thick, black skin and round heads that were indiscernible from their necks. Their eyes shined above their whiskered muzzles and frowning jawlines. He looked at her with contempt in his expression.

"Oh yeah, how were tya able to guess that?" He took heavy breaths as he spoke as though labored. He reached over and grabbed an old, beat-up rail gun, which looked as though it was from the first Thraxon War. Pulling a wide magazine from his side pouch, he slammed it into the side of the weapon and smacked the bottom of it with his webbed hand. In a blink, he placed it up to his shoulder. The rifle made a humming and crackling noise as it fired, dropping three more incoming Marcks that approached the cliff wall.

"Get down into that hole and follow it till tya find an air pocket a little way in. I'll be with tya in a minute." He pointed toward a hole filled with a brown, sewage-type liquid. The two looked down at it together, and then dolefully at each other; the liquid reeked of rotten eggs.

"Are you serious?" Crix asked with the underlying hope that the Hybor meant something else. He sighed and thought to himself, *does everything in Drisal smell rotten?*

"What's the matter with tya? Do what I say if tya want to survive. Now stop askin' stupid questions and get going!" Behind them, approaching Marcks littered the sky with attack ships.

"Just stay close to me; I'm a pretty good swimmer," Crix stated. She looked at him with assurance in her eyes and nodded. He jumped into the stink hole, and she followed close behind.

As they moved through the tunnel, he grasped at the walls and found them to be slimy, smooth, and almost alive. Several times, it felt like something brushed past him, but it was impossible to see in the murky fluid. Crix felt a slight tinge of panic go through his mind as his breath began to run out. The tunnel widened, and they came to a larger area. His thoughts raced; if they did not find an air pocket soon, they were going to drown in this awful place. He swam a bit further, but the pressure building up in his lungs was a warning; he had to get air. He felt her grip his calf with her fingernails.

She must be feeling it as well.

His heart banged around his chest; it felt as though it would burst if he did not find that air cavity. Unable to go any further, he swam upward and pressed his mouth along the top of the tunnel. There was nothing but slime; he was finished. Then his body snapped forward with a strong gush and swooshing motion, and in a few short seconds, he emerged into an air cavity with his bulky new friend and the fatigued woman. They both gasped, trying to catch their wind.

"Take a minute to catch tya breath, but we got to keep moving. Once they figure out what happened to us, they will call in the amphibious units to hunt for us here."

A minute or two passed, and the Hybor grabbed both of them together around their chests, and then sandwiched them against him. His skin felt like rubber against theirs, yet it was solid underneath from his muscular physique.

"Take a deep breath," he said just before he dove down through the widening tunnels and clenched onto them with one arm.

As they swiftly passed through another watery tunnel, the gurgling of fluid flushed past their ears. Crix felt his ears give way to the pressure; it was like nails driving into his eardrums. Just as the fatigue of oxygen deprivation kicked in, they popped upward into a large, faintly lit cave; its only light source was a single proton gas lamp at the far end. Around the illuminated area were a chiseled-out stone seat shaped in a reclining fashion and a neatly organized row of sharpened steel rods that leaned against the wall nearby.

The Hybor chucked his new young Mendac friends onto the smooth stone floor. He lumbered over to the stone lounger and flopped down, kicking one of his large, wide feet up on an old scrap piece of machinery. Grabbing a nearby wooden box, he placed it upon his lap and pulled out a plump, round, dark green aacor—a pungent tasting fish that Andors typically used for bait. He smashed the aacor into his mouth and grabbed up another, giving off a deep and wet belch. The smell permeated to the other side of the cave where the two rescued guests still laid from the Hybor's toss.

They recoiled back, gagging from the odor, which did not mingle well with the stink from the cavernous pool.

"Ahh . . . Mr. Hybor . . . sir, I don't mean any disrespect, but I thought we needed to keep moving due to the approaching amphibious units?" Crix was concerned over the Hybor's sudden lax presence.

"Yes, we do, but aacor is good for tya fightin' strength. Tya'll need your strength; have one. Oh, and . . . Krath's the name. Don't call me mister." He extended the box in their direction in offering. Crix and the young woman both gave a repugnant look and waved their hands in dismissal.

Krath growled to himself, "Useless youth, never appreciates good things." He crammed another one into his mouth.

Crix rolled his eyes and turned toward his new friend. "Well, as much as we've been through together, it's hard to believe we haven't had a proper introduction yet. I'm Crix." He extended his hand in goodwill. She pulled her wet hair back from her face, the right side of her mouth turned up into a sweet smile, and she gently placed her hand in his.

"Very pleased to meet you, Crix."

He waited an uncomfortable minute, and then looked side to side with a playful smirk. "And you are?"

She rolled her eyes, feeling a little rude. "Oh . . . Sorry, I'm Kerriah." A bass-horn chuckling came from Krath, and they both, at that moment, chose to ignore him. Their eyes locked onto each other.

"And you're a Tolagon, I see. I thought they were all eliminated as a result of the Emergency Preservation Initiative." She gently patted his chest, where the orb resided. A warm feeling flushed through Crix; still, he was embarrassed. He did not feel he had earned the right to carry the title. He had received the orb in secrecy, handed down with no instructions on how to use it. It was not official, and he had never received any formal training. The title did not fit.

"Well, not exactly." His face flushed. "I mean, I have an orb. In fact, I've always had it, and it's a part of me, almost like an organ in my body. But I don't feel that makes me a Tolagon. Those guys were legendary from what I've been told about them. That's not me; I'm not a hero. I'm an Andor living an unpretentious life, at least until this past day."

Krath threw his bucket of aacor down against the floor, sending the remaining aacor inside sliding out and across the floor. "Wrong!" he shouted. "Tya father was the Vico Legion Commander Corin Emberook, Tolagon of Soorak, chosen by Gabor, and with his death, has rights to name his replacement if unable to return to the Council!"

Crix's eyes widened, and he eagerly sat erect. "You knew my father? How do you know who I am?"

Krath drew a calming breath. "Yes, boy, and a great warrior he was. I would have fought at his side till my last breath. When I heard of his passin', I refused to believe it until his closest friend acknowledged it." He let out a prolonged, barking cough that added a deeper, noxious stench in the dank air. "He told me of a child . . ." He stopped, poised like a statue, staring into the large, watery hole they had emerged from earlier.

"What?" Crix's curiosity now had an unrelenting resolve. Krath disregarded Crix and slowly reached over and grabbed one of the steel rods next to him. Crix and Kerriah looked into the water and observed a shadowy figure surrounded by a faint green light in the depths, and at that moment, a splash of water flew up as a rod broke through the stillness. A flash lit up the water for an instant, which outlined three Marck silhouettes with one having a steel rod protruding from its torso.

"Over here, and be quick about it!" Krath waved them over to a section of the cavern that had a bulky chain hanging from the ceiling. Crix and Kerriah quickly complied.

The other Marcks emerged from the watery basin. Their armor was dark mossy green and accented with a black, rubber coating. As their visors broke the surface, Krath charged toward them and leaped into the water trapping their heads between his biceps and forearms. He rolled them like a Drisal flathead gorgator, and their flippered feet flung into the air above the water and back down again. The surface of the water swirled and rippled as a sharp thump came up from the depths. A sheared-off Marck leg flew up from the water and smashed into the cavernous wall. Following close behind, a head and arm clanked upon the floor. Air bubbles billowed up just before Krath burst from the surface with his arms outstretched as he landed squarely back onto the solid stone floor. With a wild look on his face, he charged back over to the chain and started pulling.

"Amphibious units! I hate amphibious units! Be ready!" he shouted while he heaved with each pull, his veins bulging from his face and arms.

"What are you doing?" Crix asked, alarmed by Krath's lack of details.

"More are right behind the three I just put down! When this opens, jump in and follow the slide till tya see light, and then start grabbin' for vines. Tya can use the flex cable I have stashed near the opening to repel to the cliff bottom."

He flexed and lugged for another great pull. A large, stone slab pulled up from the floor, revealing a secret passageway. The amphibious Marck units surfaced with rifles drawn to their shoulders.

"Go!" Krath insisted in a strained voice.

Without hesitation, they both jumped into the dark hole. They found themselves sliding through a narrow tunnel that quickly turned into a downpour of water. Behind them was a loud booming vibration as the stone slab slammed down, cutting off their way back. Now, left with complete darkness and water gushing down through the tight space, their momentum picked up as they hit a massive drop off that sent butterflies fluttering through their stomachs. The slide leveled off and opened to a brightly lit area.

Sunlight blazed from an opening in the cavern above, and long green vines draped down, dipping into the slide, and then following its steep path downward. Crix rubbed his eyes to provide relief from the blinding light; however, he was still moving rapidly down the natural slide. He felt the slippery vines under his back as he passed over them and rolled over to his belly. He grabbed one and managed to get a firm grip and slow himself to a stop. His feet dangled helplessly in the air.

It was not until the feeling of vertigo sank into the pit of his stomach and the back of his mind that he realized he was hanging off the edge of the cliff at the tunnel's exit. The drop-off was far and landed into the forest-covered flatlands below. The gushing water blasted relentlessly against him. He clenched the vine and attempted to look back up the tunnel but detected no signs of Kerriah.

Did she jump in behind me? His mind raced. *She must have grabbed hold of something.*

He leaned back to have a look down but could not get a good view without losing his grip. The water violently splashed against his face and eyes and filled his ears. He was overwhelmed.

Where is she?

Fire burned throughout his hands as he could feel his strength waning. He could use the orb's power, although he was worried the Marcks could detect his position.

It will have to be an absolute last resort.

He dangled there, clenching the vine, and with every effort, tried to pull himself up. The frail branch broke loose under his weight and sent him freefalling uncontrollably. He tumbled toward the ground. There was no time to think, and he had to use the orb's power to break his descent. Then, he instantly and surprisingly stopped with a spine cracking snap.

"Hang on there, buddy; I got tya," a familiar voice said. Crix looked back over his shoulder as he hung mysteriously in midair; it was Krath. He planted his husky feet firmly against the cliff wall and had one arm wrapped around Crix's torso and the other around a high flex cable.

"I'm usually partial to the quick way down myself, but tya looked like you could have used some tips. Almost turned tyaself into a splat of goo down there."

"Where did you come from?" Crix huffed, out of breath from the rush of what just occurred.

"Let's just say I was finished bustin' up those uninvited pests, and since they came apart a little quicker than expected, I thought I would meet up with tya guys early. That's when I spotted tya flailing corpse and dove after tya. Now I'm gonna put tya down here." He loosened his arm to drop him.

"No, wait!" Crix panicked.

"Aw, settle down, boy. Take a look down."

He turned around to see the ground was only about two meters below him. Krath let out a bellowing chuckle.

"Caught tya in a nick of time, huh?" He then dropped Crix, who stumbled forward and landed on his feet.

"Thanks for the assist. Did you happen to see Kerriah up there?"

"Who? That skinny little thing that was with tya?" He let out a phlegm-filled grumble. "Why is it always got to be up to Krath to take care of tya youngsters?"

"I'm right here." She stepped out from behind a nearby tree.

"What the . . . How did you get down here without plummeting to your death?" Crix was somewhat bewildered given that he almost had to resort to using the orb's power to save himself, yet she safely traversed the cliff so quickly.

She casually shrugged. "Let's just say I have a few tricks within me as well."

Krath chuckled at her reply. "Watch tya heads!" He gave his cable a twist and a hard snap, breaking it free from the hook above, and it dropped loosely to the ground.

"Well, okay then. I'm glad you're here. You certainly had me a little worried, but it looks like you can take care of yourself." Crix gave her an affirming smile.

Krath started walking away casually as if following a set plan. "It's about time to get tya back to Troika."

Crix looked at him, puzzled. "How did you know I was from Troika?"

Krath replied with irritation, "Well, where the heck else would you be from on this part of the world? Certainly not Drisal; tya could barely survive a day there without gettin' tyaself killed."

Crix sighed. "I suppose you have a point. Well, I suppose we should get going, though I'm not sure how the Andors are going to take to the likes of you."

"No worries, I've dealt with their kind before," Krath responded. "We'll move at nightfall and stay within the treelines; the Marcks will still be combin' the area for tya. For now, stay buried, out of plain sight." He hunkered down like a rodent, dug two deep holes in the loose soil, and then snapped some branches from nearby trees.

"Get in." He pointed to the holes. Crix and Kerriah slid down into the holes, which concealed them up to their chins when standing. Krath covered the openings with the leaves and branches. "It's not perfect cover, but if tya stay low, it just may conceal tya thermal signatures from their drones, as long as they're not right over top of tya. And don't be moving around in there. I'll come get tya in the evenin'." He took off deep into the forest with a lung-ripping cough until it was indiscernible in the distance.

As the day wore on, toward evening, an occasional, low-pitched hum would slowly pace by above them. Dusk settled in and the winds died down; the rustling of leaves from the tall trees gave way to stillness. The small, white sun dipped completely below the horizon. The second larger, red sun waned, and it produced a deep crimson shade over the region.

Crix became restless and gently moved away some of the coverage to get a better view outside the hole. He noticed something small move near the treeline. Squinting, he focused on the object. It was a small, shadowy sphere, and it hovered slowly next to a tree about fifteen meters away from Crix's position. It didn't make a sound as it slowly moved through the forest. He had never seen anything like it before, and he remained motionless with caution with the assumption that it had to be some sort of agent for the Marcks. He could see Kerriah through his peripheral vision; she appeared to notice the sphere and remained as silent as a statue.

The sphere eventually passed and disappeared in the shadowy distance. Crix slowly crept from his hole and crawled, hunkering low, over to Kerriah. "What was that?" he whispered.

"A stalker drone," she quietly replied. "They are the eyes of the Marcks. Deployed and operated by the dreaded CIC."

"CIC?" Crix inquired. She gave a sarcastic smirk.

"Boy, the Andors are a little behind on current affairs. CIC is short for Capture Intelligence Command, and their reputation is frightful. I have lost some friends to them."

"I am regretful for your losses; I truly am. Even though we share this world with Mendacs, Andors keep to ourselves, and due to the treaty, we are not subject to Soorak laws and enforcement. So . . ." Embarrassed by his lack of basic knowledge of these things, Crix felt he needed to explain himself.

"Treaty? That old thing was made during the Hiporal Era. I've got news for you; this is the age of the Marcks, and they don't care about a treaty." She was beginning to wonder about this Tolagon's overly sheltered and primitive rearing. She looked concerned.

"Well, I never even seen a Marck before today, so I would say they are honoring the treaty, at least somewhat," his whisper broke slightly into a normal voice.

She gave a frustrated sigh. "It's only because they haven't had a reason to go into your lands. If they discover that you have the orb, they will wipe Troika out to get it. You're kidding yourself if you think otherwise."

"What do they want with the orb? I mean, it's not like a Marck can use its power anyway, right?" He pointed at his chest in reference.

"To keep its power from being used against them," she paused for a few seconds, "and also to get it into the hands of their unsanctioned leader, Zearic."

Crix's curiosity perked up upon hearing that. "Zearic? But the Marcks are self-governing. They're not supposed to be under anyone's direct control."

She stood up and dusted off her hands. "Well, it appears they are, and by the worst possible tyrant there is. Zearic is a ruthless power monger, and he wasn't about to let an oppressive force such as the Marcks exist without getting his hands behind the controls! The people of this system have been tricked, and it's time they wake up while there is still a chance at taking Zearic down.

That ship I crashed in was the X88T, a prototype designed to system jump without the need of portals through its own internal Nurac gravity drive. I 'liberated' it from Zearic as it was being transferred from the Scientific Propulsion Labs for his inspection."

Crix's eyes widened. "That's fantastic! I mean, for the UMO to have the technology to build a fleet that can travel independently to other systems without the need of those stationary portals. But . . . wait! You stole it from Zearic?"

She gazed at him, exasperated. "You're still not grasping what is going on here. Zearic's intention is to mass-produce the prototype so he can scour the galaxy for Eesolan, the Luminar homeworld, in search of the white orb. He was able to narrow their homeworld location by means of torturing members of the Luminar emissaries that voluntarily stayed behind as peaceful advisers. The few that he didn't kill were driven into seclusion. Fortunately, the Luminars dismantled the gammac corridors that could lead them to Eesolan soon after the Thraxons used them to get here. Don't you understand what would happen if the white orb fell into the hands of a maniacal tyrant such as Zearic?"

"My guess is that would not be good." Crix shrugged his shoulders.

"According to the Luminar legend, whoever possesses the white orb could summon Cyos, the living nebula from which all orbs were spawned. I have no idea how they have determined this, but that's the legend, and that's enough to have everyone on edge. The white orb itself is allegedly too powerful for anyone to wield as the Tolagons have. It would kill anything that merged with it and has reportedly done so with the Luminars that have attempted it," she explained.

He rubbed his chin lightly. "Yes, I have heard the stories of Cyos and its mythical world-decaying capabilities. Its lore has even made its way into the inner regions of Troika, scary for sure. I have always assumed it nothing more than stories used to frighten children. I would have never thought something like that would have really existed."

He then grasped the seriousness and reality of the situation. "If it does exist, this Zearic could use it to instill fear and terror into any system he wanted to control." Crix looked concerned. "So now what? Since they've recovered the crashed prototype, what's your plan?"

She gazed up and into his eyes with a sudden sense of awareness. "I think you're the key."

His eyes widen. "Me?" Crix responded, shocked.

"Yes. There is a reason, whether fundamentally or spiritually, that you have bonded to the orb undetected all these years. I believe unseen forces are in play all around you. Forces for which you haven't crossed paths with but are destined to, and they will lead you to your purpose."

A hissing crept out from the woods. "Psst." They both turned into the direction of the dark undergrowth and brush. "Pssst." Krath waved them over. Together, they crept over to him, taking care not to step on anything that would make too much noise.

"The woods are crawlin' with stalkers," he whispered.

"We know, we encountered one as well," Kerriah replied.

"Well, at least tya weren't sighted because if tya were, we would be knee-deep in Marck scrap metal trottin' around all over the place. It's not safe to travel through here in the open. Lucky for tya, I know another way that'll require a little swimmin'." He led them down a hill, and then they followed a dry creek bed for a short distance.

The chirps and whistles of nighttime creatures fell silent as they hurried through the mesh of vines and low-hanging branches that led to an opening in the woods. The weeping trees leaned inward to a large pond that had a greyish green layer of soot, almost velvet in appearance, which covered the surface. Green and brown vines weaved in numerous directions across the pond. As they approached, the surface swirled in various directions as serpents fled from its edge and into the water.

Realizing what Krath had in mind, Crix stopped. He thought to himself, *not again.* "No . . . no . . . no! You have to be kidding me. I'm not going into that cesspool."

Krath turned around with a hidden smirk regarding his squeamishness. "Lad, we have to. There's no other way to get to Troika undetected. Besides, we need to get tya some good ole fashioned culture."

Crix placed both hands atop his head in disbelief. "Ohh great, just what I needed to be cultured by, slime and parasites." He noticed that Kerriah appeared to be unfazed by the idea as she stood there staring at the pond as though studying every possible scenario.

Krath cleared a chunk of phlegm from his throat before dipping his hand into the thick water. "Deep at the bottom of this pond is a small opening that leads to an underground river. That river leads to the inner reaches of Troika at Lake Medu. It's a long way, and the two of tya cannot make it without assistance."

"Okay, what's your plan?" Kerriah asked.

"Well, the way I figure it, I can swim fast and hold my breath for a long time, long enough to make it to Troika through this underground system. I have done it before. Tya two can't. But if I pull tya and tya have some oxygen, we should be able to make it." He looked over at Crix. "Tya'll have to use the orb to create an oxygen bubble around tya both. I've seen Corin do it before, so I know it can be done. The Marcks should lose your orb energy signature so deep underground. We can't travel in the open with the stalkers and Marck patrols scourin' the area for us. We'll have better odds underground."

Crix squatted down and swiped his hands down his face. A sick feeling suddenly drained his strength. "I don't know. I just started using the orb's powers a day ago and have never even tried to create an air bubble before. I don't know . . . I just don't know." Crix could feel a deep pit form in his stomach, and his brain raced with anxiety.

Krath slowly approached Crix and placed his hand on his shoulder. "Lad, tya have it in tya. I seen tya father do unbelievable things, and I know tya can too."

Crix turned toward Kerriah; she had an uneasy look as well. That struck him deeply. Although he had only known her for a short time, she was important. He knew he could not let her down. He understood that the Marcks capturing her, or worse, was not an option. The spirit and honor of his father were on the line now, and with a calming breath, he came to the affirmation that he could and would do this.

"Okay, I can do this. Just stand back a minute so I can test this out first."

"Do what tya need to, but be quick about it. Once tya start using it, we're going to be overrun with all sorts of recycled electronics buzzin' around here givin' me a headache."

Krath and Kerriah both stepped back from Crix. He closed his eyes and tightened his fists. A bass hum and a bluish glare intensified from around his body. A crackling began drowning out the hum and a blue glare strobed. With a blinding flash and a loud snap, the spectacle ended.

Crix was down on one knee; his left hand was intensely clenching his chest as if in pain, and he was propping himself up with his right. Adrenaline rushed through his body. His arms quivered and twitched. Kerriah ran over to comfort him and placed her hand on his back. Just as she made contact, she jerked it back.

"Ouch!" she yelled and looked at him with astonishment. "Crix . . . are you all right? Your body just shocked me."

Crix sat back still holding his chest and breathing heavily. "My heart started racing, and I couldn't stop it. I'm okay now. I think I can do this. I think I know what to do now." He got back on his feet and stretched out his arms to the sides. He took a deep, low breath to slow down his nerves. A blueish arc formed on each side of Crix. Then, encompassed in a flawless globe of blue light, Crix exhaled forcefully, and the globe expanded. He placed his arms down, and the globe dissipated instantly in the air.

Krath took an impatient glance over both shoulders. "Tya got it now? The Marcks are gonna be bearing down on us any minute."

"Yes, let's get going." Crix motioned to Kerriah. She moved to his side and snuggled against his chest. "Hang on," he whispered.

"Hang on there before tya get all lit up again." Krath pulled a section of rope from his knapsack and looped it through Crix's belt loops and around his waist. Then he tied the other end across his own shoulder.

"Okay, do tya thing," Krath grumbled.

Crix again formed a perfect, blue globe, but this time, it was around both himself and Kerriah. Now connected to them, Krath dove into the pond, snapping the blue sphere in behind him. The globe was a success. It kept the water repressed while holding a life-supporting air pocket.

Kerriah clung tight against Crix's chest as Krath pulled them through a crevasse at the bottom of the murky pond. He followed it, entered a tunnel, and then went into a large, black opening under the lake. It was a frightening sight as they passed into complete darkness. The temperature dropped as they continued to travel deeper into the strange, underground river.

Crix strained to keep the globe intact, and Kerriah held as still as possible. She did not want to distract him from his efforts. Crix felt her heart beating as she held him tight. Bizarre images strobed into his view, images of glowing-eyed creatures with long, red fangs. He managed to shake each one-off, but they continued to change, and each one was more horrific than the first. His focus had to remain steadfast, and he took captive every thought no matter what was happening around him. He understood that one tinge of fear or straying thought could affect the orb's power and collapse the globe.

The blackness around them was ominous, and at one point, there was a deep, metallic echo, as though a large bell rang inside the mysterious depths. That sound, coupled with the sights unseen, sent a creeping chill down Crix's spine.

After a while, they took shorter breaths. Their lungs felt heavy as the air started to run thin inside the globe. Then, without notice, they felt a strong force pulling upward toward the surface. Relieved but shaken, they found themselves floating in a cool stream of fast-running water. Bright green moss hung from decaying trees that lined the banks.

We made it.

Crix looked at Kerriah. She looked directly into his eyes, raised her eyebrows, and cocked her head to the side as if she never had any doubts concerning their plan. The water tossed the globe around and splashes of water smacked against its blue walls. Krath flung them upon a grassy bank, and Crix collapsed the globe, hoping it was quick enough to avoid Marck detection. They drew deep breaths, taking in the cool fresh air; its sweetness kissed their lungs with relief.

Kerriah curiously observed something different about Crix. She noticed a small bit of white hair on his head that she did not recall seeing before.

"Looks like you have got some white hair," she pronounced as she remembered that all Tolagon's hair eventually turned white as a side effect from using the orb. Crix brushed his hand above his ears as though trying to feel the new change in color.

"You know, if you keep using the orb, you're going to go entirely white, don't you?" Kerriah smiled.

Crix had never heard of this side effect. He had very little understanding or knowledge about this new power. Tolagons were somewhat of a taboo subject in Troika as there had never been an Andor Tolagon. Therefore, the Andor populace mostly considered the topic unworthy of mentioning during common discussions and teachings. He wondered . . . were there any other side effects that he did not know about or understand?

CHAPTER 6

W e should now be on the eastern edge of the Draylok Province of Troika," Krath announced. He felt a small grumble in his stomach.

"Wow! We're not too far from my home! That was quick," Crix said. He was excited to be home and to be close to what was familiar and safe. He was not going to miss the hostile lands of Drisal but was grateful for the new friends he found, especially Kerriah.

"The natural flow of the water carried us quicker than I expected, would have been quicker had I not run headlong into that strange hunk of metal down there. Sure would like to know what that was." Krath rubbed an apparent, large bump on his head.

"I believe this stream feeds into Lake Medu. I really need to check in with my keeper. He hasn't seen or heard from me for nearly two days now, and I'm sure he's going to be worried. Besides, I'm starving, and he'll cook us up something. He never misses on making a great meal for guests," Crix explained. The thought of having a home-cooked meal, sparked his eagerness to get back.

Krath immediately perked up at the thought of food. Grinning and patting his stomach. "Let's get movin, the sooner, the better." Kerriah nodded in agreement, while preoccupied with inspecting the underside of her belt.

***

The white sun broke across the horizon as they set out across the grasslands of Draylok. The lands were rich in deep green grass with a peppering of spiraled trees, which corkscrewed high into the cranberry-tinted sky with umbrella canopies. It was simple yet impressive. While traveling, they passed Andors working in fields of ort grass and golden beru grains. The beru grains grew to around waist height of the common Andor and were one of the most highly utilized food sources in Troika. The Andors were always friendly in gesture, but today looked at them with concern in their eyes.

After a while, the rolling fields turned into the wooded region of Hemlor, and then this area led them to a canton of sparsely clustered homes with steep, triangular rooftops. The whimsical rooftops were a mixture of dark wood and thatch with large, black pipes protruding in a swooping curve from either side. The small clusters of homes gave way to a much larger and denser population of Andor households until they found themselves in the heart of the residential community of Hemlor.

The entrance of the community had a series of light-russet stone roads that twisted around the warm, rustic homes like snakes that cozied amongst them. Smoke from burning wood drifted gently by in the cool, crisp, evening air. This heavy peat aroma lent to the rustic mood of the township. Children's voices echoed from various directions, and occasionally, an Andorian child would dart by and pause, startled by the sight of the interlopers. Andors considered interlopers to be those who did not belong.

One small girl, chased by several others, ran squarely into Krath. She looked up at him, and he offered her a tender grin. She staggered back, horrified, and then let out a wild shriek before running back in the opposite direction. Her friends followed in her wake as her light-blue mane, fastened with a ribbon, disappeared behind a fence.

Krath shrugged. "Guess she was overwhelmed by my handsome mug. Probably headin' home to set me up with her momma."

Kerriah rolled her eyes. "More like going to get a club."

"Hey there!" Krath grumbled, taking offense to her remark.

"Come on, my home is just a little way down here." Crix picked up his pace, and then stopped suddenly.

Krath lumbered up behind him. "What's up, kid?"

Crix gave no reply for a few seconds as he stared forward in frozen apprehension at a group of youthful, male Andors bouncing a humming sphere between themselves. One of the Andors was exceptionally tall and pranced around with an air of cockiness while knocking the others back to gain control of the sphere. Then he stopped with the sphere balanced, still in his hand. Yet the other Andor continued to grasp at it, and then he looked over and noticed Crix. His facial expression was that of anger or even hatred.

"Uhh . . . let's cut through here." Crix pointed awkwardly to a path between two homes that led to the back courtyards. "It'll be quicker."

"Hey!" the voice of the Andor boomed out. "Where do you think you're going, Chiro?"

Before Crix was able to step into the grassy lane, the Andor charged toward him with his entourage following in close step. They were dressed similarly in black, V-cut t-shirts with a red, circular emblem embroidered on them displaying the letters TZ Five. The hostile leader kept flexing his lean muscles and pulling at the waistline of his pants. Andors, with their equine facial features, tended to have a regal appearance when calm but could look intimidating when angered, as this particular one was right now.

The Andor youth stopped nose to nose with Crix. His breath reeked; it smelled like pungent dra cabbage and caused Crix to take a step back. The Andor flicked his jet-black mane back over his dark-toned neck and stepped intentionally on Crix's foot, pressing down firmly.

"So . . . where were you yesterday?" He asked with a half-grin and a tone of satire in his voice. "Not that it would have made any difference in the punishment we handed to your pathetic excuse for an annexis team." He swung around for a second to give a smug look back at his group. "I was looking forward to putting a serious hurt on you personally. Humph, we figured you were probably cowering since I rang your bell last time we met."

The Andor stepped back and violently shoved Crix into Krath. "That's okay because I just had to let it out on your buddy

Tirix instead. His shattered leg should put him out of annexis forever." He let out an obnoxious chuckle, the kind that draws out feelings of pure loathing and ill will toward the source of such a clamor.

Crix was trying to control his temper. His thoughts sunk deep over the news that his best friend Tirix was hurt by this wretch.

Krath growled, irritated by having had someone shoved into him. Crix's brow scrunched. "Akhal, why do you have to be such a dunderhead?"

"A what? What was that?" Akhal shouted. His eyes bulged as he got so close to Crix that Crix could feel his breath on him.

"Dunderhead," Crix replied, gritting his teeth. "Look, I just want to get home." He was growing frustrated by this encounter.

"Home? How many times do I have to explain this to you? This is not your home. Troika are lands reserved for Andors, and you still don't look like an Andor to me." He looked around and gave out a nagging laugh. "Further, these things you have tagging along with you don't look like Andors either. What is it that you have against Troika? You want to defecate its lands with all manner of parasitic species?" He looked over at Krath with a scowl.

Krath puffed up, his arms cocked out to either side. "Look here, pal, I don't know tya, but those are fightin' words as far as I'm concerned. Besides, I'm not thinkin' tya are a friend of Crix's, so I don't know who's going to keep tya from gettin' hurt. I know it won't be those bright-eyed fawns behind tya." Krath gave a piercing stare into the Andor's eyes while swaying his head slowly back and forth intensely. The other Andors behind him all inched back to a safe distance.

"Krath . . ." Crix placed his hand on Krath's back. "This is my problem, not yours."

"Ya well, it's gettin' real close to being my problem as well," Krath snapped.

"Pfft . . . Take your best shot, gramps." Arrogantly, Akhal turned back to the group for support, and then as he turned his head back again, he felt the force of a sledgehammer cracking him in the chin. His body lifted up a meter or two from the ground and landed, unforgivingly, on his upper back. He laid there groaning, motionless, his forehead furrowed, and Crix noticed the state of confusion in his eyes. The other young Andors looked at him with shock then completely scattered from the area.

"What the heck happened to Andors? The ones I used to know were tough and strong spirited! These cocky, weak-backed youth remind me more of your typical Mendac." He paused to clear his throat. "Not faultin' tya guys."

"Believe me, those thugs don't represent the best of Andors, not by a long shot. I suppose every species must have its cretins," Crix replied in defense of his adoptive species. Krath gave a low exhale in an expression of his deep feeling of pessimism for the Andor race.

Akhal slowly started to get up to his knees, and then, finally, to his feet. Still holding his chin, he looked at Crix. "You're going to pay for that, Chiro. You and this refuse you brought with you."

Krath stepped in his direction with an authoritative growl. Akhal was not willing to risk another blow and sulked away, disappearing amongst the clutter of dwellings.

CHAPTER 7

They continued down the winding road until they came upon a well-manicured yard with a pristinely maintained Andorian dwelling centered upon it. A contrasting, light-wood awning protruded from the narrow front door. Light smoke curled up from the leftmost stack and merged into the smoke from adjacent dwellings. A metal fence surrounded the front yard, and Crix flicked the latch across the top to open it. It smoothly glided open without even so much as a timid squeak from its hinges. They entered the homestead, and Crix announced their entry aloud. There was no answer.

"Keeper Haflinger!" he called again. "Huh? He's got to be here somewhere. He left the door unlocked. He would never leave the door unlocked if he wasn't home. In fact, he's probably the only Andor in Troika that's neurotic about keeping his doors locked. Troika's relatively free of crime and most don't even bother."

He walked cautiously through the rustic, squared vestibule. Several heavy-grained timber beams lined the area, and the ceiling glowed with champagne-thatched wood. Crix looked around and quickened his pace; Kerriah and Krath followed. He felt something was amiss. As they entered the main living area, the floors creaked with every step. The furnishings were bulky in appearance with dull, black, metal hinges and rivets; they looked primitive yet durable. The dry air was warm; a slight aroma of burnt wood and dust filled the home. Shafts of light from the tall windows cut into the darkness and dispersed across the middle of the floor. It was quiet. In a dimly lit, far corner, a life-sized wooden statue of an Andor stood guard. It wore a murky tan and green uniform, tattered and weathered in appearance.

"That looks familiar." Krath motioned toward the uniform and then resumed scanning the room.

Crix smiled, feeling a sense of pride and respect for his keeper. "Haflinger was a Morak Sergeant and fought in the first Thraxon War." As they approached it closer, the light glistened from a curved blade that fastened across the front of the uniform.

Krath leaned in toward the statue for a closer look. "Yep . . . seen quite a few of those rotten, smelly, black critters from the war get the wrong end of one of those. I'll give them Andors this; they're friggin' lethal with those tectonic blades."

The grinding of heavy wood sliding across the hard floor echoed across the room as Crix pushed open the door at the back of the dwelling.

"Haflinger!" he shouted as he rushed out the back door. Startled by the commotion, Krath and Kerriah followed close behind. They both stepped outside and watched as Crix knelt down over a grey and white Andor that was lying on the ground disorientated. The Andor's thin grey arm slowly reached up and made contact with Crix's cheek.

"W—where have you been?" he asked Crix in a withered voice. "I thought for sure they must have found you. I was going to purge the Tolagon relic." Crix grasped his hand and laid it down on Haflinger's chest.

The old Andor was shaking. His hand was frail and cold. The many years of keeping this child's identity, the bearer of the blue orb, a secret and comprehending the ramifications of their discovery had weighed greatly upon him. The stress was too much. The thought of Crix's capture was the tipping point for his well-worn heart, and he used the last of his strength to cover up the evidence that would bring destruction to his beloved nation.

"No, just relax, I need to fetch Agon. Let me get you to your bedding."

The Andor closed his eyes for a moment and shook his head. "It's too late for me, young one. The time has come for me to join my ancestry in Mothoa so my spirit can be one with the Equus, our great guardian and father." He pointed to a spot on the ground near a smoldering hole. This was where he had, earlier, dropped the important relic before being able to place it in the hole with a thermal purging cube. Haflinger kept these cubes for this specific purpose. Crix noticed the cube had recently burned out.

"There . . . there you will find the most important item I can ever give you." As he gasped for air, he continued to point at something on the ground near the hole. It was an onyx bracer inlaid with a blue signet. The dark bracer had bright-white lines swirling across its surface. Crix reached over and grasped the bracer from the ground. At that moment, as he touched it, the white lines formed into shapes on each side.

"What is it?" Crix's thoughts felt jumbled and confused.

"Opens the place of your destiny, the . . . location . . . phan . . . tss." Haflinger exhaled his last breath as his hand lifelessly dropped into Crix's lap.

"No! I've . . . I've only been missing for two days!" Crix cried out as he buried his face into Haflinger's chest. "What am I going to do now? I have no one." His voice was quiet and muffled, his head still down. Crix always felt like a stranger in Troika. Kerriah knelt down and tenderly placed her hand on his shoulder.

Sympathetically, Krath looked at the young Mendac kneeling beside his keeper. "Tya're time here in Troika is at an end. Tya were never meant to settle here permanently. It's time for tya to take up the mantle of what tya're destined for."

Crix turned angrily at him. "You keep telling me this, but why me? Why does this . . . this thing, this burden, have to fall on me? I never asked for it. I didn't want it!" Crix thought about how he always lived around the orb and its responsibilities. His whole life, he'd struggled to claw out whatever form of normalcy he could attain. He, as a Mendac, even began viewing himself as an Andor physically, mentally, and genealogically. His emotions ran wild as everything he knew was changing.

***

The local magistrate arrived to gather Haflinger's body. Crix stood at the front door speaking to the respectful appearing figure of Andorian authority clad in a long, brown trench coat with black boots. A light rain picked up to a steady pour. The magistrate's wide-brimmed hat formed thin streams of water that drizzled down its creases. His voice was stern and commanding but with an undertone of sympathy.

"Crix, I feel for your loss. Your Andorian keeper was a friend of mine and a respected member of our community. Sadly, as you know by law, only natural-born Andors can inherit or own Andor land and property. You will have to leave the premises as Haflinger had no other Andor family to pass on his estate to. The Troika local assessor will seize the property.

"Normally, you would have one day to vacate, but out of respect for your situation and Haflinger, I will postpone this requirement for as long as I can. I figure I can get you a week to find out where you can go. In two days, we will have his funeral rite prepared, and of course, you are welcome to attend and pay your last respects. It will be held at the Third Altar of Equus, on the eve of the day. If you're hurting for a place to stay, I can make space for you at my farm until you find something permanent.

"I know you and Tirix were planning to enlist with the Moraks. You would be more than welcome to stay until you were accepted and training completed." Crix looked down and said nothing in response. "Well, good luck to you, son." The magistrate grasped Crix's hand and gave it a firm shake then turned away into the rainfall.

"You're coming back to Teinol with me as soon as we get your affairs in order here," Kerriah said as she slowly snuck up behind him, having overheard the conversation with the magistrate. Crix looked back at her with broken eyes. "Sorry, I couldn't help but overhear what you were just told. Krath is right; this chapter of your life is behind you now. There's a whole new world out there for you to experience, and I have a feeling your adventure is just about to begin." Kerriah spoke with optimism and hope. However, Crix remained quiet and provided very little discussion for the rest of the evening.

As they bedded down for the night, a storm rolled in, and the rain violently pounded against the roof as if twenty angry giants were banging away with their clenched fists. The thunder cracked continuously throughout the night, keeping their sleep light. The home seemed empty and hollow.

CHAPTER 8

The next morning, Krath and Kerriah awoke to the commotion of Crix pulling on a padded jumpsuit and calf-high sport boots. Kerriah noticed an emblem displayed on the back of the suit, a red inverted triangle underscored with a horizontal line. Hundreds of light tubes were weaved throughout the one-piece suit, which gave it a faintly reflective shine. He tightly fastened it with metal buckles that went from his throat down to his lower torso. As he sprung up from the chair, he snatched up a grey helmet and started toward the door.

"I'll be back in a little while. There's food in the cupboard if you guys get hungry."

Kerriah stepped around him, swiping her index finger around his collar. "Hey! Where are you going dressed like that?" Crix could not help but smile. She was beautiful.

Eagerly, he started to explain the details of his favorite pastime. "Well . . . it's called annexis, and it is a popular Andor hard-contact sport in these parts. I play the forward, the person that has to get the other team's two batons and attach them to our own base for the win." Crix's voice quickened. "The best part is the setting. The arena is in the interconnecting Barrillian Vortex. Also, it can get pretty intense since the opposing team is trying to knock you senseless in order to keep you from completing your objective."

Krath now looked interested and snapped his head in full attention to Crix's explanation. "This is beginnin' to sound like my type of entertainment! So tya get to bust some heads?"

"The Barrillian Vortex? Hmmmm? I have heard of Andors jumping down into that for some sort of sport. I always thought those were rumors or, at best, exaggerated stories," Kerriah added.

Crix grinned and then continued to clarify. He enjoyed explaining how things worked. "Yes, that's part of it! An abnormal barometric pressure system underground from a source unknown feeds two naturally formed vertical tunnels, and that creates a wind vortex. This condition gives those who enter a weightless effect!" Crix gestured with his hands as though he was weightless.

"The two vortex tunnels converge at the lower center called the blind zone because, at that level, there is almost no visible light. The team's bases are located over the tunnel entrances. It's a crazy and unpredictable game as traversing the vertical tunnels can get fast and tricky, especially since the opposing team's sentries are looking to take your head off with their quorum sticks to stop you from reaching your goal. Luckily, I have two of the best guards around!"

Crix's tone changed as he stared down at the floor. "Unfortunately, Tirix was playing forward in my absence and got roughed up by that unfriendly individual you met in the street yesterday. He has a broken arm and leg." Crix snarled his nose and clenched his teeth at the thought of Akhal. "My team is currently in the midst of a championship series against TZ Five, Akhal's team. We were one game from winning the series before that crushing loss two days ago. Today's game decides the championship. I have to be there." Crix fidgeted with the helmet he was holding.

Krath bounced up with eagerness to go watch, but Kerriah placed her hand up to stop him. Crix looked at her and hoped she would understand.

"Wait, are you sure you're up for this?" she questioned. "I mean you just discovered that your only family member is dead and that you're to be evicted from your home. That's on top of everything we just went through. This just seems irrational that you would want to go play some game right now."

Crix looked down again and kicked at a loose plank on the floor. "I know it seems senseless from the outside, but I have to do this. I already let my friends down. At this point, they are all I have left in Troika. I can't do it to them again, or I will just lose myself and all things that tie me to my childhood." He was not ready to succumb to grief. He wanted to push it aside and deal with it another day.

Kerriah touched his arm and looked directly into his eyes. "I get it. It's just that I . . . we," she looked back glaring briefly at Krath, "we cannot have you get hurt over something like this right now. You have to look at things from a bigger perspective now."

"I am! I—" Crix shouted in frustration over this lecture. He wanted to explain but could not. He just needed to make things right. His life was spinning out of control, and this game was something that he could still do for his friends, win something that was important to them. "Look, I understand that you don't get what's going on with me right now, but I have to do this regardless of whether it's right or wrong!"

Kerriah dropped her grasp of his arm and let out an exhausting sigh. "Fine."

Krath looked at each of them, and then resumed his enthusiasm over watching a full-contact sport. "Well, little buddy, let's get goin'. We can't have tya lettin' your buddies down again on our account. Besides, I could use a little spectatin' leisure time." Crix quietly sighed. He felt an elevated sense of pressure at the thought of his newfound companions watching the big game.

"Sure, if you guys want to watch, I could probably get you into the player's zone," Crix hesitantly replied.

"I wouldn't miss it for anything," Kerriah assured. "But we are going to have to go there under concealment. Marck agents, searchers, or satellites could possibly detect us here in the open. We should take extra precautions," she reminded them both and tapped her finger to her chin while trying to devise a plan. Kerriah was always thinking two steps ahead of everyone else.

Crix placed his hands on top of his head, exhaled, and then turned to leave the room. He returned in a couple of minutes with two dark grey cloaks in his arms. He threw one to Kerriah and held the other up, eyeing it against Krath's big frame.

"Hmmm, not sure how this is going to fit your husky build. I think it will, though you may look a bit silly." He snickered.

"Hahaha, go ahead, make fun of the old guy, real cute." Krath snatched the cloak from Crix.

"We had these from a funeral rite we attended several years back." Crix remembered attending this funeral with Haflinger. It was for one of Haflinger's oldest friends.

Crix could not believe Haflinger was gone. He shook his head as if trying to shake out the memory. He could not think about that right now. He needed to focus. The two slipped on the heavy cloaks, and immediately, Krath's split down the backside as he attempted to cinch it around his broad shoulders. Kerriah looked away to hide her smile from Krath.

"Well, at least I can breathe now," he said as the torn garment hung to his knees and elbows, giving him the appearance of an overstuffed doll.

***

They arrived via public transport carts pulled by droona beasts. When the locals saw Crix in his uniform, they gave cheers of admiration. Upon their arrival, the crowds were already standing around tiered, circular catwalks above the two tunnel entrances of the Barrillian Vortex Arena; they were roaring and chanting with pure crazed excitement.

Underneath the crowd noise, there was a heavy rumbling from the vortex as the air pulled in and pushed out of the two massive holes below. Crix and his new friends' eardrums pulsated with the continual changes in air pressure as they neared the interconnecting arena. Krath dug his finger in his left outer ear and muttered something under his breath.

Kerriah was amazed at the sights and sounds of this event. At random times, long funnels of air shot out from the gigantic holes, and the crowds cheered in anticipation. She found herself mesmerized by all the activity and excitement. The large spectator girders, constructed from timber, encircled the vortex openings from high above, and some spanned crisscrossed allowing a direct, downward view into the lighted tunnels below.

As they approached the tall, wooden gate to the player's concourse, it groaned open slowly and revealed an off-limits area. Before them stood two stout Andors that blocked their way.

"Crix!" One of them greeted him, and then looked over at his odd-looking travel companions with a surprised look on his face. "Are you ready for the big game? I know your team sure missed you at the last engagement," the robust Andor inquired.

"As ready as I'm going to be, Claynor."

"Well, I'm sure they'll be happy to see you. They are over there by Vortex One," Claynor said. The other Andor stood firmly while staring hard at Krath and Kerriah.

Crix casually popped Claynor in the chest with the back of his hand and motioned to Krath and Kerriah.

"Claynor, these are my friends visiting from off territory, and they've never seen annexis played before. Do you mind if they join me in the player zone for an up-close experience?"

Claynor sized them both up. "Hmmm, I don't know. They're a strange-looking lot. Off territory, huh? I typically don't allow outsiders in the player zone. In fact, I don't usually let outsiders in at all." His lips flapped in a loud exhale. "Okay, just this once. I don't want any trouble in there, understood?" He pointed authoritatively at Krath and Kerriah.

They both nodded in agreement. He stepped aside and allowed them to pass. As Crix passed by, Claynor shouted, "Hey, Crix. I'm real sorry to hear about Haflinger." Crix solemnly bowed his head in reply and continued walking toward his team. He could feel the tightness of grief build up in his throat, but today, he would concentrate on the game and his friends.

At Vortex One, the five players of team Gears gathered around with their helmets under their arms, strategizing the forthcoming game. One of the sentries, Alta, looked up and noticed Crix.

"Crix! All right, now we have a game!" he shouted, excited over seeing him. The other team members walked over to express their relief that he was there, except for Tirix. He remained back with a look of contempt on his face.

"What's wrong with Tirix?" Crix appeared concerned.

"Well, you're not exactly his favorite Andorian alien resident right now. After missing the last game, I suppose you can't blame him. Akhal put a real hurt on him. His leg is in bad shape. Your no-show weakened our team. But hey, I just want to win this thing today and maybe put a little hurt on Akhal, if possible," Clyde, the bulky guard for the team, replied with a wink. "Also we are a player short, so I brought in my cousin Caspi for the guard position. Caspi is no Tirix, but he's no greenhorn either. He should be able to hold his own out there and cover your flank." Crix looked over at Caspi with skepticism. Next to Clyde, Caspi was relatively small for a typical annexis guard.

"Not to worry, Crix, I won't let you down." Caspi defended his small stature. Crix shook his hand and observed his bright tan hide and muscular build, which gave him a youthful, athletic appearance; however, his neatly braided silver mane and soft hands seemed more like someone who would enjoy reading books rather than smacking people with quorum sticks. Crix was unsure how he could help, but they did not have any other option.

"Okay, well, I suppose we don't have any alternatives at this point," Crix responded. "Give me a minute." Crix walked over to reconcile with Tirix but received an ice-cold greeting.

"What do you want?" Tirix mumbled with his leg propped up in a splint. He was wearing a drab green shirt torn near the neckline, his normally deep red skin tone appeared washed out, and his thick, black mane was unkempt.

He looks bad. He doesn't look like himself, Crix thought, and then whispered, "Tirix, I feel terrible for letting you guys down. I really do, but there is something larger than any annexis match going on right now. Besides—"

"No! You know what? Just forget it! I don't want to hear your sorry excuses anyway! This is the most important series of the season and probably the most important one for us ever! You couldn't even let us know where you were so we could at least take a forfeit! Instead, we got it handed to us in a bad way, and now, I'm out for the final game! We could have finally stripped the championship title from those lowlifes!" Tirix's chest constricted rapidly, winded from his angry rant. He was not able to see past his resentment of the unfair loss due to Crix's absence. He only wanted to stew in his rage and unhappiness.

"We still ca—" The loudspeakers introducing the teams and playing up to the crowd interrupted Crix. He looked at Tirix and then at the team. "Let's get into position, guys," Crix commanded his team, having to leave the relationship mending with Tirix for later.

Together, Crix's team placed on their helmets and took their positions around Vortex One, their assigned base and entrance to the arena. The Barrillian Vortex Arena had two entrances, one for each team. Each entrance opened to a tunnel that leads to the blind zone, and then over to the other team's tunnel. TZ Five, Akhal's team, took position over Vortex Two. The game was about to begin.

All players clipped their belts to suspension cables that anchored to the top of their vortex entrance. They leaned inward over the tunnels while the anchors kept them secure. An annexis official placed the individual scoring batons via long hooks to a permanently fused pole across each entrance, and each team had two batons. Directly above, the crowds peered downward from spiraled decks built of sturdy timber. The players' adrenaline started to surge.

As Crix looked straight down into the gusting, wind-filled holes, he thought about Tirix, wishing he were there alongside him. The view down would give anyone not well experienced in the sport a sickening pit of dizziness within the stomach. Each team member grabbed a quorum stick, clenching it with both hands, prepared to defend their batons and attack the opposing team.

Kerriah and Krath stood on the lower maintenance tier of the observation deck. It provided a closer view than that of the regular spectators. They could feel the waves of vibrations under their feet. Kerriah looked down into the tunnels as the powerful air gusts spouted, swirled, and reverberated below her. She raised one eyebrow questioningly and looked over at Krath. "These guys must be nuts."

Krath just continued to stare intently, almost jealous that he was not latched onto the edge of the vortex tunnel. "The thrill of danger and a sport cross all species. 'Sides . . . I could think of much worse things they could be doin' with their time. Like listenin' to some blabbering government politician flap his lips, idolizing idiots, or starin' at their comm devices like lifeless machines." Kerriah gave him a smirk and shook her head.

"I still think they're nuts," she repeated and rolled her eyes.

Four ceremonial Andors positioned further back from the tunnels held red flags high in the air. Loud horns blasted out above the cheers of the crowds. As they lowered the flags, the players released their clasps and dropped perilously down into the two tunnels. From a spectator viewpoint, their bodies became smaller as they fell deeper into the vortex, with the exception of the sentries. These two team members leveled out and took advantage of the prevailing air gusts; their job was to hover near the top of their tunnel to protect the team's two batons, which hung on a pole suspended above their entrance.

Deeper inside, Crix and his two guards skillfully pointed their bodies downward into a diving position to reach the blind zone faster. The blind zone was the center point where the two vortex tunnels joined. These players fought against the constant pushing and pulling of the powerful underground winds created by the abnormal barometric pressure system, and each focused on reaching their objective—retrieving the other team's batons—while not being smashed into the jagged sidewalls of the tunnel.

Crix noticed that Caspi had already fallen behind and lagged too far to offer any protection from Akhal and his guards. Through his helmet comm, Crix shouted at Caspi, "Caspi, you have to keep up. We can't get separated!" Caspi did not reply.

The light faded behind Crix as he continued to dive deeper into the tunnel, and the hundreds of tubes woven in his jumpsuit began to glow. He and his other guard, Clyde, quickly reached the bottom of Vortex One. They gracefully sprung up from the lower joining iron grid within the blind zone and propelled themselves toward TZ Five's entrance and their two batons. This was a fast-moving game. A spike of adrenaline jolted through Crix as he realized that they reached the blind zone before Akhal. They were in the opposing team's tunnel, Vortex Two. Caspi was still not answering, but that did not keep Crix from being excited. He felt like nothing could go wrong. He was on the move and charged up.

However, he did not revel in that feeling for very long. A jarring blow struck the right side of his helmet. It was Akhal. He fixated on Crix, filled with hate and vengeance. He continued swinging his quorum stick repeatedly with great ferocity and kept Crix pinned up against a protruding rock. Akhal was enraged. The rock dug into Crix's shoulders and back. He felt a shredding pain but ignored it. Akhal twisted his body and used the vortex's wind strength and pressure to gain momentum for each forceful blow. Crix realized he was in trouble. He needed his guards. *Where is Caspi?*

Emerging from the darkness, Clyde swooped in and knocked Akhal away, which gave Crix a second to recover. Crix, not seeing Akhal any longer, darted up toward his primary objective of acquiring the first of two batons needed to secure their victory. Crix maintained his concentration and kept his eye on the prize. He kept his body centered in the middle of the tunnel, where he was able to gain the most speed from the strongest air drafts. Still, Akhal was right behind him, reaching to grab his foot.

Then, all of a sudden with great speed and strength, Caspi fiercely drove Akhal into the tunnel wall with the end of his quorum stick. The silver-maned young Andor was excited to prove himself to Crix.

Now furious and seeking to destroy, Akhal focused his fury on Caspi. He lunged toward the new player and angrily ripped the quorum stick out of Caspi's hands and flung it away like a piece of scrap. Caspi was shocked; Akhal had moved much faster than he had expected. At that moment, Akhal propelled himself from the tunnel wall and into Caspi, smashing him against the far side. He viciously dragged Caspi's head down the rockface. Caspi's helmet cracked and buckled under the stress until the young Andor finally lost consciousness.

Akhal abandoned Caspi's limp body in the center of Vortex Two's tunnel. His helpless figure flopped around like a twirling leaf in a windstorm. An Andor arbitrator, posted in a narrow offshoot within the tunnel, took notice of Caspi's unconscious body. The arbitrator sent out a single beam of light across the tunnel to indicate the recall of injured players and a pause of the game. Clyde witnessed the unnecessary roughness, rushed over, and secured Caspi's body to an extraction line, and the rest of the players directed themselves out by riding the vortex gusts upward.

***

Back out on the players' concourse, Clyde pulled the crinkled helmet from Caspi's head to check his injuries. The other players of team Gears ran over, concerned about their fallen teammate.

"Are you okay, Caspi? Caspi?" Clyde slapped him across his face in an unsuccessful effort to get him to respond just before the annexis medic on duty nudged him out of the way. The medic placed a beam of light into Caspi's eyes and then called for a gurney. From across the concourse, a conceited grin filled Akhal's face; he had taken down another Gears player.

Clyde observed this act of defiance and was about to spout off a strong response when he was interrupted by the medic. "It looks like he's suffered a severe concussion. We need to take him to the infirmary for a series of internal imaging scans," the medic told the team, and then proceeded to load Caspi onto the gurney.

Enraged by the thought of what Akhal had done to Tirix and now Caspi, Clyde tossed his helmet to the ground and charged at Akhal. He wanted payback. He wanted to settle the score. He wanted to hurt something or someone. He was able to make contact and knock Akhal to the ground; then, all of a sudden, an oversized Andor grabbed Clyde by the throat, lifted him off his feet, and cruelly slammed him to the ground. This Andor was part of the security team at the arena. Before he could do any real harm, the other team members of Gears pulled Clyde back. He kicked and shouted as they muscled him back to their side of the concourse.

"You dirty, no-good sack of droona dung! I ought to tear your arms off for what you've done to Tirix and Caspi!" Clyde, being a large Andor, was not easy to restrain. Akhal dusted himself off and walked back over to his team with fire blazing in his eyes.

"Clyde, we still have a game to win. That's why we're here, and the best thing we can do for Tirix and Caspi right now is beat these guys," Crix said as he tried to refocus his anguished teammate back into the game. Clyde's body shook with adrenaline and twitched with fierce anger. He could not stop staring in Akhal's direction.

Crix understood how Clyde felt, but he also understood the importance of remaining calm and focused. He learned many years ago, living amongst the Andors as an outsider, how to choke back the emotions and move forward with life. Haflinger told him to keep his head down, wait, and to keep control of his desire to use the power that was inside of him. Today, he used this skill to get his team focused and be the leader they needed to win the game.

"Crix, how the heck are we supposed to do that now? We're short a guard once again," Clyde snapped while scowling back across the concourse.

Crix stared at the ground as if he was in a deep thought. "I have an idea. Give me a moment. I'll be back." He sprinted off to the maintenance tiers, leaving his team guessing at what he had planned. Clyde was exasperated and flapped his lips as he exhaled.

"Well . . . hurry! The match will resume in fifteen minutes, player short or not!" Clyde shouted. Thinking about Akhal, he started to pace like a predator that was waiting to kill its next meal.

Crix found Kerriah and Krath watching the events unfold from the lower maintenance tier.

"That was brutal; is your teammate okay?" Kerriah asked, though it was difficult to hear her as the air gusted up from the powerful vortex. Then, for a moment, he could not help but notice how striking she was as she stood there at the edge of the tier. Her hair was tousled from the wind with her milky white cheeks and emerald eyes peeking through her jet-black hair as it lay across her face. The exquisite site sent a tickling sensation fluttering through his heart. He was mesmerized.

He shook his head as if to release himself from a trance. "Caspi should be fine, though he won't be back in the game. Kerriah, I need to ask a favor of you." Crix paused to feel out the tone of her reply before asking.

"Sure, what do you need?" Kerriah responded, intrigued.

"I need a guard, and one I can depend on." He was not sure what it was that tugged at him to ask this of her considering the danger involved. Her reply was expected, yet it still took him off guard.

Her eyes widened. "Wow! I'd love to, but I don't know anything about this crazy sport you guys are playing! I'll likely do you more harm than good." She was always interested in trying new things.

"Normally, I would agree with that statement, but there is something about you." He stopped and started again, but more deliberate, more careful. "You just seem like . . . like, there is nothing you wouldn't excel at." He shook his head again and rolled his eyes. "What am I thinking? I shouldn't be asking you to participate in something so dangerous just for the sake of winning a game. I apologize for even mentioning it!" He turned to walk away, placing his hands on his head in a state of confusion over why he even asked.

"Wait!" she stopped him. "I can help! I want to help. You're right. The whole time I was watching you down there, I was feeling this strong desire to participate, and the more I watched, the more it looked familiar to me. That's how things have been for me my entire life. I'm just surprised that you noticed." Kerriah looked at Crix with pure joy and amazement. She was elated that he understood.

"I knew it! Okay, are you sure? You just saw what happened to Caspi. It can be hazardous to your health." She nodded with perfect assuredness behind her eager smile. "All right! All you need to do is keep Akhal and his guards off me. Let's get you suited up. We haven't much time." Then, over the loudspeakers, the announcer called out a ten-minute warning before the game resumed.

Krath watched Kerriah walk away with Crix and chuckled to himself. He then crossed his arms and had a smug smile across his face. "These guys must be nuts." He snorted and nodded his head, referring to Kerriah's previous statement.

***

Near the team staging area, Crix approached Tirix, who sat upon several wooden crates. "We need your uniform. We have a substitute guard to replace Caspi."

Tirix glanced over at Kerriah and rolled his eyes. "You have to be kidding me! Akhal is going to eat her for lunch."

"You have to trust me on this, just let . . ."

Tirix interrupted him before he could finish. "Ha! She'll be lucky if she doesn't get killed in there, and then you can have that weighing on your conscience as well."

He hopped down, reached behind one of the crates, dragged out a faded black bag, and then shoved it toward Kerriah. "There you go. It's likely going to be a little loose on you, so roll the sleeves and legs up as tight as you can. And that's all the advice I got to give." He then hobbled grudgingly away. The announcer called out the five-minute warning.

"Quickly, you can slip this over your clothes. I'll meet you at the vault," Crix said.

"The vault?"

"It's the rim of the vortex tunnel where we tight line ourselves in for the jump!" he shouted as he was walking away, hurried in his steps. They did not have much time left. He needed to inform the team and officials about the new player. She hastily fitted into the jumpsuit the best she could, giving its large size to her smaller frame. With her sleeves and legs rolled and belted as much as possible, she looked like a little girl that was wearing her father's clothes. She hurried back over to the vault as she heard the countdown finish for the game to resume. Crix and his team unsnapped just before she reached the vortex opening, and they were off as the game started once again, this time with a player short.

Kerriah was unwavering. She charged forward, grabbed a quorum stick from a nearby rack, and dove straight into the vortex without a thought or view below. She boomed past the two sentries that were hovering stationary, guarding the team's batons. Staying in the center and pointing her body in a diving position to maximize velocity, she was able to see Crix and Clyde ahead in the distance, although they vanished from her sight as they entered the blind zone and into the blackness. She tried to tap her comm unit in her helmet to announce her entry, but it failed to respond and instead threw out some static feedback.

As she entered the darkness, she sensed a presence swoosh past her. Then the air pressure suddenly shifted, catching her off balance, and sent her slamming down into the protective iron grate at the base of the treacherous blind zone. Beyond this grate, the Andors believed, was the unknown source of the vortex winds; these powerful air gusts generated from somewhere far below. This protective gate had kept players from disappearing into the deeper tunnels. For a few seconds, the pressure was so intense that she felt like her body was going to pull through the bars. Then, almost as quickly as the unyielding pressure restrained her, the airstream pushed outward again, releasing her from its oppressive grasp. She soared upward until she could see a peek of light from TZ Five's vortex entrance far above.

Kerriah was strategic in her movements and observed her teammate's tactics. Clyde aggressively used his quorum stick and pushed hard against one of the opposing guards, and further up, Crix bounced from wall to wall in an attempt to throw off their sentries. The walls of the cavern, though jagged with sharp rocks, optically melted away from the speed of her ascension. She kept her aim on Crix with a deep, intense focus. She figured out that the trick to rapid ascension was to time the upward air gusts, and then to flatten out her torso to capture the strong winds.

Kerriah started to feel as though she might figure this game out when one of the opposing team's guards smashed his quorum stick into the side of her head. The immense shock echoed through the inside of her helmet. Her eardrums cried out, and dark spots filled her vision as she flew back and glanced off the cavern wall. The guard stayed on her, swinging at her from both sides of his quorum stick and following through with a miss and a jab to her chin, whipping her head back. She fought to remain alert and conscious. He flipped around her with the agility of a dancer; it was obvious that he was a seasoned veteran of this sport. She rebooted herself and continued forward.

Kerriah looked up and noticed a ledge that jutted out of the cavern wall and twisted like a hook. Seeing this overhang, she intentionally hugged close to the wall while the TZ Five guard was right at her heels. He took one reckless swing at her in hopes of knocking her into an uncontrolled spin. He missed.

Kerriah felt the wind gust around her body, but she had no fear, only focus. She was perfectly calm. She continued to head directly for the overhang at high speed. Then, she used her leg strength to kick away from the wall, just narrowly avoiding a nasty collision with the rocky protrusion. However, the guard's overzealous pursuit caused the fast-approaching overhang to go unnoticed, and he plowed directly into it, smashing his helmet and shattering his visor. Dazed, blinded, and vulnerable, he withdrew himself from the game.

In the tunnel below, Clyde swiftly dispatched his opponent and shot up to assist Crix. Crix snatched the opposing team's baton and bolted down the center of the tunnel with the two sentries following him and gaining speed. As they flew past, Clyde and Kerriah converged on the sentries and promptly took them off Crix's tail.

Far below, Akhal, who now had Gear's baton clasped through his belt, was on his way up from the blind zone when he noticed Crix coming back down. Both Crix and Akhal passed one another within the Vortex Two tunnel, and each returned their captured batons to the score pole above their respective tunnels. Over the loudspeakers, the announcer stated each team secured the first of the two batons—a tied score.

The game continued. As both players descended into the tunnels, Akhal and Crix found themselves facing each other. Akhal took a wild swing with his quorum stick and connected with Crix's chest. The powerful blow sent him sailing into the unforgiving rocky wall. The air left Crix's lungs and his strength melted away. Dazed, he dropped his quorum, and his body wilted deeper into the cavern before he could recover. The attack packed an unusually vicious punch.

Next, Akhal jetted out after Kerriah. Awaiting his arrival deeper in the tunnel, she gripped her quorum stick in a defensive posture. As he approached, he swung violently in her direction, but her reaction time was remarkable as he swung and thrust to no avail. Akhal kept missing his target. He was enraged. She noticed that his efforts appeared somewhat labored. It was as if his quorum was heavier than normal.

Something is different.

At that moment, he swooped back, swung through in a downward chopping motion, and though she blocked his attack, her quorum stick surprisingly snapped into two sections.

"How, what . . . ?" she stated. Then, his pear-shaped end connected squarely on top of her helmet and sent what felt like a bolt of electricity all the way through her spine. With a dented helmet, Kerriah was briefly stunned.

Watching from above, Clyde—after dispatching the other guard—soared through the wind gusts toward Akhal to assist Kerriah. He whipped his quorum stick over Akhal's head, and then against his throat. Clyde pulled him back just as Akhal was about to swing a finishing strike on Kerriah. Then, Akhal squirmed to one side and performed an illegal underhand swing to Clyde's crotch, forcing his release. Akhal began swinging wildly in the appearance of one that has taken this event far beyond just a game. Clyde was able to block one of his attacks with his forearm; he then buckled over in pain, grasping his crushed limb. Akhal had broken his arm with one strike.

Kerriah, holding two ends of a broken quorum stick, remained hovering at a safe distance. She chimed in over her comm-equipped helmet; the blow from Akhal's quorum stick must have got it working again. "Something's different with his quorum stick."

In a growling yet cringing tone, Clyde responded, "It's weapon's grade. The bastard is trying to kill us." Clyde was livid.

Shaking his head and taking a deep breath, Crix regained his strength, and then dove down to catch his quorum stick before it became lost in the blind zone. "We need to call off the match. They'll be disqualified," he replied.

"No! I want him to feel this defeat and not squirm out of it over his cheating. Crix, finish him. My arm's broken, but you can win this still." Clyde's tone was stern and resolute. He painfully made his way to an offshoot.

Kerriah continued to keep a safe distance from Akhal, who had a depraved look on his face. In spite of this, her response was surprising. "Crix, he's right. We can take this guy. Secure the last baton; he's mine." She focused on his quorum stick and calculated his next move.

Come on, boy. Take your best shot.

Impressed by Kerriah, Crix smiled and pushed past them, cutting skillfully through the center of the vortex with amazing speed. This grabbed Akhal's attention, and he turned in pursuit of him.

"Big mistake!" Kerriah shouted just as another reverse gust from the vortex pushed out with perfect timing for her attack. With an aggressive pounce onto Akhal's back, she shoved the broken end of her left-hand quorum stick into the bottom rim of his helmet and twisted herself up and over his shoulders, prying the helmet from his head. She then mercilessly smacked him with the right-hand quorum stick. He let out a whimper, and then withered helplessly, all the strength and motion removed from his body.

Akhal flailed like a sheet of paper rippling through the wind. A sucking gust pulled his body down into the bottom grate located in the blind zone. The TZ Five sentries gave up protecting their now baton-less base and took hot pursuit of Crix. Even though they noticed, they completely dismissed the peril of their team's leader. Crix had virtually no time to secure the baton before the arbitrator paused the game due to Akhal's lack of consciousness. As Crix made his way up to secure the win, he noticed that there was no call to stop the game and he felt something . . . something calling him downward. At that moment, he turned, taking a diving position back to the bottom grate.

Kerriah followed through, keeping their sentries from coming back at Crix. As Crix approached the grate, he opened his arms and legs wide to slow his descent. He dropped his quorum stick, which disappeared into the blackness below. The faded view of Akhal's limp body pressed against the iron grate like a broken doll meant one thing. The arbitrator failed to see that he had lost consciousness before he entered the blind zone. It was clear that his bare head had slammed against the heavy grate as streams of blood poured down across his face. Crix grabbed Akhal's limp body and secured him around his arms.

"What are you doing?" Clyde called out over the comm as he attempted to watch from the nearby offshoot and was trying to figure out why they had not won yet.

"As awful as Akhal is, I cannot allow him to die here so we can win this. We're better than that," Crix answered.

"You're never going to be able to get back up the vortex carrying him. Just call for a stinking line, and they'll just be disqualified."

Crix disregarded Clyde's plea and attempted to make a push out of the blind zone. He tried repeatedly, but each attempt resulted in him slamming back down against the old iron grate. He managed to strain back up to a knee as the vortex sucked him back down. His body became frozen against the downward pressure. His muscles began failing, along with his nerves, from fighting the harassing, thunderous boom of the air passing through the grate.

Maybe Clyde is right on this. The only way to save Akhal is to call for a line and let us take the disqualifying loss. I know, though, we can still do both. I have to try.

Crix attempted to make another push for the surface, awaiting the next reverse pressure flow to give him the upward pop needed to free him from the oppressive grate. Then it came. The deafening hum turned to a barometric swoosh followed by a mighty belch. The pressing downward force turned to weightlessness, and then a sudden pop upward. He struggled to maintain momentum from the outward air pressure when he felt a push against his feet.

Kerriah gave a needed assist—just enough to get him moving upward again. Crix, elated, flattened his body out as much as he could to maximize the push from the continued upward gust. The weightless effects took greater hold as he neared the middle of the cavern and the pressure balanced out. Somehow, against all probability, he managed to make one more push to reach the top, and then attach Akhal to an extraction line. Victoriously, he latched the second baton to the capture bar of his team's base, forming what the Andors referred to as the dual of clubs.

Clyde and Kerriah emerged from the vortex cavern as the crowd above roared with excitement. Kerriah ran over to Crix and gave him a quick, firm hug.

"You did great! I honestly didn't think there was enough force to carry the extra weight of both of you, even with the push I gave you. But you did it!"

Crix took a small step back. He appeared pale and drained. "No, me either." He dropped his head, not looking as joyous as those around him did.

Then Clyde ran over and slapped Crix on the back with his good arm. "This is my guy! Victory is ours!" he roared as he pranced by the other team, his arm extended and pointing at them in a gloating manner. Crix remained quiet.

He observed Tirix sitting up by the crates. A smile had fought its way upon his face, and he painfully struggled up to his feet. Crix lifted his head and nodded toward his friend. Tirix nodded back. Crix's heart filled with hope again that they could always be pals. He then walked away from the crowds, struggling with his thoughts.

What have I done?

CHAPTER 9

That evening, back at Crix's home, he lay in bed with his mind unable to settle long enough to be restful. His head stirred over the big game earlier that day, the loss of Haflinger, and his finding of Kerriah crashed in Drisal. It was much to take in. He felt overwhelmed by everything.

Down the hall, he could hear Krath snoring like an old piece of machinery that needed maintenance. It was so loud at times, Crix felt as though someone was slowly sawing through the foundation of the dwelling. Underneath this restless racket, there was a gentle knock on the wood doorframe to his bedroom. Crix always liked to keep his door open as he hated the confined feel of his small bedroom. He rolled over. There Kerriah stood with a concerned look on her face.

"I can't sleep." She massaged her thumb across her forehead, trying to gain some focus. "Krath's snoring is shaking the place apart, and I'm worried about you. You've been very quiet since we got back."

Crix pulled the covers up close to his mouth like a child confessing to his parents. "I think I did something stupid today."

"Stupid how? You were amazing. You won and saved Akhal at the same time. Your team and the crowd absolutely loved you."

"I couldn't get up that vortex carrying Akhal . . ."

"Yet you did," she interrupted, now troubled over what he was about to tell her.

"No, I couldn't. After you gave me the push that accelerated me out of the blind zone, I almost instantly drifted downward again. I couldn't make any kind of adjustment to fight that, and an extraction call would have forfeited the match. You see, some of the most highly skilled annexis players tested the vortex, and the most weight that could ever traverse back up the vortex under any conditions was two hundred and eighty pounds." Crix was explaining what happened as if he needed to hear himself say it aloud. Kerriah patiently waited and remained silent.

"Akhal and my combined weight would have been around three hundred and seventy pounds. Clyde is okay. He's two-sixty and makes it up pretty well considering, but his biggest weak point is his slow accent compared to others. There was no way I was going to get both of us back up to the top like that, even with the strongest upward gust." He stopped to sit up and pulled his knees up to his chest. He was calculating everything in his head.

"What are you saying then?" Kerriah asked, even though she knew the answer.

"I used the orb." With a loud, disheartened exhale, he continued. "Until a few days ago, it's been easy to not call upon the orb's power because I never really had to before. Now that I have used it . . . it's already becoming instinctive. It's like moving my arm, as if I have been using its power my whole life. I was determined to get us to the top and win, and that's what I did. The best way I can explain it is when you knock something over, and your reflexes automatically act to catch it without a thought. I should have called for an extraction, but my vanity wouldn't let me. Now, I'm worried sick for Troika; have I doomed us? What will become of it once the Marcks trace the energy signature here?" Crix's eyes were troubled and his heart hurt for the possible future of Troika.

Understanding the likelihood that Zearic had triangulated the energy signature and that his worry definitely had legitimate merit, she moved close to comfort him. At that moment, it was all she could do. She sat down next to him and put her arm across his back.

"Maybe they didn't pick it up; it's possible that the force of the vortex disrupted the energy enough to mask it from their orbital detection systems." As soon as her words came out, she knew that it did not sound logical or convincing.

Crix is smarter than this.

"Whatever happens, don't blame yourself. There are times we are forced to make split-second decisions, and some are good and some bad, but we make them and must stand by them." She looked out the window and into the nighttime sky of Troika. "Still, we need to think of our next move, and we can't take any chances. We have to get you out of Troika right away."

"No!" His voice elevated. "I can't leave them to a fate that I brought upon them. I have to warn them . . . help to defend them. It's my responsibility to protect them now."

"It doesn't matter. You and the orb are too important to let fall into Zearic's hands. If the Marcks come, the Andors will have to deal with them on their own." She sighed. "Let me think this through. Try to get a little rest. I have a feeling we are going to need it." Crix watched her leave the room. His mind was full of everything and nothing all at the same time.

What have I done?

In just a few short hours, the early morning light broke across the rooftops of the Andor dwellings. Crix suffered through a dreadful night of tossing about trying to fall asleep before exhaustion took its toll. He awoke to the sound of Krath and Kerriah talking close by.

"Urrmm," Krath cleared his throat, interrupting their conversation. "Looks like he's beginnin' to show signs of life," he muttered to Kerriah. "Hit the deck! We're gettin' outa here ASAP!"

"Wha . . . what?" Crix rubbed his left eye to clear his hazy vision.

"Tya heard me right. Grab tya gear, and let's get goin'! We're gonna be knee-deep in Marcks 'cause of that stunt you pulled yesterday; in fact, I'm stumped why we aren't already." Krath started kicking at his bed to hurry him up and was clearly not giving the warm comforts that Kerriah did hours before. Of course, comforting was not Krath's style.

Crix looked over at Kerriah with a miffed look in his eyes. "Sorry, Crix, he needed to know the situation we both discussed, and we have concluded that we need to get far away from Troika. At least, until we're sure everything is clear," she explained.

Crix snapped up out of his bedsheets. "Well, don't you think I could have been included in this conversation? I know you two think I'm just naive and sheltered, but I may have some input that's worth listening to," he retorted.

Krath rested his fists on his hips. "Tya mind is not clear regardin' this, kid. Too emotionally attached to the Andors to make the right decision here. If the Marcks descend upon Troika lookin' for tya, the worst thing is to be here when they arrive."

"He's right, Crix. We should have left last night when you told me, and that was my mistake. The only reason I can conclude as to why the Marcks are not here already is they did not detect the orb's energy signature, or they are planning something massive. I fear the latter to be true, especially since they are already aware of its presence in nearby Drisal. I would have to assume they are proactively scanning for it here."

Crix sighed and placed his hands on his head. His mind was spinning with thoughts. "Where will we go? Can I still attend Haflinger's funeral this evening?"

"I'm sorry, no. We can't afford to stick around that long; we have to get going now. I have some friends back in Teinol that have a mutual disregard for Zearic and the Marcks. They have a secured area we can stay in for a short while, until things cool down some," Kerriah said.

"Okay, what are your plans for getting there? I mean, it's not like Troika has regularly scheduled flights out to Mendac cities, aside from sabe mineral cargo shipments, which will not arrive for pickup for another week. Andors keep a relatively isolated existence, and normally, the only transport that leaves here at all is diplomatic trips for Grand Chief Isomar." Crix firmly crossed his arms, waiting for their reply.

Krath and Kerriah looked over at one another and shrugged almost at the same time. Crix's mouth dropped open with disbelief. "No!" He did not intend to give in on this subject. "We are not going to steal the Grand Chief's transport. That's where I have to draw the line. It's disrespectful. Besides, that transport is located in the Stablet Alcazar, and you're not getting anywhere near that. It's protected by Morak elite guards, who are sworn to protect his palace with their lives."

Kerriah pressed her lips tightly together in rebuke. "Okay . . . what's your plan to get us away from here quickly? Walk?" She stared intensely at him, waiting for an answer.

"Well, no, obviously, but there has to be another way."

"How far away is it?" Krath's voice rose. This discussion was already poking through his thin veneer of patience.

Crix looked nervously at Krath for a few seconds before responding. "The Alcazar is located in the mountain region of Crein, and that's not easy to get to on foot. Although by sky carrier, it's about two hours from here. The sky carrier is the only practical way to travel between the Troika provinces."

Krath jumped up, grabbed his pack, and started heading toward the front door. "Where are you going?" Crix blurted out with the slim hope of stopping him.

"I'm goin' to the Alcazar, and so are tya. That's our ride outta here, and the meter is runnin', so let's get movin'."

Although he was exasperated and uncertain, Crix knew they needed to leave, but stealing the grand chief's transport did not sit well with him. Yet, he decided to follow their lead, given the respect of their experiences, and he was outnumbered two to one.

***

The sky carriers were a primitive and continuously running transit system that operated between the five Troika provinces. The system consisted of two fastened-together, cylindrical dirigibles that carried round, open-air platforms beneath them. A single pilot sat upon a raised seat at the rear of each platform.

The sky carrier station was nothing more than a simple, rustic ticketing booth with a short line of Andors awaiting the next carrier. The carriers touched down smoothly and flawlessly for only ten minutes at a time before lifting off to make way for the next arrival. At any given time, a continuous line of four to five carriers could be visible in the clear Troika sky. Water stains seeped down the patinated sides of the lightweight metal carriers. They were very quiet; in fact, the only noticeable sound they made was a long hiss as they lifted off from the ground. This fit well with the older generation of Andors, who were adamant about living a low-tech and quiet existence.

Crix, Krath, and Kerriah boarded a sky carrier destined for Crein and the Alcazar. As they rode, they observed the peaceful, natural, wooded Andorian countryside. There were only six Andors onboard with them, who intentionally acted as though they did not notice Crix and his companions. It was difficult to tell if it was out of politeness or uncertainty that made them keep such a distance, but either way, it was apparent, and it made Kerriah feel uneasy, so she stared out into the woods below and tried to ignore them. Only the elderly Andor pilot would give them a suspecting glance from time to time, though he never spoke a single word as the transport passed over kilometers of thick woods.

The wooded lowlands of Hemlor slowly changed over to the rocky, mountainous highlands of Crein with Andorian homes clustered into the rocks and hillsides. The dwellings looked similar in appearance to the homes of Hemlor. However, these homes appeared casually tossed onto the side of the mountain or even windswept there from some great storm. There was no uniformity in their layout; rather, the rugged terrain decided where each house found its place.

The hiss from the metal carrier picked up tempo and intensified as it went upward to climb above the rocky summits. After clearing a steep range, the air cooled noticeably and gave a slight tickle when it curled across the skin. The ascending landscape leveled off to a field of tall and narrow, rock-like towers, so close in proximity the sum of them had the appearance of an old, dead forest turned to stone.

"I believe the open field on the other side of the Pillared Forest is the Alcazar." Crix pointed forward, but he was not quite certain. The dense forest of stone pillars became increasingly sparse until they reached the sky carrier station on the far side of the open field. The carrier slowed, and the hissing started again and grew louder as the carrier approached their destination. The platform gently touched the surface, and the passengers quickly exited via a small section of latching side rail. Right behind them, about a dozen or so Andors urgently boarded before it departed once again.

Posted at the station entrance stood two dark, cloaked Andors wearing navy-shaded chest plates. Looking statuesque and towering in appearance, they wielded great, curved blade weapons. Steam blew out from their nostrils as their warm breath hit the cool mountain air. Their chiseled faces, bulging muscles, and large veins perfected the look of forceful Andor protectors and appointed guardians of the land. They were not to be trifled with and would not react well to outsiders approaching their post.

"Moraks, as we near the Alcazar, we are likely to see more of them," Crix whispered.

"They wield such primitive weapons, yet I don't think I want to get on their bad sides if we can avoid it," Kerriah noted while sizing up their blades.

"Tectonic blades aren't as primitive as they appear. They are infused with Ghoran crystals and will seriously mess up the individual that comes in contact with one," Crix warned with a whisper.

"Ghoran?" Kerriah asked.

"Shhhh!" Crix tried to get her to quiet down as the Morak guards looked at them with interest. He started to become uneasy.

His neck became tense, and he found himself trying to stand taller than normal.

As they approached the station's exit, one of the guards lowered his blade, blocking their passage. "What's your business in Crein?" he questioned, noting that they were foreigners. Outsiders were generally not welcomed in Troika and even less so in Crein.

"We are here to have a look at the stone forest of Mothoa; we have heard so much of it, and . . . we just want to have a look at it with our own eyes." Crix clumsily offered a last-second, pitiful explanation. He was not very good at being deceitful.

"You've seen it. Now be gone to where you have come," the Andor's strong voice commanded in an unyielding tone.

"We were hoping to get a closer look than this. Can't we just walk out to the edge of it?" Crix's voice was childlike, though he hoped they would not notice his nervousness.

"No one is allowed to enter the sacred forest except for Andors that have departed from the living realm with honor. Now go back to which you have come before I have you shackled and hung from a barstil tree!" The Andor's tone was even harsher than before. Crix looked toward the forest.

"Wait justa minute there, buddy. Them's fightin' words where I'm from . . ." Krath barked at the Morak guard before Crix quickly placed his hand up to stop him.

"Look, I've lived in Troika since I was a child, and my keeper, Haflinger, was a Morak during the first Thraxon War . . . Well, he died two days ago, and I wish to pay honor to the lands his spirit will inherit. That's all." The two Moraks looked at him as if looking directly through him.

"Then why are these two here?" one of the guards asked while pointing to Kerriah and Krath without even looking at them.

"I tell you what. Can we at least just hang out in the small wooded area between here and the Alcazar and view both from afar?" Crix asked as respectfully as he could.

The guard let out a forceful exhale. "There's no law that says you can't. However, be warned, don't try anything illicit or inappropriate while being in the area," he responded with an insolent tone.

Krath smiled. He knew they were about to do exactly that.

CHAPTER 10

L ooking through his antique field glasses, Krath observed the
perimeter of the Alcazar. The majestic stronghold of the
Andors sat atop a plateau with a massive U-shaped reflecting pool
at its base. The pool surrounded a statue of a strange, mythical-like
creature, the likes of which Krath had never seen before. The
Alcazar had five, tall, narrow spires that reached into the sky with
the tallest at the center. Grey and weathered, it was easy to tell that
this structure had stood as a representation of Andorian fortitude
for countless generations, long before the settlement of Mendacs
on Soorak. Surrounding the structure was a series of smaller towers
with openings near the top. These perimeter defenses had Morak
Sentinels positioned inside, each armed with heavy turrets. The
chain-driven guns fired electrostatically charged barbs capable of
incapacitating both organic and robotic invaders. The Morak
Sentinels were the elite of the Morak forces and had always held
the honor of protecting the grand chief.

"Well . . . where the heck is the transport bay in this place?
Wa—wait a second." Krath panned halfway down the cliffside.
"There tya are. Very clever of them to camo it against the cliffside."

The grey and black granite texture created the visual illusion
of a solid rock face. Concealed within this illusion was a cutout

section that the transport used to access the underground landing bay. At first glance, most untrained eyes would miss it.

"Okay, you found it, so how do you propose we get in there?" Crix questioned.

Krath lowered his field glasses and looked over at Crix with annoyance. "Since a direct assault is out of the question, we climb."

"You can't. Take a closer look at the cliff wall, and you'll see why." Crix gestured toward the Alcazar. He wanted to prove a point.

Krath gave a scowling grunt and looked back through the field glasses at the cliff. He leaned his head forward a bit as if to get a more focused look. "Humph . . . Well them sneaky Moraks. So they lined the cliff with razor spikes, even used camo to help maintain a neat and tidy view."

The razor-sharp spikes peppered the cliffside like tiny hairs. Crix gave a gratified smirk and crossed his arms. He wanted Krath and Kerriah to realize his worth and that he had knowledge that could help them. "So you see . . . we can't get to that hangar."

Krath bit at Crix with the sharpness of a feisty dog. "Now tya look here. I've been patient with tyar negativity, but my pa—" Crix cut him off before he could finish.

"But there is an alternate way in." He pointed his finger in the direction of the stone forest.

"Now that's my boy. Let's have it, and be quick about it," Krath said with an instant reversal in his tone and a big grin on his face.

"It's through the most sacred place in Troika, the inverted Crystalline Forest of Mothoa. The entrance, I think, is just after that steep cliff we flew over in the sky carrier at the very thickest portion of the forest of stone. In fact, the inverted forest is directly below those stone pillars. From there, the old rumors say, there's a tunnel into the lower levels of Alcazar."

"Well, let's get to poundin' feet. We have no time to spare standin' around here flappin' our jaws." Krath shoved his looking glasses back into his pack.

***

Surrounded on either side by natural rock walls, the pillared forest was nestled neatly between a steep cliff drop-off and the open field leading to the Alcazar. They snuck their way into the forest of stone by belly crawling through the taller grass until they reached the first pillars. There wouldn't be time to waste as the curious guards might question the length of time they spent in the small patch of woods and begin searching for them.

Inside the forest, the cool, crisp air filled their lungs with a sparkling energy that pulsated throughout the sacred land. The towering behemoths of the stone forest produced an eerie feeling. The deeper Crix and the others traveled inward, the more densely packed the pillars became. A strange sense that they were attempting to crowd them out and wanted to prevent them from going further fell over Crix. Eventually, the forest's sparse patches of bright-green grass dispersed into a smooth stone floor, and the light dimmed to near darkness from the unforgiving pillars.

Kerriah rubbed her arms for warmth. "This place is beginning to give me the creeps." It was already chilly in Crein, and it felt even colder within the stone pillar forest.

Startled by a strong gust that weaved through the pillars and produced a squawking scream, the three nearly jumped out of their skin, even Krath.

"I don't like it either." Crix's voice echoed through the narrow, stone maze. "This area is forbidden, and it would not bode well if we were caught here. According to ancient lore, the stone pillars have some significance with the inverted Crystalline Forest below. The specific details of which have been kept mostly secret."

It was difficult to shake off the feeling that someone or something was watching them. Then, Krath's shoulder brushed up against one of the pillars, causing it to release a dreadful wail as though he had awoken a tortured soul from within. He stopped and curiously placed his hand on the pillar. He needed to set his mind at ease that the noise did not actually originate from within its core. The wailing came out again and intensified until he removed his hand. The awful noise had an unnerving curl that was reminiscent of a suffering animal. Crix and Kerriah stopped and looked over at Krath with immense concern.

"All right, guys," Krath said, "I think we may have a problem."

Crix's face turned ghost white. "What did you do?" he whispered, worried about the response.

"I just brushed up against this thing, and it started ballowerin' like a sufferin' beast."

"Aww, great!" Crix appeared stressed as he motioned at them to get away from the pillars. "Please, just try to keep as far from them as possible."

"Sure thing, buddy, but there's not much space to keep clear with when tya're my size, and it's gettin' tighter as we go on. If it keeps like this, I'm going to be pushin' my way through these things."

Kerriah took a close inspection of a pillar and cautiously blew air onto it in hopes of getting a benign reaction. "What's the story with these, Crix? Are they some sort of living organism?"

"I don't know. The common Andor is given little knowledge of Mothoa. A limited group only knows its true secrets. There are, however, many old myths and tales. I just don't know which to believe," answered Crix as he looked up to the tops of the stone pillars.

Kerriah crouched down to examine the base of the pillar. "Well, I'm not one to buy into myths or folklores, but . . . if they hold any bit of information that could be important, I would be very interested."

Crix looked down and took a deep breath. "The one that stands out in my mind right now is the tale of Suros. As the ancient myths go, he was a great Andor chief who gave his life to destroy the rogue faction led by his brother Tersik." Crix pressed his palm against his forehead, ran his hand through his hair, and grabbed the bottom of his face. He strained to recall the details of the story. He exhaled loudly with stress in his voice. He had taken for granted the old stories and did not think he would ever need to recall them for a serious purpose. The younger generation of Andors had not had the ancient lore passed on to them as staunchly as the previous ones had.

"I don't recall the story exactly, but Suros was pretty much the unwavering example of Andorian honor and bravery. When his power-hungry brother, Tersik, turned against him to rein terror upon the Andor civilization, he sacrificed himself to save Troika. This secretive lore casts over this hallowed ground, as well as these pillars, and this was the epicenter where the conflict finally ended. No one ever enters here, and those that have . . . never come back. And here we are trouncing right in the middle of it." Crix meant to be sarcastic, and yet, he was still concerned over what their fates might be for such an ill-mannered defiance.

"Hmmm . . . that's a real nice story and all, but I just wanted to know why these oversized sausage tubes are wallerin' at me." Krath poked his finger on one of the pillars. "Problem is . . . now tya got me a bit scared." He gave a mocking smirk and started heading deeper into the pillar forest. "Come on! Our favorite walking scrap army will be here soon, so we got to keep movin'." Crix reluctantly jogged to catch up with Krath; Kerriah followed close behind him.

Within moments, the daylight unexpectedly grew into pitch-black darkness. A shiver settled over Crix, and suddenly, he became short of breath.

"Krath? Kerriah?" he called out and waited.

TOLAGON

He was unable to see anything and swung around desperately, banging his elbow into one of the pillars. A horrible, painful shrill screamed out from the once-silent piece of stone. Crix detected no other sounds within this space and no replies from Kerriah or Krath, only an eerie silence mixed with the throbbing thump of his fast-beating heart. It pounded—pounding so loud he was positive someone or something would hear it. He moved his hands blindly around to assist his lack of sight. The only thing he felt was the irrepressible stone pillars, and each time one was touched, it executed that awful shrill that echoed through the forest.

Where are they?

Thoughts raced through his mind, and he tried not to succumb to the overwhelming feelings of fear and uneasiness. He wanted to take captive every thought. A whispering hiss fluttered from all directions as though something was searching for him. His throat tightened, his stomach felt constricted, and his eyes were unable to focus. Then, at that moment, an icy hand grabbed his shoulder. He helplessly yelled out and awkwardly spun around. There was nothing there: no light, no sounds, not even a wisp of a breeze.

A sizzling, like that of searing flesh, echoed through the narrow maze of stone, and a dark blue light poured out from behind him. He turned around again to find himself illuminated. The intensity of the light blinded him, and it turned from blazing blue to bright white. Now, instead of complete blackness, he witnessed pure white and total silence. Then the white light slowly dissipated into achromatic shades of both black and white. He began to identify the shapes around him.

131

For a moment, he caught a glimpse of a massive creature, similar in shape to the statue he had observed near the Alcazar's reflecting pool. The creature was a lengthy, globule form. Its flesh swirled as if storms brewed within it, and near the top of this being resided an expanse, which held a perfect void of both color and light. However, there was one thing Crix found to be most extraordinary—the creature had a great stone beard. The massive beard consisted of hundreds of giant, stone-like pillars similar to those that he and his friends had encountered in the forest.

The creature took notice of Crix. The mysterious void on top of the being turned toward him, and though it was without light, he felt it stare into his soul. A deep profoundness and quiet solace within this giant sent an uncomfortable chill that rushed down Crix's spine. It seemed strange that such a great being would even take notice of something as small and insignificant as Crix.

The white light around the creature abruptly shattered away and returned to blue. Then, a tall, dark Andorian figure stepped out from the illumination while the massive titan inquisitively continued to watch. Fog poured from the Andor's eyes, blending into the sea of blue. His black armor glistened around his massive shoulders and forearms. The helmet molded to fit the shape of his head with a round emblem protruding from the top. His silver mane blew out from the bottom of his helmet as a strong breeze whisked up, bringing with it a sulfurous odor. The Andor advanced fluidly toward Crix, brandishing a long, curved blade in his right hand.

Going against his inner desire to hide the orb and not expose its location, Crix prepared to do what was necessary to defend himself from the uncertainty of this warrior's intention. As the Andor came upon him, uncomfortably too close, Crix held his hand out, ready to give this Andor a suppressing blast of orb power. His hand popped and crackled with blue energy then diffused back to normal. Crix turned his palm around with a look of confusion before trying once again. Blue energy surged from his fingertips and swirled around his hand, and then nothing.

Strange?

"There is no need to conjure your enigmatic powers against me, young Nathainian. I assure you that your efforts would only be in vain." His voice shook the ground with a boom which was so grave the words were unintelligible. Yet they filled Crix's mind, and he understood with perfect clarity.

"I know all there is to know about you and where your destiny lies. As you are beginning to comprehend, any living force cannot harm me, including the cosmic power that dwells within your body as it too is living. The wholeness of my power is connected to this land for which you behold."

"Are you—" Crix inquired, shaking with trepidation.

Before he could finish, the Andor swung his blade around and plunged it into the stone floor with a thunderous crack.

"Enough! You will not speak but listen only! There is nothing from your tongue that could enlighten me, and there is much for you to learn. Even as you seek passage into the forbidden Crystalline Forest of Mothoa, the enemy hovers overhead in its vessels of steel, ready to sack the great lands of Troika. My influence over this region has allowed me to place time in repose for a transitory moment. This brief juncture will provide you the knowledge regarding Troika's origins, which is required for you to clear this portion of your journey." He paused, and Crix slowly dropped to his knees as if this figure somehow inaudibly commanded, and he obeyed.

"I am Suros, and I have guarded Mothoa and its secrets for countless generations. All who have attempted to pass without warrant into these hallowed grounds have fallen to my blade. Listen to my account, and you, Nathainian, will be the first to pass with your body and spirit intact."

He stepped out in front of his implanted blade and raised his arms toward the sky. Behind him, a cone of light blasted out from the blade. This light gave an ethereal illustration to the blackness of the sky. The massive, bearded creature moved through the emanating light from beyond the blackness and behind Suros. A mouth appeared on the great creature, and it opened as wide as the cone of light from Suros's blade. The blade's light bent around and turned into the creature's mouth. There was an intense flash, and then everything looked different. The land was barren, devoid of life and vegetation. Huge geysers burst nitrogen high into the airless atmosphere, filling the skyline with a murky hue.

"What you witness now is Troika, or as your kind would refer to it as Soorak, before the time of the Laggorns and their reshaping of this world. To understand how we received the world we have today, we must visit another distant system from long ago, a system that was the birthplace of the Laggorns."

The scene changed to a system that surrounded a cerulean star. "The Laggorns once reigned over the living system of Auroro where, under their influence, life somehow flourished beyond the bounds and atmospheres of the planets. The exact origins of the Laggorns are not fully known. I only know that when the universe was very young, a great power deposited into that system. A power that I do not understand, though I accept. When it settled, twelve Laggorns emerged.

"At first, they were without shape, as shape was insignificant to them. The Auroro System consisted of thirteen worlds surrounding a massive, blue star. The radiant energy from this star ignited the power within these beings, and they became aware of each other and their surroundings. As thousands of years passed, their intellect thrived in what far exceeded anything we could comprehend. As such, they collaborated and agreed to focus their abilities to create a flourishing and wondrous system."

As Suros narrated, the images continued to transform; the Laggorns appeared in the Auroro System as luminescent hazes of violet, forms that represented the Laggorns in their earliest embodiment. A view of each world within the system faded in and out, displaying landscapes that flourished and spawned bizarre shapes of animal and vegetation lifeforms. Suros continued.

"Eventually, the Laggorns took physical forms for the benefit of the species they created so that those species could recognize them. In time, they reshaped all the worlds of the Auroro System. As many millennia passed, their abilities and love for creation grew so strong that they could no longer remain within the confines of these thirteen worlds and their natural limitations. So they created life to withstand these boundaries and filled the voids of space between the worlds."

Crix noticed the planetary skylines changing from blue and black to a flourishing kaleidoscope of color and imagination. The lifeless space between these worlds filled with their creations. Uncountable lifeforms streamed across this blaze of imagination and danced with joy and abundance.

"They knew not suffering and were protected from environmental harms that would have ill effects on the living as we know it."

Suros paused as if to take in the wonders that maybe he had only seen a limited number of times. "To look into these skies, to travel this system, would have taken even the most mundane soul and instantly turned him into a master visionary. Alas, from the great blue star that once sparked their wondrous abilities, it was also to be responsible for their eventual demise.

"The colors in the sky rippled and then turned grey. A brilliant blue and red flash pulsed across the skyline, and a spear of energy that spanned light-years thrust deep through the heart of their great system, devastating everything as their blue star exploded.

"Of the twelve, four were in the outer reaches of the Auroro System at the time of this cataclysmic event, working to expand their wonders when the smaller thirteenth world they were on was broken apart and expelled into deep space. The four Laggorns bound themselves together and went into a dormant state for one hundred ages.

"They hurled through space without direction until their dormant mass happened upon the dual star system of Oro, which awakened their dormancy. The fourth being, Trias, the Laggorn of the seas, never awoke, and its great force expired as it fell upon our neighboring moon of Thale where its surface engulfed with water, and its last vestige of power set forth unto that world. The other three, the Laggorns of the winds, the beasts, and trees, placed themselves upon Troika. There, they began their reshaping of this world. Limited by the lesser stars of the Oro System, they had not the power to cast beyond this local world like before. In time, their powers ran short, and their once infinite lifespans waned; they could feel their days numbered. In a final effort to preserve their kind, they chose to merge their remaining powers into one.

"The Laggorn of the beasts, who we call Equus, would be the one to carry on for the next millennia. As the other two passed and the centuries crept by, the Laggorn of beasts became lonesome. It decided to create an evolution of its most beloved beasts, the Andors, the great equines. This creation, this race, was the one that made the Laggorn the most pleased.

"Equus admired their majestic coats that glistened in the daytime light and shimmered in the lucid glow of Oro under the nighttime sky. They had strong, chiseled faces and dark eyes that looked up at the Equus as though they could speak to it through their expressions. Equus gave them knowledge and speech. However, seeing them run on four legs was no longer fitting for a creature of higher intellect and noble spirit; as such, it altered their posture to walk upright and gave them hands to bear tools and build creations of their own.

"Time passed, and the Andors evolved as a species under the Equus's care. They formed a nation built on principles, stoicism, and honor. A deep history of great leaders emerged, and their lands never knew of war or cruelty. The nation's grand chief would always turn to the Equus for counsel and pass this wisdom unto his nation."

The scenes continued to play out in the background as Suros progressed through the journey. Sites of great halls and towns of wood and stone emerged. The Andors adorned in fine clothes strolled about contently.

"It was the golden age of the Andor as each had a cup that was overflowing with prosperity. In the time of the eighth millennia, a grand chief was born from the greatest of all grand chiefs . . . Litore. Litore founded the elite Moraks, which heroically repelled attacks from the beasts of the neighboring land of Satore. At the time, it was not fully understood why the Equus allowed these creatures to attack its beloved Andors; however, it was evident by later generations that it was preparing them for their future—their future void of its counsel and protection.

"Litore had two male offspring with the eldest being Tersik, who was to inherit the title of Grand Chief. Tersik, however, was spoiled and greedy. He plotted to overthrow Litore and later raised a rebellion to kill Equus with the flawed mindset that he could steal its power and knowledge for himself. When Litore discovered Tersik's plot, he banished him, setting the youngest offspring as the new heir.

"Tersik's madness only grew, and he used his cunning and persuasiveness to scour the countryside of Troika and create discord. Sadly, Litore's affection for his firstborn allowed the coup to continue for too long, and by the time he gave a decree to have Tersik assassinated, the rebellion was inevitable."

The scenes behind him faded in and out faster and faster as he progressed through the story. Tersik appeared as a hulking silver-coated Andor with a matte-black mane. He wore silver-plated armor and helm, and his eyes were wide with madness. He stood atop a smoldering heap with his blade in one hand, clutching the garment of a Morak warrior whose body hung limp. His insurrecting force swarmed in raiding towns and cities, leaving smoke and ash blanketing the skies behind them.

Suros straightened his stance, looking upward as he finished his story with strength in his voice as if speaking to a crowd of many. "In the final battle, Litore and the youngest gathered the remains of their warriors, and two mighty forces collided in what would appear to be the end of Troika. At the end of the ensuing conflict, the last vestige of the nation of Troika was the highland temple of the Equus.

"Tersik was intent on destroying the last of the Laggorns, and he made a final push to take the sacred region. As the warriors fell, Tersik reached his youngest brother on the battlefield. Blinded by rage and jealousy, his unstoppable bloodlust incapacitated the youngest, and he prepared to give the deathblow with his curved blade. However, his blow was stopped by Litore's blade, which pierced his armor and into his shoulder. Tersik fell only for a moment; however, his strength and aggression proved too much for Litore to defend. As the youngest regained his composure and came to his father's defense, Litore commanded him to go to Equus. He did as commanded, and Litore eventually fell to Tersik.

"Temporarily content with Litore's death, Tersik paraded his battered body in celebration, dragging him naked before his troops in a motion to degrade his image. During this celebration, the youngest sought Equus as his father commanded him. He found the being weak and its lifeforce waning. Equus observed that the youngest was pure in heart and a suitable leader for the Andors, so he bound with him, giving him much of the knowledge it held and its remaining life force.

"Before Equus expired, it gave a gift to the youngest to pass on to all future Andor generations. This gift would be the basis of its power, its beard of stone pillars. The pillars are what remain of the Laggorns when their power at last expires. What's left in them dispersed into the beard, and when the other Laggorns of Troika passed, their beard essence was assimilated into Equus." The sky rumbled above them, and Suros gave a casual glance upward, and then continued his story.

"A pact was struck between Equus and the youngest. They would forever be united, and through the remaining power of the Laggorn, the youngest would eradicate Tersik's army and restore the lands of Troika. Equus gave the youngest the remains of its life, wisdom, and strength. It then collapsed to the ground; its body dissolved to where only the beard remained, implanted here always as you see them today, above Mothoa."

The scenes turned to the young Andor; his body radiated with a blackish shimmer that pulsed in rhythm with his heartbeat. He hovered above the great pillars as the approaching army of Tersik scaled the mountainous plateau. The youngest allowed Tersik's force to enter the pillar forest, and he cast a dark barrier around them. When some of them tried to flee through the darkness, their bodies wilted, and their life pulled from them, leaving only withered, pale corpses. Their life force sucked into the surrounding pillars, trapped there forever.

Upon seeing this, the others fled inward to the densest portion of the stone forest. The youngest replicated his form many times until Tersik's forces were outnumbered twenty to one. Each incarnation wielded two blades, and each swarmed in and massacred the remnants of Tersik's force. Bloodied and shocked, only Tersik remained wielding his blade and was still driven with wrath.

"My brother," the youngest said as he lowered himself down, phasing out his replicated forms, "I feel sorrow for you. You were given so much, but now so much is lost. Yet you still clutch onto the culprit of your losses, your jealousy and greed." Tersik drew back his blade, grasping deeply with both hands behind his head in a readied attack stance.

"I don't know what you've done with the Laggorn, but its power was to be mine!" he snarled with such loathing in his tone that his voice cracked. "Now, I will slay you and take from you what is mine." The youngest looked down with regret, took one step back, then leaned forward and screamed a horrid shrill out at Tersik. Tersik's body folded back and merged into the pillar behind him.

The scene faded, and Suros slowly stepped aside, revealing a pillar tinted in black. "Here lays my brother, his life fused permanently into the beard of the Laggorn as is his ancient army. When you touched it, his spirit trapped within shrieked out."

"You? You're the youngest?" Crix looked perplexed as though he was assembling the details in his mind.

"Yes, and you are uncertain because the truth was intentionally obscured. As you are now aware, the true story was concealed from the greater masses in an effort to trivialize the pillars and their importance, to keep the enemies of Troika from ever targeting them. If they were to ever be destroyed, Troika as we know it would be lost, as all our power and ancestry from our very beginnings rest here.

"I had lived and ruled over Troika for several generations before my own passing. The power of the Laggorn kept me unnaturally vital and strong. However, I could eventually feel the burden of this power taking a toll on my own morality. Such power will always corrupt any lesser being over time. It is in the pillar of my brother that I eventually stored most of the Laggorn's power and knowledge. From this stone pillar, a crystal-bearing tree grows beneath, which is the reservoir that ultimately contains this all-important, life-bringing element." The ground rumbled beneath their feet and whooshing reverberated overhead. Suros looked upward with a troubled gaze. Crix shook his head as if to gather his thoughts.

"I—I have so many questions."

"No!" Suros stopped him. "There is no time. You must save the crystal and preserve Troika's future, or it will be forever lost." Suros pointed toward a small clearing in the forest. "Follow the path to a small opening that will lead you down into Mothoa where you will find the Inverted Forest. This is the forest grown from the stems of Equus's great beard and is where all deceased Andors rest their souls. Take the narrow tunnel into the forest and look for the tree that bears the crystal that is shadowed. Use this, and only this, to cut away the crystal." He pointed to a small, V-shaped cutter that lay on the ground near the base of one of the pillars. "It was made from the blade of Tersik's own sword, and it's the only thing that can release the crystal safely from its branch. Then, make your way to the grand chief's transport to keep the crystal from this invading force." The ground shook again but with more ferocity than before. Faint and distant voices steadily emerged . . . They were familiar.

"But I'm not Andor by blood. If I touch the crystals, won't I die?"

"No! Do as I have commanded, and you shall survive. Do this for Troika." Suros snapped his attention upward again with even greater alarm on his face.

"I will do it." Was there any other answer he could have given? After all, this was his fault. His heart weighed heavily, but his mind focused.

"Now, go quickly. Troika is under siege; I will repel our adversaries as long as possible." He faded out into the distance, and the nearby voices became loud and very close to Crix.

CHAPTER 11

W here in the backside of a droona beast have tya been?"
Krath grabbed Crix's shoulders, trying to get his attention.
He was raw with irritation. "Troika's under attack, and tya're lolly
poppin' around like a trite kid in these forsaken pillars! Let's get
going to that transport now!"

Kerriah appeared looking slightly out of breath and fatigued
behind Krath. "Oh, good! Thankfully, you've found him! There is a
massive line of Marck shock troops making their way into the Pillar
Forest."

"Yes, and by the sound of things, I doubt that the grand
Andor's Alca—pain-in-my-backside is going to hold out for very
long," Krath snarled.

"I know the way in. Come on!" Crix darted down the path
that Suros directed him to with the cutter in his hand.

Above them echoed a thunderous crack chased by a shriek
and ground vibrations. Debris and mangled Marcks clattered down
sporadically from the sky. The shadow of Suros whisked above
them, piercing the hover-disk-equipped Marcks with his saber as
they swooped by, firing in his direction. The Marcks were unable to

overcome his blinding speed. More and more of these metal adversaries found themselves at the end of his unleashed wrath as he skewered and dismembered their bodies with overwhelming precision.

Kerriah dashed to the side, avoiding the splash of scrap metal from a Marck hover disk that crashed nearby. "I don't know who he is or where he came from, but I'm glad he's on our side, or at least, it appears he is at the moment!" she shouted above the commotion.

Crix and company approached a path in the stone pillar forest that had a sharp downward pitch. It snaked around and ended at what appeared to be a steep wall. Crix stopped to look down the path. The sight puzzled him.

"He said it was here, but this leads nowhere." *Did I miss some important detail from Suros?*

"What? Who said what?" Krath grumbled then looked over at Crix with a goaded expression. "Boy, tya may be the offspring of Corin, but if tya keep at these games, tya're gonna end up with a knot on your skull. Now, I thought tya said you knew where tya were going?"

"Is this a joke?" Crix irritatingly kicked away a small piece of metal scrap. The metal piece tumbled down the steep path and appeared to pass through the wall. Crix took a couple of cautious steps from Krath.

"Okay, that was strange." He then decided to slide down the path with one leg pressed forward into the ground while leaning back to keep his balance against the sharp decline. As he approached closer to the wall, he felt a sudden draft and a strong smell of turpentine mixed with a hint of mustiness beneath.

"Would tya hurry it up down there?" Krath yelled from atop the slope.

Crix tried to lean forward. His supporting foot caught some loose rock, and he stumbled, attempting to catch his balance against the wall. He felt a strange numbness course through his limbs as he fell through, helpless. He could hear Kerriah scream his name as he flailed down into blackness that emerged into a faintly lit chamber. His body took a cushioned bounce off an invisible energy field, which emanated directly above a circular formation of violet- and crimson-tinted crystals. He remained suspended facedown above the crystals. A tickling sensation went from his head to his big toes as though hundreds of fingers were gently twitching over every inch of his body. A subtle ringing felt like something was trying to worm its way into his ears. He pushed his hand down but could not penetrate this unseen field between him and the crystals. He rolled over until he fell away and landed on the floor.

Around him, giant stone figures of armor-clad Andors lined the perimeter of the circular chamber. A large archway led to a dimly lit area that was mostly indistinguishable. The ringing faded from his ears as he moved away from the center formation. The smell of turpentine was thick in the air, and close by, he could hear the sound of a strong exhale. Then, a cold, steel bar hugged his throat tightly.

Two armor-clad Andors emerged out of what appeared to be thin air wielding long, metal staffs with glowing, crimson crystals at each end. Their helms were majestic and tall, and their metal plates were cast charcoal black, which made them nearly invisible in the low light. The two Andors converged upon him as another restrained him from behind. An armored knee jammed Crix sharply in his spine, while the bar snugged across his throat with enough force to labor his breaths.

At that moment, a familiar voice from above howled louder and louder before it stopped right next to them. The Andors looked over to see Krath hovering facedown above the crystals.

"What the heck?" he grumbled while flailing his arms around as he tried to grasp something solid. He looked over to observe Crix. "Tya better be lettin' my buddy go there 'cause when I get outa this fix I'm in here, tya'll be feelin' the sensation of my fist on tya noggins," Krath snarled.

One of the Andors turned toward Krath with his staff pointed in his direction. The attached crystal crackled and blazed. Krath popped off and belly-flopped squarely onto the floor. He slowly got up with one hand clenching his back in pain.

"Why you dirty—"

Another voice wailed from above and interrupted Krath. Kerriah stopped short of the crystal formation, and then the unfriendly Andor zapped her off the invisible field as well.

"Who are you? How many more of you are there?" one of the Andors questioned in a deep, stern voice.

"Now tya listen here," Krath stormed at the Andors with his arms cocked forward and fists clenched. The Andor raised his staff, and a red flash filled the chamber, blinding them. After a few seconds, their vision returned to a chamber filled with Andor Morak warriors, who quickly restrained Krath and Kerriah.

"Stop!" a booming voice echoed from above as the room illuminated in a deep blue. Suros hovered above, and the Andors promptly snapped into a militant, upright stance upon seeing him. "Allow them to pass as I have granted them passage through Mothoa and to the tree of Tersik."

The Andor warriors looked at each other in bewilderment before dropping the three from their vice-like clutches.

"Yes, my loyal servants, the most sacred of all our trees, the one that holds every vestige of power and knowledge of Andorian Civilization. We are under siege, and these mechanized foes are resolved to our destruction. They are many with more forthcoming in a continuous stream of marauding, and we cannot repel them all on this day, but we can delay them long enough for the Tolagon to keep safe our future."

A thundering overhead gave way to dust and small rocks falling from the ceiling high above. Suros turned to illuminate the archway before them. Beyond it revealed a massive hall that appeared to have no end as the light dissipated into the distance. Glistening above the hall were great hanging vines clustered with crimson- or violet-colored, tetragonal-shaped crystals. As light passed through the crystals, they gave off a sparkling resemblance of the nighttime sky with dueling stars.

The Moraks stepped aside and gave way to the strangers. Crix and Kerriah walked cautiously into the great hall. Their eyes scanned the high ceiling, and their mouths dropped open in wonderment.

"Tya better keep tya grubby mitts off me," Krath barked at the now passive Moraks in the chamber behind them. He followed his companions into the hall and casually dusted himself off.

Crix stared upward, his mouth wide open. "The Inverted Forest of Mothoa is amazing. It's more than I had ever imagined it to be." The childhood descriptions did not come close.

A soft and persistent whine came from a thousand different sources above them. "The noise is maddening in here." Kerriah shook her head and rubbed her ears.

The cavern trembled with a thunderous boom from above. The ensuing vibrations caused crystals to rain down from the trees, creating a chorus of wind chimes tussling in a gentle breeze as they pinged off the stone floor. Out of nowhere, two modestly dressed Andors flanked in and grabbed up the crystals. They gently placed them into wooden boxes.

"The sacred crystals are pieces of our life spring, where all Andors relinquish their spirit upon death. The pillars above capture their spirits, and the roots of those pillars preserve them for all time. This is the last gift of the Laggorn." The bluish light emerged again with Suros standing before them. "These fallen ones are quickly harvested and used in many ways to power Troika. Yet the one tree, the tree of Tersik, contains the mystery of our civilization. From its crystal, all questions are answered, and a rebirth of our species becomes possible. This is from the power that created us.

Hear me now: the Andor will once again be masters over their own world.

"You, Crix, will harvest this crystal and take it away from here until that time has come. For reasons that I cannot explain, I can tell you that taking the crystal will not be an easy task, for no one has ever attempted to approach it without a great loss to his or her inner strength. However, I have long known that it is you which would be the crystal's harvester. Now go! We will hold back the intruders and see you safely to the Grand Chief Isomar's transport."

Crix and his companions hurried deep into the subterranean great hall that resided beneath the Crystalline Forest with their eyes trained upward, scanning for the mysterious crystal. It felt like a daunting task as the mystic trees were many and their vines intertwined into thickets in some of the denser sections. The glowing crystals dimly illuminated the subterranean great hall, which spanned as far as the faint lighting would allow them to see.

"There!" Crix pointed at one of the thickest parts of the vines that webbed across the high ceiling.

Kerriah and Krath looked deeply to pinpoint Crix's find. They cautiously moved ahead to get closer to its proximity, finding it difficult to believe that he had found it so quickly. Hidden deep within the forest of inverted trees, the almost black crystal hung tangled amongst twisted vines from a crooked, grey trunk. The dark purple crystal was longer than the others were, and it had a faint illumination deep within its core. The vines cradled it as though they were protecting a child.

As they approached the tree that held the darker crystal, the whining sounds misted away into the distance. The grounds above shook violently, and the inverted trees rained crystals from their branches.

Kerriah impatiently paced back and forth, not happy about the delay. "I don't really understand this whole crystal thing here, it seems to me that we need to be focusing on getting to that transport ASAP."

Krath firmly posted his fists at his hips, his large chest pushed outward as he drew in a deep breath. "Well, boy, tya gonna get that thing so we can get outta here or just continue to stare at it till our recycled buddies join us down here?"

"Yeah, it's so high up there that I'll have to use the orb to get it."

"Crix, just do it. They will know we are down here, but if we are down here too much longer, it won't matter anyway. Besides, I have a feeling that mystic Andor can help us . . . hopefully." Kerriah was not one that would normally believe in the supernatural; yet, it was hard for her to deny what she had witnessed with her own eyes.

Crix nodded, and then snapped into a blue glow. He raised high into the air near the tree that clutched the Tersik crystal. As he reached into the vines to grasp it, he was stunned with an overwhelming feeling of despair and sadness. He pulled back, struck by such a feeling of deep sorrow that he could not help but weep. He had never felt so extinguished mentally. His thoughts went to the darkest of places, places that he had never been. He felt livid, sad, and bitter all wrapped into every sweeping thought.

Why does he have to do this anyway? Getting pushed around by these . . . whoever they are. It's his fault, though. They will all suffer and die because of him. He doesn't deserve to live . . .

"What's wrong with him?" Kerriah asked. Krath just grunted and shrugged his shoulders. "Crix are you all right?" she persisted. He slowly faded, having difficulty shaking off the feelings of despair as if a cold, bony hand clenched around his heart so tightly that it held his soul captive. A rumbling shook the cavern hall so violently once again that Krath and Kerriah found it difficult to stay afoot.

An explosion collapsed a portion of the ceiling. It continued to crumble downward as a large, metal dome smashed a hole from the surface above. Fragments of trees tumbled to the floor, and the immediate area was showered with crystals. Two giant hands plunged through the fracture from around the dome extended by long, scaly tubes. The hands turned back, placing themselves against the flat of the ceiling. They gave a push, dislodging their hosts from the stubborn rock above.

The metal dome pushed further inward.

"Please, Crix! Hurry!" Kerriah pleaded.

He looked down at her, and the feelings of despair melted away, its clutching grip unraveled. He swung back up to the grey tree with his focus anew and began tearing away the vines to get to the crystal. He tried to reach for it, but as he got closer, the despair snarled back into him. He withdrew his hand.

The metal dome finally smashed through the rocky ceiling and crashed to the floor below. A huge Marck rose slowly up from piles of rock and dirt. The dome was the head, and its legs and arms extended outward from its bulky torso. The top of its head grazed the tips of the inverted trees. A single, large, glowing red circle in the center of its head scanned the cavern.

Witnessing the destruction, Crix plunged recklessly into the mangled vines and grabbed the crystal with one hand while cutting away the vines with the tool that Suros provided. He blacked out, overtaken by visions of a Laggorn and bizarre foliage followed by an exploding star. He observed a shadowy Andor with fire blazing deep in his eyes. He pulled the crystal from the tree's vines, and his vision cleared. The strange feelings of despair departed. Ahead of Crix, a large, domed- headed Marck shredded through the lowest hanging trees, its red eye cast a glow upon him, and it charged forward.

More Marcks poured in from the newly created hole in the ceiling. Some dropped from cables and others from hover disks.

"Away with you, interlopers—you whom have desecrated the sacred hall of Mothoa. Now behold your foolishness," Suros called as he appeared from the darkness and cast fistfuls of crystals down upon the cavern floor.

He drew his blade, and it ignited into deep blue flames. The floor shook, an eerie shrill echoed out from beneath the ground, and a maze of boney spines ripped up from the earth. The spines interweaved with red and blue veins, and then took the shape of flesh. Before them now stood a small army of ancient Andor warriors from generations past, each in different adornment representative of their era and tribe. Suros dove forward and slashed at the oncoming Marcks, and the Andors followed behind, swarming the uninvited guests.

Crix and company sprinted down the hall and deeper into darkness, weaving through the melees that were emerging all around them. More Marcks continued to pour in, and another domed head crashed through the ceiling above. After a lengthy trek, they finally reached a split corridor at the far end with two passages, one to the left and one to the right. The squared right passage had a large header with ancient Andor symbols above it, and the left passage was round and appeared to narrow.

"Which way?" Kerriah stopped and took a closer look at the Andor symbols. "Neither," Crix replied. He pulled the dark crystal out from his pack and held it in front of the passages. The two passages vanished and between them appeared a steep stairway leading upward into darkness.

"How tya know that was there?" Krath inquired.

"I'm not sure. For some reason, I just knew," Crix explained. He thought it must be the crystal, or possibly some other influence. Either way, Crix was certain this was the right path; there was no doubt in his mind. He had no reservation about his choice. Krath dropped his head down and rubbed the back of his neck bemused.

Behind them, in the distance, they could hear the battle as it moved closer and another metal dome punched through the ceiling close by. "They are onto us," Kerriah said. Together, they dashed up the steep incline through the hidden passageway.

The steps led up to a large square chamber that was dark; it was difficult to tell its scale and size with certainty.

"Well, where now?" Krath asked. He was confused as to why they were in a dark empty room while hoping it was not a dead end. Being a Hybor, Krath had keen sight in the dark due to life in the murky depths of Thale and could see that the chamber had no distinguishable features or exits. He gave a growl of discontent.

Crix, still holding the crystal, cupped it in his open palms and extended his arms forward. An unsettling, dim light filled the room and revealed its secrets. The walls and ceiling were filled with hundreds of small holes of many different proportions, the largest of which one could fit a normal-sized fist. Kerriah cautiously approached the wall closest to her and rubbed her fingertips across the holes.

"For some reason, I don't like the looks of this." Her voice quivered nervously.

All at once, black vines rapidly crawled from out of the holes and scaled across every section of the wall and ceiling and eventually blocked off the stairway for which they entered. The vines continued to weave their ways in and out of each other and slowly filled the room. The three of them huddled close to the center of the room in an attempt to keep a distance from the encroaching vines.

"What the heck are we supposed to do now?" Krath barked at Crix.

"I'm not sure exactly," Crix replied as he stood strong, clenching the crystal. "I feel compelled to just stand here and do nothing."

"Do nothing!" Krath shouted. "We're supposed to just stand here and become plant food? Tya must be tuggin' on me, buddy, 'cause I'm not goin' out like that!" As one of the vines neared Krath, it curled out as if it attempted to grab him. Krath snatched the vine and twisted it; the vine was rigid, and even with his strength, it would not bend easily.

"This thing won't break." He struggled against it with both hands, the muscles in his arms strained with tension.

Kerriah ducked and spun away, avoiding several of the grabbing vines. However, as she backed too close to the wall, one snatched her ankle and pulled her down then dragged her across the floor as other vines seized and subdued her limbs. Her struggle against them proved futile, and the strength of the vines was too much for even Krath. They overtook him as more and more vines grabbed hold and pulled him up to the ceiling. He howled lividly over his situation, while he squirmed like a restrained beast in an effort to free himself.

The vines circled Crix but never made a motion to grab him as he kept his ground in the center of the room. One of the larger vines coiled back and pointed directly at Crix's face as if it were looking at him with unseen eyes. It turned and circled around his head before stopping again by his face.

"What do you want?" he asked, speaking to the vine.

The vine pulled back as though startled by the sound of his voice. Two more vines crept in and touched the crystal Crix was holding but snapped back as soon as they made contact. The two vines drew back and formed into an insignia, one that looked vaguely familiar to Crix. An insignia of two stars joined at the corners with a column behind them. Then, he recalled noticing the same insignia on Suros's armored shoulder pads.

"Suros!" he shouted.

The vines stopped and moved in from every direction before pulling Crix off his feet. The stone ceiling slid open and pulled the three upward in a twisted web as they intertwined themselves in and out, moving them up, and then forward. Crix struggled to keep hold of the crystal and, at the same time, not to be mangled in the snaking vines.

He yelled, "Stop!"

The vines stopped all at once, as though they responded to his command. "We just need to get to the Alcazar hangar."

They started moving upward again, and then to the left and forward. They could see nothing but felt pinching and scratching all over as the vines continued to transport them to their destination. They moved for a short while with small cracks of light sliding by as they traveled through the underground passage. Heavy stones were grinding beneath them; then, full illumination swiftly emerged. The three of them dropped into a brightly lit room; the vines withered back into the ceiling and vanished from sight.

As they got back to their feet again, they found themselves in an observation room overlooking a hangar area with a regal, pale, greenish-grey ship located in its center. At the far end of the hangar, two giant, star-shaped columns lead to an opening. Emerald dyed banners, each embroidered with a unique insignia, hung from the moderately adorned walls. Crix took notice, once again, to one of the insignias that were the same as what Suros had on his armor.

"There's our ship," Kerriah quietly asserted, thrilled at the thought of flying once again. As she stood up, Krath grabbed her by the back of the head and pulled her back down below the window opening.

"Yep, but we are going to have to deal with those two soon to be headin' to the scrap yard buddies over there first," he whispered, pointing over at two Marcks that had an Andor guard subdued with his hands behind his head and face to the floor.

"I see that . . . What exactly did you have in mind?" She turned to look back at him but realized that he was already down a staircase to the right, eagerly trotting off toward the Marcks without an apparent care or worry.

Crix peered over the ledge for a look. "Has he lost his mind?"

Kerriah, with her hand over her mouth and a troubled look in her eyes, replied, "I believe that went a long time ago."

Metallic screams and blasts echoed across the hangar, followed by metal spinning across the stone floor. "Whatcha waitin' on? Get down here," Krath yelled from below.

Crix and Kerriah started their way down to Krath when they were stopped by a bulky, Morak warrior that dropped in from somewhere above them. His appearance was battle weathered with blisters across the left side of his face. He grabbed Crix and tossed him almost without effort against a nearby wall. Kerriah planted her heel into his knee, causing him to flinch just long enough for her to slide past him. She hurried over to where Crix laid clenching his ribs, still trying to shake off the massive jolt he had just taken.

Displaying complete control over his emotions, the steadfast Andor warrior charged at them, the look in his face cold and menacing. A blinding flash and an image of Suros emerged before him and sent the Morak to an instant halt.

"Child . . ." Suros said, "you have fought bravely. However, these three are not our adversaries. Your enemies are there." He pointed to the opening between the columns where a group of eight Marcks in green-tinted armor tactically worked their way into the hangar. Suros placed his two hands on the Andor's shoulders and his blisters and wounds dispersed.

"You are whole again. Now, go in defense of our kingdom!" The Andor leaped high into the air to the top of a service platform near the ship. He then dove into the Marck intruders and bashed them away as if possessed by a warrior spirit.

"The ship is there. Now, take it. I will see to your safety out of this place. Keep safe the Tersik crystal. Go!" Suros's body misted away into the air as Krath ran up in his place.

"What tya waitin' on? It looks like that big ole Andor is holdin' his own against those hunks of refuse, but more keep comin'. I think we need to get goin' and quick."

The slender ship with its long, forked bow and wider aft looked properly majestic for that of the Andor Grand Chief. As they approached its clear lift tube, a feeling of hope crept over them. Krath activated a switch, calling the lift down, and they hurried on, shooting up into the ship's belly.

A gleaming, concaved, metal door groaned open to an area highly polished and ornate. A series of tall-backed chairs, padded with black velour and dark, metallic, brushed steel, lined both walls on each side. In the center of the room sat a trim and judicious Andor, who leaned forward with one elbow rested upon his knee as though sizing up the group that had just arrived. His long face was pure white, and his mane was a stark contrast of dark grey. He wore a tall crown of brass with a circular emblem in its center that matched a standard above his chair.

Flanked by two heavily armored Moraks, which bore the same circular emblem on their chest plates, the crowned Andor sat up and let out a deep grumble before speaking.

"So . . . this is Crix, son of Corin Emberook, I presume. Well, I am confident that you have in your possession the Tersik crystal, as Suros has promised, or else you would not be standing here before me now." His voice was gritty and difficult to understand.

"Grand Chief Isomar, I take it?" Kerriah cut in, unimpressed with his title.

"Hmmm . . . and who is your haughty companion?" The Grand Chief responded. Kerriah braced her fist at her waist and took a swaggered stance in preparation to deflect any potential insults.

Crix took a slow and humble bow. "These are my friends and have aided me in my journey here, Grand Chief. I stand here humbly before you."

The Grand Chief arose and grasped his staff with a crescent edge at the top. He popped it hard against the floor. "Yet, you came here to steal my ship, did you not?" His voice raised.

Krath stepped forward defensively. "Now, tya look here. I'm not one for kissin' the hiney of any—"

"Silence!" The Grand Chief's voice roared out so forcefully that even Krath backed down from his advance. "There is not time for you to interject your views, only that you will take my ship and get the crystal far away from here. The great prophecy long predicted this, though I, as most Andors in this age, have chosen to deny it until now. The rebirth of our ancient lineage will come from what you now hold in your possession, and you are the instrument for its safekeeping. These lands are forsaken now, and I will sacrifice myself as my ancestors once did long ago to ensure its survival."

He paced toward the lift tube with his two guards falling in behind. "Take my ship and leave these lands to safety." The ship shook, and a rumble echoed from outside. He looked upward. "Our destroyers are upon us. We shall repel them!" He placed his hand upon Crix's shoulder and looked squarely down at him.

"There is a place of perfect alignment, the forgotten world where all has died. That is where we will begin anew. When that time comes, it will require the mystic abilities that you inherited to awaken the crystal from its sleep." The ship shook so hard it felt like it nearly capsized. Crix looked at him, confused. For now, he would just try to remember these words with the hope that one day, they would become clear.

The Grand Chief turned and disappeared behind the cylinder door.

"Ookay, let's get this thing in the air," Kerriah said, still in slight puzzlement over the scene that just played out before them. She hurried through an arched door, and then a lengthy hall that led to a cockpit with four seats.

"You know how to fly this, right?" Crix asked, troubled that he had not considered this until now.

Kerriah smiled at him. "I can fly anything that's flyable."

Crix exhaled his built-up anxiety and nodded several times with relief. "I knew that; somehow, I knew that."

She is going to be good at everything she does.

Outside the ship's window, they observed the Grand Chief and his guards hacking and slashing away at Marcks that swarmed into the area. Kerriah fired up the ship's engines as if she had flown it a hundred times before. As the engines whirred up out of their slumber, the guards outside became overwhelmed and fell to their relentless attackers. The Grand Chief's crown dropped from his head and clanked to the floor; blast wounds riddled his body. He threw down his broken spear and drew his blade for one final engagement. In his death rage, he sliced the head off one last Marck before he slumped to the floor, never to rise again.

Crix was horrified as he watched through the viewport and witnessed the great Andor Chief fall. "Kerriah . . . we have to get going!" The Marcks outside were all turning their attention back to the ship.

"Got it!" She tapped several switches and pushed the throttle forward. The ship rose from the hangar deck, and the nose dipped forward slightly before moving steadily forward through the two massive columns. They thrust out of the hangar and kept a low altitude to avoid detection as they pushed their way out of Troika.

"This is my fault." Crix's face was long as he observed the distant landscape of Troika blackened in smoke with flashes of war sparkling throughout. "All my friends, everything I know . . . Gone." He dropped his head in sorrow.

"No," Kerriah said. "This was inevitable as Zearic and the Marcks tighten their grip over the Oro System. All worlds and species will fall victim to his insanity eventually. However, you saved Troika. You have that crystal, right?" Crix slowly nodded.

An explosion rocked the rear quarters of the ship. "Dang it! I just knew it!" Krath barked. "We picked up several Marck scrappers before we left the hangar. I'll take care of these chumps." He then stormed off to the back of the ship with his fists pumping with every pounding step.

Two more explosions severely rock the ship. Then a large, shocking explosion jarred the ship upward, knocking Crix to his backside. Kerriah gripped the controls as alarms sounded, and the ship tilted sideways and into a spin. Somehow, she was able to regain control, for the moment, though the ship was on a downward descent that she could not stop.

"What is going on back there? The stabilizers are no longer responding!" Crix jumped up to call the doors open for a look. As the door swooshed open, a gust of swirling wind and fire threw him to his backside again. He crawled back up to his hands and knees to witness a large section of the ship's midsection missing. The rear of the ship was gushing flames and debris as the remaining midsection eroded away before his eyes.

"Get back!" Krath shouted as he bounded across from the back of the flaming ship and into the narrow passage with Crix.

"One of our party crashers decided to blow himself and half the ship up with a fusion detonator! Luckily, I was able to use his buddy to shield myself from the blast!" Krath yelled over the crackling of the ship falling apart while dusting himself off nonchalantly.

"The ship is going down, and Kerriah is struggling to keep control of it!" Crix shouted.

Krath appeared annoyed by the news. "Awww . . . no kiddin'? I mean we just lost the whole back half. Do tya think we really needed it?" He pushed Crix aside and tromped ahead to get back to the cockpit.

Kerriah looked back and noticed the concerned looks on their faces. "I've lost forward propulsion, so my guess is that we are in bad shape back there."

Krath strapped himself in the seat next to Kerriah. "Tya can say that all right. How we are lookin' for a good ole crash landin'?"

She gave a long sigh as she took in the situation. "I need to find a way to crash out of Marck visibility . . . There!" She pointed toward a lake of murky water below. Tall reeds and purple flora surrounded the dark lagoon. The fertile, black soil around the lake had darkened its waters to the point that there seemed to be no visibility below the surface.

"If we crash there, the ship will sink into the dark water and disappear with the water smothering the smoke and flames." Fortunately, her father was a thorough flight instructor. He had made it a point to teach her how to emergency land a ship in nearly any scenario he could imagine in the event that it was ever necessary. This would, of course, include crash landings. It was here that the years she spent surveying with her father would once again pay off in her flight skills.

She guided the ship down as steadily as she could as it violently approached the lake below. "Brace yourselves, this is going to hurt!" she yelled as the ship gave out a screech then a deafening crack from its belly as it smacked against the watery surface. The impact knocked them forward; loose items zinged through the cabin like missiles past their heads. Black water gushed inward from all directions, and the ship pulled down into the lake.

"That's it! Get out!" she ordered, taking full charge of the situation.

Krath kicked out the remaining portion of the compromised cockpit window. The incoming water blasted into the ship along with a strong, pungent smell. The water was laden with organisms, both large and small. The slithery lake critters whisked about, frenzied from the sudden commotion.

Incapable of fighting against the inward gush of water, Kerriah and Crix submerged into darkness. They were both blown back against the inner wall of the ship and pinned against it with what felt like the weight of a concrete slab pushing into them. The gushing water swiftly released its vice-like hold on them, but there was little hope to find their way out in the murky, black water as the ship's nose dipped downward. Then, out of the darkness came Krath. He easily snatched them up and kicked his way back to the surface.

Krath pulled them up on the shore. His eyes' membranes closed and opened several times to clear the soot from the lenses. The three leaned back on their elbows of the muddy lake edge and took a moment to gain their thoughts. The ship's tail was the last thing still visible before bubbling into the depths of the dark lake.

On the shore, serpents slid away, and jelly-like critters oozed back into the water for safety at the presence of the three disturbing their leisurely day in the sun. After the three sat quietly for a moment, Crix looked over at his two companions and exhaled deeply.

"I honestly don't know how we are still alive, but thanks. I mean, I just want to say thanks for you being who you are. I can't image who else I would want here with me at a time like this . . . aside from Haflinger." Crix ran his hands through his hair and rested them on top of his head. "He would have something wise to say right about now. Something that would just make you know that this all has a purpose." He lowered his hands and stared off into the distance.

"No worries, buddy, I'm sure wherever tya keeper is right now, he's lookin' down on tya with a big smile of pride. Besides, I ain't goin' nowhere," Krath responded. Never having any offspring of his own, he felt deep warmth settle over his normally reclusive inner self that came in a fatherly sort of way. For Krath, Crix was a child he had an overwhelming need to watch over and protect from harm.

Krath glanced over at Kerriah. "How in the heck did tya learn to fly like that, little Mendac?"

She leaned over onto her elbow to answer. "Well . . . my father. He felt it was important for a woman to learn to fly a ship beyond the confines of skyway pipes. He was always amazed at how quickly I took to his instruction; it just came natural to me. I later used this skill to dodge Marck blockades for the insurgency."

"Very good . . . tya turned me into a believer. Well, let's have a quick look around here and see what we have to work with." Krath stood up. The reeds were tall, and he pushed some aside in an attempt to get a better view. Air spurted out from a distance and quickly caught his interest. He pushed further into the reeds and pressed down more. The random spurting drew in closer.

"Krath?" Kerriah whispered. Krath pushed his arms deeper in and folded down a large section of reeds.

"Dang!" he whispered loudly in his gravelly voice. "Jet-propelled Marcks and a whole mess of them." A wall of Marcks hovered just above the reeds, scouring the landscape for their prey.

"There are too many, run!" Krath stomped by, giving a pushing nudge to Crix and Kerriah. They raced after him as he created a path ahead through the thickness. The spurting now turned to continuous thrusts that swarmed all around them.

They reached a hillside that was slick with mud and thicket. Without hesitation, Krath leaped down and backslid through the muddy slope, tearing through the coarse vines and thorny brush. Kerriah and Crix stayed close behind trying to benefit as much as possible from the wake he was creating. They reached a bottom and a clearing, but the Marcks encircled ahead. Dozens of Marcks surround them with their rifles drawn. A metallic voice sounded off from one of the hovering assailants.

"We want the boy, the one in possession of Tolagon weapon. Send him forth, and your lives will be spared to hard labor within the mines of Dispor."

There was only one reply in Krath's mind, and he did not need a second to consider. "Tya can take your propositio—" he lashed out just before a plasma blast ruptured directly in front of him.

"You will receive no further warnings," the voice proclaimed. A Marck ground assault ship dropped down directly above them with a loud boom. The ship darkened their view of the sky with its crescent shadow.

"Guys, our odds aren't getting any better here," Kerriah said, affirming the obvious. Just as she got her words out, a vertical beam of white light drew up directly in front of them. It was about four meters in height and broke open into a rectangular doorway. The light from the doorway blinded them and gave off a soft hum that pulsed. Krath took several cautious steps back, unsure if it was a new Marck weapon.

A distant and solemn voice called out from the light source. "Enter, there is safety here." Krath tilted his head, somewhat puzzled. "No time, come quickly," the voice persisted.

"Wait just a minute there; I know that voice. If I'm correct . . . then . . ." He paused and then motioned for his two companions to follow.

"Halt!" one of the Marcks warned.

"At this point, we got nothin' to lose here. Come on!" Krath dashed into the illuminated field and vanished. The white light flickered for a second as he passed through. The Marcks closed in just as Kerriah and Crix leaped into the doorway. It gave out a loud pop and crack just before it closed, leaving the Marck force without its prey.

CHAPTER 12

Crix stumbled back up to his feet after his hasty dive into the gateway. Everything was blindingly bright, so he rubbed his eyes to adjust, and tears poured out from sensitivity.

"Kerriah?" he called out.

"Quickly, put her over there in the suspension field," a gentle voice unfamiliar to him spoke out.

"Put who where? I can't see anything. My eyes can't adjust to this light." Crix, frustrated, started to feel around for answers.

"Hold still there, boy." Krath placed a pair of light-filtering lenses over Crix's eyes. The intensity of the lights dimmed and became clear. "There tya go. Tya see, Plexo's kind likes it to be good and bright for some reason. Lucky he had these things handy for us."

The slender, translucent being with long arms and a heart-shaped head stood up straighter as if to gain composure. "Well, I designed my ship to mimic that of my homeworld of Eesolan," he said in a soft, eloquent voice as he motioned his hands over a twinkling array of various colors dancing in the air, which swirled in chorus with his hand's movement. The swirling colors appeared to control bright beams of light all around Kerriah's suspended body.

Plexo placed the back of his hand against her forehead. "She is beginning to come around. Fortunately, she was only stunned as their intent was for captives and not casualties."

Kerriah's eyes opened, and she squinted while placing her hand over her eyes. She slowly removed her hand and looked around. "Wha . . . what sort of place is this?" she asked. Crix, Krath, and Plexo looked at her with amazement on their faces. "What?" She was confused by their expressions.

Plexo moved so fluidly that watching him created the illusion of a spirit and not a physical entity. He approached Kerriah and leaned in to take a closer inspection of her.

"Astonishing . . . Most peculiar indeed. Your natural eyes have adjusted so quickly to the illumination here," he said with almost a question to his statement.

A being from the distant diplomatic world of Eesolan, Plexo was gifted with a heightened sense of logic and scientific reasoning. This was an inherited side effect of his home world's encounter with a nearby gamma-ray burst. It wiped out most of their populace many centuries ago. A ghost-like appearance and the gift of enhanced focus and vision graced the survivors of that terrible tragedy. This vision allowed them to see things beyond that of normal eyes and minds.

"Well, yeah, why shouldn't they?" She looked over at Krath and Crix whose eyes had a strange, opaque look to them. "What the heck is wrong with your eyes?"

"Well . . . well . . . normally, I would coat your optic lenses with a temporary synthetic filter, but in your case, it does not appear necessary." Plexo put down his optic augmenter and placed his hands together with delight in his face. "You are an interesting one for sure; time permitting, I would be delighted to run some tests on you. With your permission, of course."

Kerriah appeared irritated. "Look, I'm not for being anyone's science experiment, got it?"

Plexo took a cautious step back from her. "Very well. I'm sure you have many questions as to where you are, and at least for two of you, who exactly I am. Let's start with who I am first.

"As Krath has already pointed out, I am Plexo, a Luminar as you may have guessed, sent as part of the second envoy from Eesolan. My primary directive was initially to design and construct this system's first Komeectram-driven intergalactic gammac corridor sequencers, or commonly known as gammac corridors. I was later drawn into service as the Vico Legion's chief scientific officer during the dreadful Thraxon War. As the UMO turned over to Marck control, I went into temporary seclusion while I made numerous modifications to this ship. Modifications that gave it a more home-like feel, as well as technologies that would better allow me to observe Marck activity undetected, amongst other things."

Only one portion of what Plexo told them perked Crix's attention. "So you knew my father as well?"

"I most certainly did, young Emberook. We can speak more of it in a little while, but first, please allow me to show you around." Plexo spoke out a command in an alien dialect, and the wall at the far end of the room faded away as if it were never there. The room opened into an eccentric laboratory that had no visible floor or ceiling. Swirling colors and small spheres darted around as quickly as nighttime insects attracted to lights. At the center of the massive lab was a large, white, spherical control center with six teardrop seats that dripped from the underside.

Plexo stepped off into the lab as if he stepped onto an invisible floor. His body appeared to skip across the area, much like a vision from a dream. So much so that Crix had to give his eyes a good rub, but the optic augmenter prohibited it.

"Come, my friends, do not be afraid. On Eesolan, we have learned to control gravity even in our simple, everyday movements, and I have longed for that freedom again ever since leaving. Recent developments have allowed me to recreate it here. I can assure that you will not get hurt. The feeling has an energizing quality that you will learn to appreciate."

Kerriah looked at him skeptically. "Recent developments? Care to explain what you mean by this?" Plexo intentionally avoided the question by changing the subject.

"Follow me, please; we have to get you cleaned up quickly as your soiled attire is at risk of contaminating the fragile elements here." He skipped across to the far side of the lab, waving for them to follow, and then called out a command that revealed another room behind a disappearing wall. Nobody followed him.

"Aww . . . well . . . considering what we've been through the past few days, does jumping out into this void really seem so bad?" Crix turned and gave a forced smile just before taking a leap of faith into the lab.

His whole body felt a tickling sensation that started from his belly and pulsed outward through his body. The feeling gave him a slight shiver at first and then was followed by a heightened sense of calm and awareness.

"Wow! This makes me feel like a child again!" he shouted back to Krath and Kerriah. "Plexo is right; this feels unbelievable!" He began spinning and leaping around with a smile cemented on his face. Even though he should feel traumatized after the ordeals that he had endured over the past number of days, including the demise of Troika and the death of Haflinger, somehow, this artificial force was making him feel joyful and full of energy. Crix took in deep breaths. The air smelled and tasted sweet, just like when he was a child.

Upon seeing his instant bliss, Kerriah leaped out, joining him, and they danced around and giggled as if their years were instantly halved.

Krath scowled and mumbled under his breath. "I never much liked being a kid. What the heck is wrong with just walkin' anyway?" He reluctantly stepped out with the rigidness of a Solaran grit ox in his stride. He fought back the joyful feelings and kept his tempo moving toward Plexo, yet he could not help but crack a slight grin as he reached the other side.

"Quickly, you two," Plexo called out to Crix and Kerriah. "These instruments are highly sensitive to contaminants." Crix grabbed Kerriah by the waist and swung her around, both of them smiling and feeling more carefree than they had in years. Looking into her deep green eyes, he felt his heart melt, a feeling he had never before experienced.

"You know, you're truly remarkable. I feel as though when you're near, there is nothing I cannot achieve." Crix was entranced in her stare.

"I . . . I have to say that I have had similar feelings since we met. Crix, there is truly something different about you, and it is not just the orb. I find that I want to be wherever you are." Their heads drew closer, and warmth flushed over them both. She had never had good relationships in the past. The egos of her male suitors had always been a point of contention, and her natural abilities were typically too much for their frail self-esteems. This had caused her to become more standoffish to advances. However, Crix did not appear to suffer from this underlying jealousy; maybe it was his rearing in Troika. It didn't matter why; she was willing to let him in, but he needed to take the initiative.

"Hey! Get tya butts over here before Plexo shorts out!" Krath cracked out in a startlingly loud voice, which broke their grasp from one another.

As they entered a triangular room, Krath gave a slight chuckle.

"It felt nice, did it not?" Plexo asked, not expecting a reply.

A device with intertwining metal rods rose up from the floor. The tops of the rods were embossed with unfamiliar symbols. Plexo said several more strange words, and a drawer slid out from the wall.

"Here are some loose-fitting garments that you can wear while I reconstruct your current apparel. These garments can also be worn through your cleansing process." Plexo handed them each a white, long-sleeved top and trousers. The material was so light to the touch that it felt just a bit more substantial than air, yet was still opaque.

"What's that 'bout cleansin'? I'm not one for cleanin' up and smellin' pretty. I personally like a little stench; it adds to my charm," Krath protested while rubbing his gritty chest, causing flakes of dirt to break off.

Plexo looked at him with disgust in his face. "Well, I find your odor to be offensive, and the filth is detrimental to my instruments on board this ship. So please, if you will, place these garments on, and I will show you to the cleanser. If you require privacy, stand up against the wall to the far right of the corcybliator and place your palm against it," Plexo instructed.

Crix and Kerriah each took their garments and walked over to the wall, placing their hands upon it. As they did, walls emerged around them individually, and like most of the walls there, they poured out like fluid before taking their solid forms. Krath just dropped his pants and shirt in the main room and began to change into the white garments.

Plexo looked over at him appalled. "Simply revolting! You have no self-dignity, do you?"

"Nope. None whatsoever. What about tya? Tya just run around in tya birthday suit all the time; why are my parts so offensive?" Krath replied as he ripped the top fitting it over his large torso.

"As Luminars, we don't have any distinguishable reproductive organs protruding from our bodies, and we keep ourselves properly cleansed, so there is nothing to be offended about," Plexo explained with his head deliberately turned away from Krath.

Kerriah and Crix emerged with their white garments on and their old ones in their hands. "Now place your soiled garments in front of the corcybliator," Plexo said.

They placed their clothes as instructed, and he told them to back away. As they stepped back, the floor where the clothes sat rose up. Plexo said an indistinguishable word, and a swirl of color appeared before him. He pushed his fingers into the colors, and the clothes separated into their individual pieces. The pieces one-by-one broke apart into smaller and smaller fragments until they were mere molecules floating in the air. Then, with a snap and a loud swoosh in the air, the molecules merged back together, and the garments dropped down and then were lowered back down to the floor.

Without hesitation, Kerriah leaned down, picked up her clothes, and held them up inspecting them. "Amazing, they look better now than when they were new." She placed them up against her body to make sure they would still fit.

"The corcybliator breaks items down to the molecular level and reconstructs them, removing all impurities, and at the same time, discovering conceivable methods to improve them without compromising the original purpose of the item itself. It's a highly intellectual instrument," Plexo explained. "Now, before you put those on, I must ask you to step onto that concave section of the floor over there. I believe you all will fit if you stand close together."

Krath moseyed over to the edge of the cavity and peered up at a cone-shaped device that was only a meter above his head. "So what sorta contraption is this?"

Plexo looked discontentedly in Krath's direction. "That, my Hybor friend, is the source of freedom from parasitical microbes and offensive plumes of stench that emanates from your hulking frame."

"Hybors like to have a little reek to us. In fact, our females prefer a stinkier male." Krath blew under his arm in the direction of Plexo.

Plexo scrunched his face in utter revulsion. "Please, just step into the cavity as this will only take a few seconds."

They snuggled together in the cavity, and Plexo swooped and swished a small batch of the floating colors. The cone beeped several times in rapid succession until it sounded like a continuous, high-pitched tone. Black and white rings shimmered downward rapidly over the three. Then, all of a sudden, the beeps halted and the rings faded. They looked at one another curiously as their appearance had changed slightly. The air was devoid of any scent and was now completely sterile. Their skin had a smooth glow and appeared more youthful.

"The Volcrum purifier not only neutralizes and draws away all contaminants from your bodies; it also does the same of all your dead skin, thus your enriched appearance. This is as clean as you will ever be," Plexo explained.

"You look really handsome Krath," Crix joked as he elbowed Kerriah.

"Shut tya mouth before I give tya a good wallopin'. This is humiliatin'. I need to find a good ole pool of stagnate marsh to take a dip in just to regain my dignity back." Krath stomped over and snatched up his clothes and angrily thrust them back on. His normally cracked and crusty flesh now appeared smooth and shiny.

After getting dressed in their original attire, Plexo led them back to the main lab and to the teardrop seats below the spherical control center. "Take a seat and try to clear your thoughts. I would like to show you something."

Krath, already irritated, snarled out, "This ain't gonna do anythin' like scrub out my guts, is it? Cause I just about had it."

"No, no . . . certainly not. This will tap your consciousness into my observation drones, which I have scattered throughout the system. This is the most efficient way to get you caught up with what has been occurring and what you need to be prepared for," Plexo replied.

Krath chuckled. "Observation drones? How tya getting' those past Marck detection systems?"

Plexo paused for a few seconds before answering. "Well, I must admit that I have lost a few of them. Fortunately, I have them programmed to self-destruct if they are ever compromised to keep my location here a secret. The biggest problem I have had to date is simply getting a view of Nathasia.

"The Marcks have the planet so heavily quarantined that it is virtually impossible to get within any sort of observational distance of it. In fact, they have shrouded the planet with a light disruption cloud, which I have yet to find a way to penetrate. I find it quite intriguing; you cannot observe the planet with even the most powerful optical sensors. All they return are shadowy distortions. There is also a sizable Marck armada there, and a rather bulky ship that my sources have informed me is responsible for generating the disruption cloud. It's been this way for almost three years now and has me gravely concerned." Plexo stopped and took a deep exhale, shaking his head and looking slightly fraught. "Anyway, it would be better if you see for yourselves. Now relax and tilt your heads back into the seat."

A few seconds went by, and there was a sploosh as narrow beams of light poured down from the small tubes in the sphere above them and contacted their foreheads. Their bodies instantly went numb, and they found that they could no longer physically move. Plexo's voice came from inside their heads, similar to a voice that would be in a dream.

"I would have warned you of the side-effects, but I was worried you might not understand that requisite for Arc Stasis. For your minds to be unrestricted enough to travel, you must give up your body temporarily. You see, Arc Stasis projects your minds through the observation drones. This connection gives you the exact view, smell, reverberation, and feeling you would have if you were actually there.

"It's quite an extraordinary device I must say, and one I've spent much time in recently. That is how I was able to locate you. Of course, you spotted my first drone near Drisal and aptly evaded its presence. Fortunately, when the attack began on Troika, I located your transport breaking out of the region, which brings us here." Plexo paused for a few seconds. "Let's have a look first at what is happening to certain areas of Soorak right now."

Their minds felt a sturdy pull as if being drawn through a duct, unable to resist its attraction. The blackness slowly pixelated into a vivid, panoramic view of a small township filled with a mix of clear and opaque domes. A cityscape of white and red cylinder-shaped buildings sketched across the horizon in the distance. The only noticeable sounds were the whistling of auto-tracers and zipfoils flashing through the skyway pipes high above and the groans of the wind occasionally gusting between the structures. The air, however, had an abnormal smell. The scent was not particularly strong, yet it was subtle and similar to rubber or the toxic chemical that would come from melted plastics.

An occasional resident would walk by at times with a subdued expression on their face. These rigid figures neither smiled nor frowned nor spoke; rather, they stiffly trudged by as if in a trance. Something just didn't feel right, and there was a sense of emptiness in everything around them.

"Do you notice something that's flawed here?" Plexo asked.

"I've been in isolation for a long while, but shouldn't these shops and eateries be full of folks this time of day?" Krath responded.

"Precisely! There is no one around aside from a token roamer for a very logical reason. These Mendacs are no longer a . . ." Plexo paused and then shouted in frustration. "No . . . no!"

They turned around to observe a resident standing mere centimeters from them. Garbed in formal work attire, he stared directly at them as though he could see into their minds through the drone. His eyes flashed a blazing orange light, and his mouth opened slowly letting out a shrieking buzz. The terrible noise was loud and had an irritation level similar to that of an alarm system. Their view went black in an instant.

Plexo sighed. "It appears that my drone was detected and destroyed once again, hence breaking our view of Keirtol. I'm afraid it's happening more often lately."

Crix squirmed in his seat. "What is wrong there? What were you about to tell us?"

"The township of Keirtol is no longer a town, rather a test subject for a secretive plot to Marckanize all living things in the Oro System."

A deep feeling of confusion poured into Crix's thoughts, as he started looking to Plexo for reassurance that what he just saw was not real. "Those people are no longer alive? They have somehow been transformed into a sort of Marck? Why and who would want to do this?"

Krath interrupted before Plexo could reply. "Tya can bet it's that worthless bag of dirt Zearic and his corporation Sinstar, who has also illegally taken control of the Marcks, even though he denies it."

Plexo confirmed Krath's assumption. "I'm afraid you may be correct. Though my probes have not been able to get close enough to him to either confirm or deny his involvement, I suspect he is not alone in this."

"Really? Who else would be behind it?" Kerriah asked.

"Ohh . . . I believe the Marck Central Core is at play here . . . the queen."

"Tya what?" Krath was not excited to hear the answer.

"Yes, from what I have been discovering from the little bits of information that have leaked through my sources, this central core actually has a persona of a queen by design. I know little else of this queen, but you can be assured that if Zearic is working with this persona, who thinks itself a queen, that the relationship must be a contentious one given that Zearic sees himself as our assumptive monarch. This possibly strained relationship could work to our advantage, as dismal as it appears on the surface." Plexo explained his theory.

"Ahhh . . . great," Krath grumbled. "Just what we needed, someone else that thinks themselves better than the rest of us. What's worse is we created this one."

"I may add that Keirtol is not the first town that this travesty has befallen upon. There have been several others, and the pattern suggests that a smaller community was used first, and then followed by larger ones. I fear the next will be a major metropolitan area. The pattern I have observed thus far is that the leaders are transformed first, making it easier to apprehend the remaining populace, individual by individual. If anyone were to suspect something was happening, with whom would they file the complaint? The local Marck control station? I'm afraid the citizens of the Oro System put themselves into a grave position when they created this supposedly independent Marck security force."

"Not everyone agreed to this," Krath said.

"Nonetheless, I need to show you more. As you may recall, I mentioned Nathasia, and I will show you what I have been able to see." They all closed their eyes and leaned back into their chairs. The pulling sensation ran off with their minds again, and the scene pixelated into a view of a grey planet. The sight of it was haunting, a hazy green shroud poured over the planet, spilling out a short distance past its spherical lower edge. Hovering above it, an immense ship with a device that looked like a giant trident hung beneath it. A green shadow appeared to emit from the trident, and many other warships there kept their distance, though still lurked nearby.

"As you can see, I cannot get a view of this quarantined planet. My drones are swiftly destroyed if they get anywhere in proximity to the garrisoning fleet that surrounds it so meticulously. There is something malevolent going on there, and one thing I'm certain of, whatever it may be, it will not be pleasant for any of us. There is a more important reason that I show you this cursed world." Plexo paused as if to wait for inquiries that failed to come. "The yellow orb is there still."

"The what?" Krath snarled out in contention. "Tya know that thing was vaporized in the Meutor Valley by the Vico Legion during the second Thraxon War. Plexo, have tya lost your radiated mind?"

"No, not at all actually," he calmly replied. "There were only three of us that knew of its whereabouts, and I assure you, it was amply safe from that blast. However, I had to still play the part and act as though it was destroyed. You see, the orbs can never really be destroyed, at least not by conventional methods . . ." His voice softened.

Deceit was not part of a Luminar's culture, and that show of dishonesty was something that Plexo grappled with for a long time. However, it was for a cause worthy enough to cast his ethics aside, but not without cost. He looked up with sorrow in his eyes.

"This terrible war has torn away pieces of me. Much the same for everyone that was involved in it."

His face appeared distressed as his memories of twenty years ago raced back. Leaving the three of them in Arc Stasis for a few extra minutes, he pulled himself out and stepped away to reflect on the painful memory of when he had to betray his sacred morality. He needed this moment. His mind was drifting hard into his woeful past.

CHAPTER 13

Twenty years ago . . .

"Plexo, do you have a read on this? Plexo, do you copy? . . . Plexo?" Corin, though relieved to see Thraxons withdrawing, was almost more concerned over the arrival of the Marcks. "I have the feeling something's gone wrong. I'm going to check on him. Stay with the legion and let me know right away if you encounter any Marcks." Creedith nodded in agreement. Floating upward, he took off over the horizon to the rear command base where Plexo was stationed.

Corin slowed as he neared the base and dropped down behind a chunk of charred wreckage. Directly above the base hovered an Elgon class transport ship with its deployment bridge lowered. Elgon transports were small ships used to deploy and extract ground forces. The side of the ship bore a familiar symbol. He had seen it before while sitting in on an early demonstration of Marck prototypes.

There were about twelve to fifteen sentry Marcks positioned around the structure. Corin cautiously approached the base, but as he hovered in closer, one of the Marcks took notice of his movement and pointed the business end of his rifle toward Corin.

"Halt, lethal force has been authorized." The blue-tinted Marck sputtered in a deep, unrefined voice as though speaking through a pipe.

"Stand down. I am Commander Corin Emberook; I'm the governing command over the Nathasian System and the Vico Legion."

Two additional Marcks approached and trained their rifles on Corin. "Halt, lethal force has been authorized." The same command was given from each in the same unrefined voice as they approached.

Memories of Marck design screens from months ago flipped through Corin's mind, data provided to familiarize himself with the new, elite, high-tech force. The original plan from UMO command control was for him to act as a commanding military advisor over the Marcks until the final transition was completed. Corin steadfastly refused that offer. The thought of leading what he referred to as "mindless metal monsters" was utterly absurd.

The Marcks before him now were security and not designed for military operations. They bore a lighter grade armor and weaponry as this made them more practical for civilian installments. They were slender with exposed, ball-hinged elbows and knees. Corin was now even more curious who was inside, but he had a deep suspicion he knew who it was.

"I guess I failed to make myself clear then. I'm entering my base, and you will stand down." As Corin continued toward the entrance, the eyes flashed on each of the Marcks, and they opened fire.

Corin rolled to the ground while throwing up a defensive barrier that defected several glancing shots. He pushed a two-fisted energy blast at the closest Marck, bursting it into shards. Grabbing up the Marck's blaster, he placed two well-aimed shots disabling the other two. From around both corners of the compound, the echoes of winding servomotors approached. Corin squatted down on one knee and positioned both arms straight and lowered his head. From around the corners, the Marcks emerged as Corin pushed out simultaneous energy blasts, blowing them into fragments that scattered to the ground.

A sturdy, metal door to the compound in front of him slid open vertically, giving a loud, mechanical whir mixed with grinding metal as the mechanical components moved against the dust and grime embedded in it.

"Commander Corin!" a stern voice called over the outdoor communicator. "Come inside and grace us with your presence." Corin knew this voice all too well. He was not thrilled hearing it come from within his science command station.

Zearic. Their association had been soured by Zearic's plot to steal the yellow orb, which had ultimately led to the destruction of the Nathasian civilization at the hands of the Thraxons. Following in the legacy of his father, Raucass, Zearic had always been ruthless and driven by a lust for power, and he firmly believed that all other species were inferior to the Mendacs.

Corin entered cautiously. He passed several security-class Marcks as he made his way down the corridor to the control center. Their heads turned slowly, following his approach and passing. He entered the command center room and observed eight more security Marcks standing by. Plexo sat on a small, metal stool in the center of the room. Several other science and engineering officer's bodies laid motionless on the floor. Plexo's head was down, and the look of dejection resonated from his face as he looked up at Corin.

Next to Plexo stood a tall, slender figure dressed in a UMO Galactic Marshal uniform. His face was creased and pitted on the left side; the remnants of old scars that cut down from his brow to his cheek. *Zearic!* His left eye shimmered red against the reflective light as he turned his head. The synthetic eye was a replacement of his original that was lost long ago when one of his immoral lab experiments went wrong. Corin's turbulent history with Zearic hit a boiling point at the start of the Thraxon invasion of Nathasia.

"Zearic, who do you think you are? You seize my rear science command post and kill my science officers! My command authority comes directly from Galactic Marshal Singsly, and I will witness your execution for this!" Corin shouted with his index finger pointed straight into Zearic's face.

"And my authority comes from Realm Chancellor Caabor himself. Singsly's command has been absolved, and full transitional command has been granted to me!" Zearic snapped with contempt, his voice froggy like someone who shouts often.

"You should have no authority!" Corin's eyes flared. "Your lust for the yellow orb has already destroyed everything around us.

189

Deceiving me into using my influence over the UMO console to defer aid to this world was your lowest point until now. I have done everything within my strength to free this world from your betrayal, and it has cost me my soul." He shook his head, frustrated. "Has the UMO become so corrupted that they would put a power-mongering sociopath in such a high-profile role?"

It's bad enough that he controls the largest Marck weapons development corporation in the Oro System, but now he is also in control of the unified and mechanized system forces? Corin fumed to himself.

Ignoring the insult and accusation, Zearic turned and pulled up a dead science officer that was slumped over a control panel. He let his body crash down limp to the floor. "As your superior, I am most grieved by your lack of subordination. You directly violated a priority one command to hold and preserve the Meutor Valley at all costs. All costs!" He violently slammed his fist down upon the panel, cracking the display. "Do you even understand what that means? The objective is worth more than your lives!" Zearic took a sturdy, harsh kick to the body on the floor as if to show his opinion over its value. "Instead, what I see is a cowardice commander that has abandoned his principal objective for the sake of self-preservation!"

"Self-preser . . . ? You don't have any idea!" Corin's face turned red with frustration. "My legion has been fighting and dying to preserve this valley and this burned-out world for six months straight, and no one has had the courage to come out here and tell us why this particular valley is so damned important!"

"Not that I owe you any explanation, but that valley held the last reported location of the lost yellow orb according to the

Nathasian official we interrogated. At least it was until you sent it to complete oblivion. Now, we're uncertain it even exists." Zearic had a look of hate and discontent pouring from his eyes.

Corin pushed out a heavy exhale in disgust. "Of course, I should have known. You're a lunatic." He was too exhausted to get further into a verbal confrontation.

All of this loss, all of this pain . . . for what? Zearic's power grab and his quest to be the unquestioned dictator of the Oro system.

"You're not even supposed to be in control of this self-governing mechanical force. Wasn't that the deal?"

"Until the transition is fully completed, they are mine! Right now, you are only slowing this transition." Zearic pulled a thermal blade from his jacket and held it at Plexo's neck. "And this piece of toxic waste will be the next to pay for your costly blunders, as the one who executed the illicit command to decimate the valley." The blade singed Plexo's neck as it burned a black line in his glowing skin. Plexo barely flinched as he lowered his head as if to accept his fate.

"Marshal or not, killing Plexo will be the last thing you'll ever do! You're responsible for far too many lives lost already. I'll bury you on this forsaken world! That you can count on!" Corin assured as he intently stared at him from across the room. The threat against Plexo instantly reignited his fighting spirit.

Zearic cracked a self-assured grin. "If you care so much for the remnants of your pitiful throng, you will back down and do as I command. The Marck force outside has been ordered to exterminate your troops if there are any signs of insubordination during the handoff of military control."

Corin, now furious, stepped back, kicked over a table, and screamed out of frustration. Scientific instruments scattered across the floor as the Marck guards raised their weapons toward Corin. His eyes welled up with seething anger and emotion, but he regained his composure. He could not live with the guilt of more lives lost because of him.

"No . . . I will take full responsibility and ownership. The destruction of the valley falls on me." He looked down with dismay. "My soldiers were following my orders."

Zearic lowered his blade. "Good, and with your cooperation, they will be spared and allowed to return to their loved ones." He stepped forward with his hand extended toward Corin. "First, you will relinquish your orb, and you will be hereby stripped of your title as the Tolagon of Soorak."

"Commander, no!" Plexo pleaded. "Don't!" It was at this moment that he realized that his deceptions were returning to inflict their inevitable toll on everyone and everything he believed in. This was not the Luminar way. His eyes welled up with tears for the first time in many years. He felt like an empty shell.

"Silence, you toxic wretch!" Zearic shouted at Plexo. "In addition, the Vico Legion will be disbanded, and you will be court-martialed for your insubordination. Perhaps the council will take pity on you and allow you to spend your remaining days in the Dispor moon as a subterranean scab harvester."

"Do as you will with me, but my soldiers and my family are to be spared," Corin insisted.

"Oh . . . they will. Now start by handing over your orb." Zearic gestured his hand out.

Corin cupped both hands together inward in front of his chest, summoning the blue orb from his body and into his hands. The blue, iridescent light emerged from his chest and gave out a high-pitched squeal as if reluctant to let go of its host.

Zearic's eyes lit up as he snapped his finger and motioned to the security Marck behind him. The Marck holstered his blaster and grabbed a clear box that had a solid metal base from a container nearby. This box was specifically designed to pacify the orb's power and keep it in stasis.

"Now, place it in the containment box for transport back to Soorak."

Corin hesitantly stepped forward and dropped the orb into the box as a white stasis field grabbed hold of the orb and held it captive. The Marck slammed the top down and then turned a switch on the side. The box let out a hiss as if drawing the air out.

"Put him in custody!" Zearic ordered. He stormed down the corridor for the exit. His Marck security units swung forward and fell in behind him one by one.

A remaining Marck pulled a shiny metal cylinder from his belt and held it behind Corin. A bright yellow ring emitted from one end to the other, surrounding Corin's midsection in a barrier of energy that gave off a persistent hum. Corin tried to turn and look behind him, and in doing so, his elbow brushed against the energy field, burning his sleeve and searing the skin beneath. He felt a push behind him that nudged him forward.

Just as Corin reached the outside door, a roaring boom shook the walls and echoed throughout the compound. The Marck guard that was leading Corin stopped suddenly and pulled Corin back. He heard metal crashing to the floor behind him, and the energy ring opened, freeing his arms. Corin turned around. Plexo stood there with his luminescent hand grasping a fusion cutter; it's arching blade popping and snapping. Corin looked down to see the Marck's headless body lying on the floor like an abandoned heap of metal.

Plexo gestured toward the door. "Commander, have a look outside."

Corin touched the tiny screen located next to the door. As the door slid open, smoke and fumes billowed inward. As the smoke cleared, he observed Creedith standing over Zearic with his tectonic blade pointing at the lower backside of the highly agitated marshal's head. The battered remains of the Vico Legion surrounded them. Littering the ground were smoldering heaps of Marck security units, along with a crashed transport that was formerly positioned above the compound.

"Commander! Please forgive me." Creedith was sincerely worried that Corin might be upset over the disregard of his orders. "I had one of my soldiers follow you at a distance when you left. When he reported that you were attacked, we came to assist. That's when we found Zearic and these Marcks carrying your blue orb. We instructed them to hand it over, and they foolishly attacked."

Corin looked over and noticed the blue orb still in the containment box lying on the ground. "Corin! You and these . . . these thugs will forfeit your lives for this treachery!" Zearic attempted to bat away Creedith's blade, but the strong Andor gave him a swift kick in the face. Blood spewed from Zearic's mouth while he inhaled dirt from the ground.

"You horse-faced dreg, the moment you so foolishly attacked that transport, a distress signal was sent to the Marck command fleet, and a rescue force will be dropping in any minute now!" Zearic snarled.

"Thanks for the warning," Creedith replied.

Plexo looked down at a small observation globe in his palm. "He is correct, sir. I am detecting a massive armored force heading this way from the south."

The Tolagon kneeled down and picked up the box containing the orb. He disengaged the stasis, and the Tolagon reunited with the orb once again. "We need to get out of here quick! Plexo, is your ship ready?" Corin asked.

"It is ready. I recently upgraded its Radiant Drive, and it should effortlessly outrun anything in the Marck fleet."

Corin and the legionnaires made their way down a narrow channel that led them into an underground hangar. A sleek, bronze ship stood awaiting its restless passengers. Plexo approached the control platform and flipped a switch. At that moment, a lurid vibration rumbled from above the subterranean hangar. Corin looked up toward the commotion.

TOLAGON

"Too late, they have arrived."

CHAPTER 14

Current day . . .

Plexo found it difficult to clear his thoughts. The sacrifice that Tolagon Emberook made that day still haunted him. He had to stay vigilant for Crix. The Oro System needed a new hero, a new Tolagon. Crix would need his guidance, and only a clear, logical mind could provide that. Plexo returned to Arc Stasis; he felt relieved when they still appeared to be preoccupied with the intimate view of Nathasia and the menacing fleet that surrounded it, except for Kerriah. She stared straight at him and clearly was not in Arc Stasis, but she did not say a word. It was as though she could see his pain and allowed him to have his moment.

They felt drawn back into their physical selves once again as their minds released from the clench of Arc Stasis. Their eyes slowly focused back to their real surroundings. Plexo calmly slapped his hands on his own lap in an attempt to regain his composure.

"Now, if things have gone as they should, you should now be in possession of the Phantos Bracer, which is a critical part of what you will need to gain access to the numinous council of Gabor." Plexo noticed Crix attempting to hide it earlier after he had changed his garments. The bracer was the last thing that Haflinger gave him before he passed, so for that reason alone, it was important to Crix.

"What?" Krath grumbled, agitated by Plexo's cryptic words.

Plexo smiled and focused his attention on Crix. "What you do not know is that the council was sealed off by the last two Tolagons before they were to resign their orbs. From my understanding, the seal cannot be opened without at least two orbs. Therefore, one of the reasons the yellow orb is important is that you will need it to gain entrance to Gabor.

"That is only the secondary reason that we must retrieve it, though. We must keep it out of the hands of Zearic. If the orbs were to fall into his hands, then all hope would be lost. With the Marck's tight control over Nathasia and all the activity that appears to be surrounding that planet, I fear that it's only a matter of time before they happen upon it."

The mythical lore was that inside Gabor contained an ancient alien race that once lived among the Luminars. A race they discovered on one of their interstellar quests many generations ago. It was from this race that the knowledge of how to control the orbs eventually came.

For a minute, they all remained in silence, trying to digest everything they just learned, and then an uncertain voice broke the quiet. "I—I have so many questions. How am I to wield two orbs by myself? Is that possible? What is Gabor?" Crix was just beginning to become acquainted with controlling the power of the one, much less two.

"When we Luminars discovered the Oro System, we were elated. However, what we found was a system immersed in a multi-generational war. Our solution was to find the best living examples of each world and bestow upon them an orb of Cyos, a gracious gift indeed. It was, however, that important, and we determined that it was the ultimate purpose of the orbs.

"The newly cast Tolagons would now be trained though Gabor. Trained to lead the way for peace and defend the system from future wars. Gabor is your future. It is the place that you will learn to be a Tolagon. It's where all Tolagons have been taught and where many of your questions will be answered.

"Each of the four orbs possesses a certain uniqueness in their powers. As you have already discovered, the blue orb has power over mass and gives its bearer the ability to create and manipulate solid objects, motion, and certain forms of energy. The yellow orb has power over thought and perception, the red over natural elements, and the green . . . light energy. Therefore, for that reason, there isn't a one-size-fits-all training for the Tolagon. Also, I'm afraid that without this knowledge, prolonged use of the orbs power, will eventually prove fatal to its host.

"As far as wielding two orbs, I only know that Tolagon Emberook is the only living creature that has ever done so and only for a short time after Tolagon Ridol of Nathasia fell in battle. So yes, it can be done, but how, I do not know, only that it must be done. You must gain access to Gabor and reactivate the council that resides there; this will give you all the rights, training, and knowledge so that you may fully harness the orb's abilities. With this knowledge, you can restore the Tolagons and their great order. I also fear that your continued use of the orb's power without this training could lead to your demise. There is no one else to teach you, no other Tolagon to aid in your journey," Plexo explained.

Crix sat there in deep thought for a moment, and then asked the only question that came to his mind. "How am I to find the orb on Nathasia? I mean, I have never even been there."

"Someone, who knows of its location, will have to escort you," Plexo replied.

He felt some relief in that answer. "You?"

"No . . . to leave my ship would be my demise. I know that statement must confuse you. You see, Luminars have extensive lifespans in comparison to your own due to our altered state of being. As you may or may not know, my world was in the direct path of a gamma-ray burst. This event changed our world forever; the radiation blast killed most, initially, but the survivors developed a heightened mental capacity and unnaturally long lifespans. We also inherited this wonderful radiance you see today." He stopped to extend his luminescent arms out and swooshed his hands around, only to notice that no one gave any positive feedback to his statement or gesture, and then continued.

"Well anyway, my species lives some two thousand or more years depending on the individual and his internal tissue regeneration rate. This tissue acts as an organic battery within our bodies. Not a battery as you know it but an organ that serves as a mechanism that collects and stores gamma radiation. However, like any battery, it holds only a finite sum of this energy. This energy maintains our life force. Internally, we know when the energy is getting low, and when we will ultimately expire, we can feel that within us. Therefore, to my point, mine has expired, yet I am still here. About a decade ago, I realized that my time here was drawing near an end. Customarily, I would have to accept that end, only there was much still to be done, and consequently, I knew I could not leave yet. In that, I found a way to preserve my existence with only the small inconvenience of being isolated here, where the energy source I found now exists."

Until now, Crix had only heard faint tales of the Luminars and certainly nothing of this detail. Plexo took on an intriguing persona: someone that he needed to ask countless questions of, but of those questions, one is the most important. "Okay, then who is my escort?"

"He is an Andor, best friend, and first officer under Tolagon Emberook."

Krath perked up, knowing of whom he was referring to. "Creedith? Yes! But I heard that he was captured and killed shortly after the Vico Legion dispersed."

"Captured, yes, but not killed. He has spent the last twenty years doomed to hard labor on Dispor. Zearic tortured him for months, yet he would never divulge the location of the blue orb. With the hope that he could find different ways to force the information from him in the future, he was to be kept alive, if you can call it that."

Krath rubbed the top of his head, still unhappy over its shiny glisten of cleanliness. "So tya thinkin' we can just do the ole jailbreak there on Dispor, eh, Plexo? That's one thing I always liked about tya, always good for some gut bustin' laughs." Krath's tone was drenched in sarcasm. "Look, I was always good with Creedith, never had any problems with Andors, and I would love to see him free of that place, but tya ain't gettin' anywhere close to Dispor unless tya an incomin' prisoner or lack a heartbeat, and then tya ain't gettin' out; that's for sure. No one has ever left that place. I mean no one. After twenty years in that place, there's really no sayin' that he's truly still alive anyhow."

They were all aware of Dispor's notoriety. The Dispor moon was a forced labor prison facility that mined scaberious, the active element required to supply self-sustained power to the individual Marck unit. There were only life sentences on Dispor, and to keep prisoners working, they used their families as collateral.

"It's also located in Sector 38; that's outside the main system, and only accessible through gammac corridor portal Delta, which I don't need to remind you is heavily fortified by the Marck fifth attack fleet," Kerriah snapped.

"Krath, if you believe Creedith is dead, then you truly don't know him as I do. To your concern, young Kerriah, yes, and I am certain you are waiting for me to say how I have planned to circumvent this obstacle, in which case, you would be correct. The power that I have harnessed here has given me the ability to deploy modified probes, which can focus that same power from my parallaxer all the way to the line of sight of the probe. This is the same process that I used to open the door for you to escape here from Troika." Plexo, in a rare moment, looked genuinely excited as he explained his most prolific creation. His audience, however, looked at him with their own personal expression of disbelief. "You do understand what the implication of this is?"

Kerriah leaned forward as if to get a closer listen to what he was explaining. "Are you telling us that you can jump us, physically, to almost anywhere your drones are looking? You do know that the Marcks have the X88T prototype that I attempted unsuccessfully to steal that can jump without the portals as well?" Kerriah said.

Plexo squinted over her second question. "Well, to answer your first question, yes, in a way. The main limitation was the power required for a long-range jump, and until now, it took the large, stationary mag infusers of the gammac corridors to create the power required for injection into the point-to-point topology. Now, it is also portable if you will." His excitement built further, and he talked faster and with less care. "Further, I have devised a way to alter the power signature so as not to alert Marck detection systems." His excitement suddenly stopped, and his expression went from a look of elation to that of someone that just took a hard shot in the stomach. He cleared his throat and sat back straight, hoping that he could plow through his clumsy words. "As for the Marck prototype ship, I'm not certain of its authenticity. To be honest, I do not believe they have the ability to design something with that level of complexity."

Kerriah just sat back and smiled. "Well, I beg to differ."

However, Krath did not let him off the hook for his slip and pressed him sternly. "Plexo, what exactly do tya have here? What is this energy source tya are keep flappin' about? Don't tell me tya have an orb here, cause tya know tya ain't supposed to have one of those." Krath grinned.

CHAPTER 15

Plexo sighed, giving up on the charade. "Well, just between friends . . . I might as well show you what I have. Please arise." He stepped off his seat and called out, "Core passageway."

The area blurred out and went dark for an instant then a high-pitched whistle filled the air, as well as a deep chill. The cold air gusted against them, and the sensation of a sharp drop filled their bellies. As the illumination returned, they were no longer seated in the main lab area; rather, they stood in a large, round space that was filled with a deep emerald glow. The glow flowed from a clear dome that sat upon a plinth in the center of the room. Six nearly transparent spiral pipes pulled in the emerald glow as they floated around the dome. There was a constant vibration, subtle yet noticeable.

"This is where my laboratories and this ship acquire their power. This is what I found." Plexo opened his arms toward the dome as if to present the glowing object to a large audience.

Krath's face scrunched and his jaw turned to a bitter scowl. "That's the Green Orb of Thale, the Hybors' Orb. How did tya get your hands on that?"

"It wasn't easy or simple, but had I not liberated the orb, it would likely be in the hands of Zearic."

Kerriah began having feelings of suspicion over Plexo's motives. After the decommissioning of the Tolagons, only a select few had knowledge of the orbs' secret locations, and their memories of these locations were supposedly erased. This gave her an escalating distrust for Plexo.

"I think you should explain exactly how you came to possess this orb," she demanded.

Plexo smiled with apprehension. "Very well, and I would expect such an inquiry, of course," By his own reasoning, he was a Luminar, and it was his people that gifted the orbs to the Oro System, so who better to be its caretaker? Who should have possession of it now, if not a Luminar emissary? He had some difficulty masking the hesitancy in his voice, and it must have shown through somewhat as he began. "For you to understand, I must first explain to you what happened to Centran, the last Tolagon of Thale, or at least how the tale was told to me."

Plexo folded his arms and took a nearby seat as if to give a lengthy tale. "At the close of what was eventually to be referred to as the second Thraxon War, Centran had just finished the concealment of the green orb just as he was decreed. After his discharge, he impatiently returned to his home with the intention to live out his remaining years with his family, enjoying a much quieter existence. However, when he arrived at his lagoon-based dwelling, his family was not as he had expected.

"His children, who at the time of his arrival were apparently swimming about in the shallows near his dwelling, took notice to Centran's arrival and swarmed over to him with the eagerness one might expect from children of a returning war hero. When he reached down to crest his eldest son's forehead, he immediately knew something was amiss.

"The child's head was cold and rigid, as was that of his other children. When the child looked upon him, his suspicion was validated. The child's eyes glared a yellow flash, and from his mouth shot a cerebral conduit that pierced through his neck in an attempt to merge with Centran's central nervous system. Centran was able to withdraw before it could make a proper connection, but his other children lanced his limbs with their fingertips, bringing him to his knees.

"He was a battle-proven Tolagon, so even in his wounded state, he was capable of fighting off and eliminating the impostors. He cried out to his wife only to discover that she was already standing upon him. She spat a cerebral conduit through the back of his head and pulled thoughts, but what they were looking for was not there."

As he spoke, Plexo leaned forward, pulled a clear bead from thin air, and twirled it around his fingers while he stared intently as he told his story.

"The concealment agents that were commissioned by the UMO to ensure orbs were hidden had already purged his memory of the whereabouts and the final resting place of the orb. Of course, the agents had vanished as well. I believe Zearic killed them for not revealing the orbs' locations. No one knows for sure, but without these agents, the whereabouts of the orbs would be lost." Plexo shook his head with disgust.

"The whole idea of dismantling the Tolagons was so poorly thought out and clearly born from desperation." He sighed, realizing that he had allowed himself to become emotionally sidetracked.

Crix still listened with his purest attention, eager to learn more. "I am sorry, Crix; allow me to continue. When Centran was brought to Zearic still alive, he attempted things of immeasurable cruelty to extract the orb's location from him. In the end, Centran passed unintentionally, leaving Zearic with only the location of Theodo, his ward. The agents had neglected the fact that Centran had a ward, and though this ward was not allowed access to the council or knowledge of its location, the location of the orb was indeed revealed to him.

"Fortunately, the ward told me of the green orb's location before he was forced by torturous methods to tell Zearic." Plexo flattened his palm and placed the bead in the middle of it. "Also, I had the equipment required to retrieve it from its hiding place. Allow me to show you."

The bead slowly started to spin and hastened in speed until a holographic image ballooned up from his hand, displaying a world swooshed with shadowy clouds swirling overhead and vast oceans tossing into waves of a violent storm. The image was so vibrant and detailed that one would think they were viewing it through the viewport of a ship on site.

"Ahhh, home," Krath mumbled, and Plexo nodded but remained silent as the image changed, pushing inward to a pinpointed location on the surface of Thale.

Clouds passed and swooshed out of view as the watery surface neared. Dark, rocky spires emerged like apparitions in the night, rising high, each coated with a smooth layer of crimson moss. The crooked spires littered the surface breaking through the murky green waters below like slender spear tips plunging through their targets. Their view neared a spire that was broken in half and then continued into the waters below. The waters were dark and visibility was limited. Giant bushy ferns that disappeared into the depths swished around like giant fingers looking for something to grab.

Krath chuckled to himself with a whistle of an old man mixed in his voice. "Watch out for those suckers; one tiny brush up against them, and they'll coil tya down so deep that even the glow fish won't find tya."

The image continued to follow the spire deeper and deeper as the base began to widen, and the sea life appeared even more bizarre. Needle-like worm creatures shot out from the sides of the spire almost as if they were attempting to attack. Krath snickered again. The view kept going deeper and deeper until there was no visible surface light, and after a few seconds, a tiny, green speck of light appeared deep in the distance. The light occasionally shimmered as though something passed in front of it. Their view approached the light. It became larger, and its illumination gave detail to its surroundings with an eerie emerald hue.

The green orb sat nestled in a circular trench at the base of the spire; a trench dug partially into the rocky side. Plexo spoke as the image stopped on the orb.

"This is the deepest part of Thale, and at these depths, even some of the densest objects crumple; however, I have a surprise here." He resumed the video stream. The advancing view of the orb stopped at the edge of the trench, and two humanoid shapes came into view moving toward the orb. Both were somewhat bulky and had the appearance of kegs stacked upon each other. The head of one rotated around, revealing a reddish light, and then turned away. Krath pushed out an irritated exhale and leaned forward to gain a better view of the image.

"What are those? They look a little like fat Marcks, but not like any I've ever seen, and what's worse is they are 'bout to get their filthy clamps on that orb."

"Very good observation, my brute friend," Plexo answered. "But those robust Marcks are my Marcks."

One of the Marcks drew a bar from its waist belt and held it above the orb, releasing a cube of energy that surrounded the glowing green sphere. Just as the orb began to rise, a dark shadow crashed down upon the Marck. The shadow turned inward and revealed two pale, glowing eyes. The view widened to reveal a long, winding figure with the body of a serpent. One of the Marcks illuminated the beast, and it snarled, exposing a mouthful of long, crystalline spikes for teeth. Blackish lace adorned the serpent's long back, which spanned outward like a net of feelers sifting for unsuspecting prey. It jerked its head away and coiled up as the bright light stung its purely nocturnal eyes.

The Marck kept the light pinned upon the beast and blasted a flashing rod toward its neck. A dark fog strewed out from the apparent wound, and another Marck dove forward stabbing into the serpent's side, slashing down with a blade of energy. The black lace folded down upon the Marck and rippled forward, dragging it into the serpent's jaws. In a show of strength, the Marck burst outward from the side of the serpent, carving and slashing away at its flesh until it exited the ruptured body of the beast while still holding the captured orb.

"Pretty remarkable, yes?" Plexo added as he shut down the video stream.

"Tya better not tell me tya have Marcks here, Plexo," Krath warned and pointed his plump finger toward the Luminar's face. "Cause if tya do, that's nothin' short of treasonous."

Plexo fanned his hand downward to settle Krath. "Not to worry, these Marcks are under my control. I happened upon some good fortune by virtue of one of my interior contacts. Through that contact, I was able to get my hands on these mostly forgotten about prototype Marcks. I can assure you that these Marcks have their homing transceivers reprogrammed to report to my own systems. They chain-relay their communication streams through an encryption system in much the same manner as the UMO Marcks do to hide the location of the Central Core System. However, my relay system is quite a bit less complex. The ones you observed in the video, were fascinating as I cannot place what their exact purpose would have been, though I do have some suspicions."

Crix's eyes widened. "What do you mean by that?"

Plexo was excited to explain, hoping that in doing so, he would enlighten himself with some sort of new theory as to their origins.

"Well . . . they were designed to withstand pressure that just seems improbable for any practical application, certainly nothing that I can think of that the UMO systems had been working on that would require that sort of pressure scale. Fortunate enough for me, they so happened to have been perfect for the Thale expedition but were well over-speced. Their design made them too bulky for combat or policing. My other Marcks, six in total, were more as you might have expected but had a couple of additional features that must have been removed from production models due to cost." He looked wearily over at Krath. "Now, if you can contain yourself, I would like to show them to you."

Krath shrugged in a manner to suggest that he could not make any guarantees. "Hey, whatever, as long as they don't provoke me, we won't have any problems."

Plexo frowned, but then called aloud, "Core passageway." That placed them, within moments, back into the main lab area.

"Tya know I'm not likin' tya movin' us around like this . . ." Krath grumbled before Plexo's next command interrupted his objection.

"Eetaks!" Spinning motors whirred as a container projected smoothly from the wall. The container had the appearance of a glass cell with nine Marcks inside standing shoulder to shoulder: three bulky Marcks resembling the ones from the video stream and six burgundy Marcks with lighter, more simplified builds. Each

Marck attached to a light-emitting cord that connected to the back of their head.

"Eetak Four, galvanize," Plexo said. In an instant, one of the slender Marcks flinched and shook before becoming detached from the cord as the cell walls slid down. Krath and the others stirred with uneasiness. Plexo took notice of their concerned postures. "Not to worry, friends, I have completely rebuilt the logic in these units, and they cannot be controlled by anyone aside from me unless I designate it otherwise."

Crix scrunched his brow. "Excuse me, Plexo, why are you referring to them as Eetak?"

"Ahh . . . yes, their names." He rubbed his chin and squinted sharply at his nine rebuilt Marcks. "I was quite pleased with them after I finished my work and wanted something clever to call my team. However, I could not get Eetak out of my mind since I observed that word carved into the foot of a single light model prototype. I have no idea what the name means, but it just seemed to be fitting. So I named them Eetaks and numbered them down from one to nine." He motioned the active Eetak over toward a wall in the distance. Eetak Four sprung from the platform and nimbly attached its hands and feet to the wall.

"Impressive, wouldn't you agree? I referred earlier to this removed feature. It is a special type of alloy. This alloy has a molecular structure that gives these Marcks spring-like characteristics and allows them to leap with the same prowess of a Nordan Forest Imp. In addition, they can attach themselves to metallic surfaces by magnetically charging themselves. Obviously, the UMO Warfare Ministry decided that having acrobatic Marcks was not a great enough gain for their intended use and replaced these abilities with the hover disks." Plexo motioned again, and Eetak Four scaled gracefully down the side of the wall like a Drisal spider and then jumped back over to the platform.

"I have retrofitted these prototypes for labor instead of battle. I used them to help construct this ship, and they did so quite expeditiously. Personally, I find them better used for labor than battle as I'm not a supporter of warring efforts either." Plexo crossed his arms, satisfied with his explanation.

"That's real funny since tya designed some of the most devastatin' weapons that we had durin' the second war."

Plexo looked at Krath with dismay. "Yes, I did what I had to in order to preserve life in these magnificent worlds. Unfortunately, the Thraxons could not be reasoned with, so war was our only option."

"Well, I'm sure you are exhausted. There is a resting chamber for you to gain your strength back. You have a very important task tomorrow, and you will need to be well-rested. I have much work still to do in preparation, so Eetak Four will escort you to your chamber. I will send for you after a while to begin preparation for your first task." Plexo immediately turned away as if lost in thoughts.

An Eetak waved them over to a bridge of light that rose upward from far below. When it reached their level, they stepped up onto it, and their weightless feeling gave way. The bridge strangely gripped to their feet as they followed into a passageway lined with transparent material.

All the while, Krath continuously grumbled to himself. "Great, now we've got ole glow rod dictatin' what we are doin' . . . followin' Marcks around, getting' pushed here, and then there . . . having to listen to him brag about the orb he stole . . . strippin' me of my fine odor. What a friggin' nightmare." He stopped complaining as the passageway opened into a large room.

The center of the room contained a low-sitting, round table filled with various foods that appeared to have been prepared minutes before their entering. Krath's eyes widened and his mood lifted. "Lectian and ego worms! I haven't been able to sink my teeth into some of those in years." He lumbered over to the table and began to throw back the food. Slurping up the slime from his hand, juices sprayed and oozed down his chin as he reached over for another fistful. The well-adorned table was loaded with vessels of dark green worms, piles of bright colored fruits, racks of meat, and pear-shaped containers filled with various juices.

Kerriah looked at Krath with abomination in her face. "Uggghh! I was just about to partake in those seared pamenilas, but I've just lost my appetite." Crix spotted a neatly stacked pile of purple fruits, grabbed two, and rubbed one against his shirt before he took a bite.

"Well, it's disgusting, but I've seen worse. Besides, I'm ravenously hungry, and it's going to take much more than that to turn off my appetite at this point. You should eat something; you're going to need your strength." Kerriah picked up a yellow, star-shaped fruit and rubbed her thumb across its rutted outer layer.

"I should, but I've always been able to go long periods without sustenance anyway, longer than most." She looked up at him as if wanting to confide about something, but she remained silent for a few minutes and watched them eat.

Around the walls were several receded areas with built-in gravlock sleeping units. Kerriah looked over to the receded area furthest from the dining table, grabbed Crix by the arm, and pulled him in that direction. Crix, with fruit still in his mouth, dropped the fruit he was holding and stammered clumsily over with her. She motioned for him to sit. The suspension zone boosted them upward like a pillow of air, and she gently settled down next to him and placed a hand on each of his arms to gain his full attention. She discreetly looked over and took note that Krath was still fully engrossed in slopping down the most pungent items on the table and casting the scraps carelessly to the floor. He hardly even noticed they moved.

"Crix," her tone was soft, "I feel . . . I can trust you, and we have well . . . you know, something between us, something I just wish we had some time with a little less chaos going on to explore." Crix set the half-chewed fruit down, and his eyes opened wide like a child as she now had his undivided and focused attention.

"Anyway, I need to be forward with you regarding me. What I just told you about food is true, more than you may be thinking. I have gone days, even a week, with hardly a bite to eat and have been barely affected; don't get me wrong, I still feel hungry and will eventually eat, but I don't get physically weak like most will, at least not as quickly." Crix leaned his head back a bit as if to take a broader look at her.

"Really? That's incredible! What about water? Do you need water?" He started trying to recall if he observed her drink anything since they met several days ago. He was intrigued.

"Not constantly, like most everyone else, but I do feel warm, at times, and a cool drink does bring my temperature down, but I do not get dehydrated like you do."

"I . . . I don't even know what to think. It's a little strange, but it certainly doesn't change the way I feel about you." An assuring smile warmed across his face.

Kerriah lowered her head slowly and then looked up again into his eyes. "I pretty much have learned to accept those oddities about myself, and then today, while plugged into Arc Stasis, while you were seeing images, I saw nothing. At first, I wanted to say something, but then I realized that the only reason I did not see anything was due to my issues, and then I was too self-conscious to say anything. So I sat quietly and listened to your reactions as to what was being observed." Crix settled back and tried to dissect in his mind what she told him. It was a difficult context in which to reply as he was not sure if his reply might come off as insensitive or even rude. He decided to tell her what his thoughts were and hoped that it would not be offensive.

"What you're telling me seems almost like more a blessing than a curse. I mean at least it's a good thing that your body can withstand starvation and thirst so well."

"Actually, you're correct in that regard and others. I've never been sick, never, and was always highly athletic and top of all my classes in intellectual scoring. Just like in Annexis, I was able to catch on quickly, where others, I would imagine, have taken years to be competent players. It's just always been that way for me. I've tried to keep this hidden from others; in fact, you're the first I've told this to. I'm sort of an anomaly, and though it may be difficult to understand, most of the time, I just wished to be normal. I don't feel like I can have relationships. This, whatever *this* is, always gets in the way . . ." Her voice quivered, and she placed her hand over her face. Crix gently pulled her to his chest and wrapped his arms around her small frame.

"I understand, trust me; I understand more than you realize." He was not about to diminish her need for him to listen. However, he was tempted to explain his youth growing up as a different species in Troika with the orb whispering strange words into his ears and many Andors unwilling to accept him into their culture. Instead, he placed his hand under her chin and gently lifted her head. She removed her hand from her face to see his eyes.

"You should have Plexo take a look at you. After all, he has all the technology here to probably find out what's making you so exceptional. Believe me, you are nothing short of that . . . exceptional."

She snapped away looking at him with disgust in her expression. "No! I'm not going to be prodded like some sort of lab rodent." She puffed out a forced breath and turned away with her arms crossed. "I really thought you would have been a little more understanding, guess I was wrong; you're just like everyone else."

Ahh man . . . damage control time. "No—no—no! That's not at all what I meant. It's just that if you better understand yourself and why you are different, it may help you to coexist with these gifts and even use them to help with the challenges in front of you."

Exasperated, she pulled away, and then innocently cocked her head sideways. "I know you didn't mean anything negative, and I'm sorry for snapping at you like that. It's something that really gets me emotionally charged, and I don't think I'm ready to hear what the truth is yet. I'm afraid of how it may change things."

Crix gently touched her back and shoulders; her muscles were tense. "Don't worry, Kerriah; I understand and have no problem with your differences at all. I want you to know that you can always talk to me about anything you need. I was actually going to have Plexo look at me regarding some of the strange things I'm feeling with the orb since I have been using it. I don't expect too much, but I need someone who knows this thing better to help me."

She brushed her hand across the side of his head, whisking her fingers through his hair. "I've noticed that more and more of your hair is turning white recently. I like this new Tolagon look. It makes you look more distinguished."

CHAPTER 16

Crix waited until things settled down. Kerriah did not appear to sleep often, so this was a unique opportunity to slip away. He looked back into the room and observed Kerriah and Krath sleeping soundly; well, Krath was snoring like an old motor struggling to start up with every breath. Crix chuckled to himself and strolled in the direction of the lab; as he walked, he felt a strange push, and the further he went, the harder the pressure became until he was unable to go any further. It was as if the air grew denser until it formed a solid barrier.

"Eetak!" he called out. Within seconds, the Eetak that escorted them into the living quarters earlier appeared moving toward him from the other side. It approached within a few meters and stopped, saying nothing.

"I need to speak with Plexo." It remained motionless for what felt like several minutes before motioning him to follow. The resistance faded instantly causing Crix to stumble forward.

He followed the Eetak for a while, and the corridor path changed. And even though he should recall its direction from earlier, it strangely felt that it was going in a completely different direction. The Eetak disappeared around a corner, and as Crix turned the same corner, he found himself inside a hangar. A bronze ship with a flat but wide hull sat waiting flanked by two smaller ships. Eetaks milled about busy with tasks. Plexo stood upon a tall pedestal with glistening controls surrounding all sides. He noticed Crix and called out.

"Ahh—Crix Emberook, so what brings the pleasure of your company? You should be resting with your companions as I have a challenging day planned for you tomorrow."

"I would like you to take a closer look at me and tell me more about this orb that lives in me," Crix replied. Plexo immediately stopped what he was doing and stepped out onto an almost invisible step that lowered him down to Crix like a bird gliding down for a gentle landing.

"What exactly do you mean?" Plexo asked, intrigued by the question.

"I mean this orb; since I have been using it, I feel different." Plexo cut him off before he could go any further.

"No. That's not what I meant. You said the orb lives." Crix paused for a long minute before responding, and Plexo moved in closer, his eyes trained on Crix's.

"I can hear it speak to me, but I just don't know if it's the orb or me going mad."

"Have you had any visions?"

Crix recalled back to his struggles to keep the orb bubble up. "I'm not sure if this is what you mean, but I did have some haunting images flashing through my sight once when I was using the orb."

"Yes, that is common with Tolagons when they overuse the orb's power. In short bursts or with minimal power usage, like levitation, you won't have any images, but when you draw upon it heavily, you will see them, and they are always frightening, from what I'm told. The great Tolagons were able to learn to suppress these images, or at least ignore them."

Crix thought back to the creatures in his visions. "I've seen these creatures, monsters that were ravaging everything around them. They looked at me as if they wanted nothing more than to do the same to me. Do you know what they could be?"

Plexo appeared distraught over this question. "It's difficult to say, but the orbs have their origins from Cyos, the great living nebula, and I could only surmise that whatever you are seeing is from some dark corner of the universe that they have once been exposed to." Eager to change the subject, he placed his hand at Crix's back to bid him to follow. "Come with me." They exited the hangar out a small door to a room filled with transparent, round tanks that contained blue and silver fluids and a single table in the middle.

"Please lay back and relax on the table." Crix quickly complied, lying back and noticing a series of light-filled conduits directly above him. Plexo placed his hands together and pulled them apart, giving way to swirls of colors, some of which Crix had never seen before. His fingers wiggled as the colors mixed and swooshed around. "Now, just clear your thoughts and try to hold still; focus on the dot on the ceiling."

A tiny, dark spot appeared on the metallic ceiling and moved in an S-like pattern so slowly that it almost put Crix into a trance-like state. The conduits snaked down closer to Crix, and light poured from them like water from a faucet. The light immersed Crix's body until it vanished from view. Only the blue orb was still visible, searing through the illumination.

A razor-thin screen dropped down from the ceiling in front of Crix. Plexo turned to look at him through the screen and immediately stepped back startled. He placed his hand on his chest in bewilderment. Plexo was not one to be easily shocked and could not recall the last time he was truly surprised about anything. He gazed intensely into the screen for a while, and then cautiously leaned in for closer inspection.

"Well, very fascinating, indeed. Aren't you full of surprises, my youthful friend?" he said to himself but loud enough for Crix to hear, though he was still entranced. "This is certainly a twist of events, but I don't think now is the time to disclose what has been made clear today." He took a few more minutes and adjusted the light intensity, panning the screen in closer and further out, trying to get as much detail as he could. He turned around and moved some color swirls around with his fingertips, and then the light drew back up into the tubes, leaving Crix as he was. "You may wake now," Plexo instructed. Crix's eyes dilated before he gave them a firm rub with his palms and then sat upright.

"I feel like I just had enough dreams for three nights' sleep. How long was I out?" Crix asked, groggy.

"Not long, though being ignited as you just were, can trick your mind into believing it has slept for many hours."

Crix waited for a minute, and Plexo continued to look him over with an intrigued look on his face. Crix could feel the anxiety building. "Well . . . what did you find out?" He asked. Plexo had no intention of disclosing what he had found at the risk of distracting the budding Tolagon, particularly at the eve of which so much was about to be expected of him. However, he would give him a fair answer.

"What you are feeling is the orb binding to your very own molecules. It is a perfectly natural thing that all Tolagons went through as they began using the orbs. As a result, the only way it can be released from you is either willingly or by death. Accord et decimate, as the old Tolagons used to refer to it. The voices are a little more difficult to explain, and I'm not convinced what you are hearing is the orb." Crix jumped to his feet.

"What do you mean? I'm going crazy?"

"No, let's just say that there are some things that will unfold soon, and when it does, you will step back and question everything about yourself. I also firmly believe that, in the end, you will be the paramount model of what a Tolagon exemplifies. But not all things can be disclosed at this time; as such, knowledge given prematurely will destroy what is to be." Crix stepped back, frustrated from Plexo's unforthcoming stance, yet understanding for the moment and siding with trusting in his wisdom. "Now go get your rest. I will send for you in the morning and bring you back to the hangar area."

Crix turned to walk away, and then abruptly stopped. He needed to get one other bothering concern off his mind. "Have you heard of anything regarding Troika's fate? Is there anyone or anything left there? I mean, did they destroy it all?"

Plexo's expression turned bleak, and he wished that he would not have to be the one to answer this question. "I am sorry, young Tolagon. The Knactor Legion does not take prisoners or leave survivors. True to their reputation, my probes have shown me only the grimmest images of Troika. Do not let this information break you or fill you with hate. Rather, use it to galvanize your own will to take on your role as Tolagon and tactically shut down these Marck forces. That is the best way to honor your fallen home."

He felt dark, and his face froze as he stared down at the floor. Crix tried to pull his thoughts from the abyss. It was hard not to fall into feelings of despair and vengeance. He knew what Plexo was telling him was the right way, but he was going to have his own internal battle to face. He looked back up at Plexo and nodded somberly before walking away.

"Crix. Before you leave." Plexo pulled his attention back from the sorrowful place for which it had slumped. "I realize this is a difficult follow-up to what you have just learned about Troika, but I feel it's worth mentioning." Crix turned back around still appearing disheartened.

"I had removed Corin's body recorder before Creedith took him back home on the day he was mortally wounded. What I had learned from the recovered video was that Corin had drawn a portion of the Marck forces away from us and, in doing so, stumbled across an industrial building filled with algae. This mutated algae appeared to feed on any energized components.

More importantly, it did so quickly. He was able to use these algae as a weapon to destroy the forces that tried to prevent our escape from Nathasia. I can't tell you much more, but this information may be useful later in your quest. When you find Creedith, he may have more knowledge to offer."

As Crix left Plexo, he could only hold his emotions together until he was out of his sight. Immediately, he broke down and cried. Tears poured down his cheeks and out from his soul. *Tirix.* He was his best friend since his earliest memories. *He's gone now. I can't believe that day, after the game, is the last time I will ever see him again. Clyde, Claynor, Caspi, everyone . . . gone.*

***

Crix returned to the resting chamber in a solemn mood. He pulled himself back together after hearing the news of Troika's destruction. All was quiet except the wet hack of Krath's snoring. He could tell that Kerriah had her eyes open.

"What's wrong?" she whispered, noticing the dejected look on Crix's face.

Crix did not want to discuss what was going on; he would rather lie down and stew about it on his own. However, he had a fondness for Kerriah, and it almost felt like his first love but a love that had never actually manifested into anything aside from his own hopefulness. His desire to be near her gave way, and he went to her willingly to share his sorrow.

"I just got back from seeing Plexo."

"And?"

"And nothing. He more or less said it's all a normal part of being a Tolagon, and the rest he cannot tell me at this time. The problem is the rest sounded like the important part."

"There's something else, I can tell." She noticed that he must have been crying.

"Troika is gone."

"I know. I'm so sorry, Crix."

She invitingly tugged on his arm. "I can't sleep by myself tonight; between everything darting around in my mind and Krath's barrage of sound effects, I need someone to lay with me." Crix slid next to her, and she cuddled up next to his chest.

She was warm, and her soft hair refreshed his senses like a breeze swirling across flowers on a Draylok hillside. He nuzzled her hair and found it intoxicating. He was at ease and dizzy all at the same time. She felt the tickle of his breath and turned around. Their eyes locked and their hearts raced. A gentle kiss chased into a deeper kiss which lasted, yet not long enough. They both knew that tomorrow might not go well, that this could be their last night.

They paused, staring deep into each other's eyes, ensuring that they both had the same thoughts. Crix studied her eyes and found something so profound. She sparkled with anticipation looking back into his. They pressed into each other softly, sharing sweet kisses. Fortunately, the salty, old soldier on the other side of the room slept as if he was in a coma.

Crix had never been this close with anyone before, and he could not imagine it to be any better. She was perfect. The excitement of her body next to his eventually settled; they both fell asleep nestled in the coziness of each other's embrace.

CHAPTER 17

Hit the deck!" Krath howled, startling Crix and Kerriah from their sleep. "Tya got about five minutes to get somethin' to eat 'cause ole glow rod has some sorta mission for us."

Crix was still a little drowsy from a short night of sleep. He pulled himself out of bed and gave Kerriah a light kiss on the forehead. "Thanks for last night; thanks for caring." She smiled in appreciation for his tenderness and gratitude.

After grabbing a quick bite to eat from the freshly stocked buffet table, they followed Eetak Four down the corridor to the hangar that Crix met Plexo in the night before. Plexo stood before them flanked by three Eetaks: two marked in deep grey with red insignias on their chest plates that displayed the image of a skull which was cracked down the center, the third heavily armored with a full armament of assault weaponry.

"Isn't that the Crimiant mark?" Kerriah asked.

"Yes, that's very observant; I have retrofitted Eetak Five and Six to look like Crimiant guards. They will be your guide for entry into the penal moon of Dispor."

"Aw, great, and what is our disguise going to be?" Krath was irritated as usual but already knew the answer.

"You're going to be their new prison transferees from the orbital prison station of Crimiant," Plexo replied. "I have a Marck shuttle that I procured by calling in a favor and have likewise marked it up with the Crimiant insignia and coded with prison protocols. This will be sufficient to get you through the guarded gammac corridor Delta and deep inside Sector Thirty-Eight." Sector Thirty-Eight was an outer system that was used primarily for mining and forced labor. There were no naturally inhabitable worlds there.

"From there, you will shuttle into the Dispor docking station for prison transfer processing. The Marcks on the far side of the gammac corridor run somewhat independent of the core since the relay systems are unable to traverse the portal. This will likely ensure you won't be recognized until the outer relays have been updated. To my surprise, they appear to be a bit lax on this. My sources have indicated this to be a weekly update. If things go as planned and my sources are correct regarding Dispor protocols, my Eetaks should be able to escort you to the third level of reparation. Creedith is supposedly held on the fourth level, so you will need to apply some of your own creativity to get yourselves sent there."

Unfortunately, no one outside of Dispor knew much of the reparation levels aside from the fact that each level was worse than the former, and that the deeper levels were for the most notorious prisoners whose life expectancy was minimal. Most considered Dispor the worst place to be of the UMO controlled systems.

"Okay, so what's the big one that's armed up to his choppers for?" Krath asked while staring cautiously at the Eetak that was hulking with armor and laden with what appeared to be every type of small to medium armament that could be squeezed onto a single Marck frame.

"Eetak Two is your cooler in this mission. Since he was one of the prototypes that could withstand extreme pressure, a characteristic that makes him particularly strong and capable of resisting quite an onslaught if necessary, I decided to outfit him for heavy assault. He will remain concealed inside the shuttle as his presence would positively alarm all Marcks stationed at Dispor. If you find yourselves in a bind or things go poorly, you are to activate this tracer." Plexo handed Kerriah a device that looked like a small dot.

"Conceal this behind your ear and pinch it hard if needed, and it will transmit a signal that will active him from up to twenty kilometers away . . . even underground. Once activated, his only mission is to wipe out all mechanized units detected while zeroing in on your position. This is to facilitate a path out for you. I have supercharged his power packs, so he will, for lack of a better term, go into a frenzy until his energy supply is exhausted, which I expect to be about thirty minutes.

"Oh . . . and please, stay clear of him. There will be a sizable amount of collateral damage, and in the end, he is equipped with a failsafe to clean up all evidence of his existence. When that happens, make sure you are a good distance away. Of course, he is there only as a last resort, and my principal design is for him not to be called upon."

He continued to brief them on the mission and assured them that the odds were better than they believed. The general mood of the group was one of anxiety folded in with bravado. Crix and Kerriah, with their youth, gained the emotional push needed from Plexo and his speech, whereas Krath stood back with irritable discernment. The shuttle door slid open, and Eetak Five and Six militantly turned before entering the small ship. Plexo placed his hand over his chest in a devoted gesture of farewell.

"Safe return, my friends. Remember that while you are away, I will use my probes to monitor Dispor. I have already passed them through the guarded portal undetected, thanks to their relative size. I have also devised a plan to recover you once you have reached a safe distance from the prison's outer detection systems."

Just before the shuttle hatch closed, Krath turned to Plexo. "Hey buddy, how do tya know Creedith is still alive?"

Plexo apprehensively frowned. "I don't, but if anyone would still be alive in that dreadful place, it would be him. Besides, we desperately need him to be." There was a faint sign of nervousness in his delivery.

Krath took a solemn breath. "Okay, that's all I needed to know." With that, the door slid shut with a lengthy hiss.

CHAPTER 18

O rdal three-six-nine, Crimiant prisoner transfer to Dispor, shuttle three-alpha-twelve requesting clearance for attachment to forward docking station." Eetak Five's crackling voice was unnerving as it communicated with Dispor's space control tower.

Kerriah ushered Krath and Crix over for a huddle to discuss the holographic image generated from a small square she held in her hand. "Okay, let's go over the basic layout once more." She went back into the details of their mission, not wanting anything to stray from the plans that Plexo had provided.

Crix snuck a look out of a narrow strip of window for a glimpse of the darkness of space. He had never been off Soorak, and the notion of space travel to another world had stirred his stomach and distracted him from the mission briefings. He wanted to look around like a wide-eyed child, to experience and soak up the sensation of space travel; he found himself woefully unfocused.

Kerriah looked up at him and cleared her throat in an apparent effort to regain his attention.

Krath cracked a large smirk. "Tya never been in space before, have ya, buddy?" Crix shook his head. "Well tya will learn to hate it like most of us, though it's sorta fun at first, but it's just a whole bunch of work and discomfort these days."

Kerriah looked at both of them, annoyed that they were not taking this as serious as she was. "May I continue?"

Krath and Crix had a look on their faces like schoolchildren in trouble before they straightened themselves back out and leaned over the hologram image, waiting for her to continue.

"Level one is the scab processing level; we will arrive there first, but since we need to get to level three, Plexo has our prisoner status as operative saboteurs. This means the law requires that we are to be directly transferred to level three, which is the lower scab mines." She paused and listened briefly to the communications between Eetak Five and the tower Marcks.

"Affirmative, these prisoners are not in the database, level three transfers classified due to insurgent risk." Eetak Five pressed on with his programmed orders from Plexo.

She turned around and finished her briefing. "We are to remain in proton shackles until we reach level three. Once there, if we discover that he's been transferred to level four, the scab hives, we will have to get ourselves sent there. At that point, Krath, it's your move, and I hope that will be enough to get us put into level four. We will wait until you make your move."

"Tya don't need to worry, slim. I have this, no problem," Krath reassured. "I'm just lookin' forward to bustin' up some of those Mark guards as we break our way back out with ole Creedith."

"Clearance granted. Proceed to forward docking station eight," the mechanical voice hummed out over the shuttle's communication system.

The Dispor moon was eerily dark, like the face of a monster on a moonless night permanently shadowed by the planet, Vaapur-9, a result of its stationary orbit. Vaapur-9 was a haunting planet, a mix of grey and black, with clouds of ash and smoke from its numerous active volcanoes and geysers spewing methane into the atmosphere. Dispor's surface appeared to be lifeless with strange, hooked, rock-like formations that littered the surface. A generation ago, an exploratory mining ship discovered an aggressive lifeform called Scaberious deep beneath the surface of Dispor. These scabs contained prodrain crystals, the principal power component in Marcks.

Scabs were dangerous when found alive and would swiftly chew through the flesh of those that stirred their habitats, and then wildly consume the minerals from the victim's bones. It was a horrifying death and suitable for the worst convicts sent to Dispor, an assumed death sentence. Kerriah had always thought of this place as vile and worthy of its collapse. The thought of having to travel there sickened her, but at least it was a rescue mission. She would be more than pleased to get someone, especially a political prisoner, out of this place of misery, even at the peril of her own life.

Surrounding the Dispor prison station were circular battlements, four of them, that housed heavy concussion cannons used to repel unwanted ships or terminate those attempting to escape. The cannons looked menacing, and it was likely their appearance, alone, had prevented their use. As they neared their approach, the protruding docking stations came into view, twelve in total with eight in the front and four in the rear. Red beacons strobed on the eighth dock, signaling their destination.

The shuttle spun around as it neared, and then quivered as it mated with the dock. A deep echo crashed down upon the upper and lower hull as stabilizing clamps latched onto the ship, which was now just as imprisoned as the living inhabitants of the grim, dark place.

Kerriah steadied her stance and tightened her core. Krath rolled his eyes. The shuttle's lights went dim, and red auxiliary lighting blinked online just as the external hatch swirled open to the long, dimly lit gangway, leading into the beast known as Dispor.

In the distance, the laboring of machinery screamed out, evidence of their poorly kept components in the harsh environment. The bitter scent of death reeked from the hot, dry air as it filled their shuttle's airlock, beckoning the new arrivals. Crix's lungs burned and his eyes watered as he peered through the pollution and flashing lights. Eetak Five and Six emerged from the cockpit wielding their rifles and stopped at the hatch. The group fell in behind them, shackled, as they proceeded inward.

The gangway opened up to a checkpoint station with three Marck units. Their soiled armor was shaded dark grey with Dispor's vertical, white, barbell insignia spanned across their chest. Eetak Five handed over a transparent card to one of the Marcks, who then turned around to slide it into a panel nearby. Turning back around, it motioned for the other two Marcks to take possession of the prisoners. Eetak Five raised its palm forward and stopped the two approaching Marcks.

"We have orders from the high authority to escort these prisoners to level three," Eetak Five said.

"That is an illegal operation; prisoners not escorted by Dispor guards are forbidden entry into the lower prison security levels," the guard replied.

"Our orders have been cleared; we will follow the facility guards down with the prisoners," Eetak Five retorted.

The guard paused for several minutes before replying. It was difficult to determine if the Marck was receiving orders during this wait or was taking time to process a decision on its own; the wait was agonizing. The Eetak's escort was part of Plexo's plan to make sure they had the support needed. All the while, Kerriah considered some contingency plans, and then the guard responded. "You may follow to level three."

With that, the guards tagged each of them with a thin piece of transparent material inserted beneath the skin on the backs of their necks.

Crix began having feelings of reluctance over what they were doing. This was not the place anyone tried to get into, and yet, that was exactly what they were doing.

This is insane. What are we doing here? Disconcerting thoughts flooded his mind.

The likelihood that Creedith was still alive seemed about as remote a possibility as them being able to escape if they did find him. Kerriah was suffering from similar thoughts as she felt like this might well be a wasted end to her efforts of thwarting this regime. Krath simply shrugged and assumed that, at the very least, he would get to bust up some Marck junkers.

They followed the guards down a long corridor, and a large door opened slowly, letting in a stale odor of toxins from the lingering air. Behind that door was another heavier door a few meters beyond. The heavy red door had black burn marks around the edges as if the foul-smelling soot and vapors that had escaped left their mark. The door screeched open, and hot air gusted inward. Kerriah felt the scorching draft across her face. The air made their gag reflexes clench from the stench of pollutants and decay.

The Marcks escorted them out to a mezzanine that overlooked into the processing facility on the moon's surface level. Their eyes strained against the bright lights in this area, and then they slowly adjusted. The three observed hundreds of prisoners clad in grimy yellow jumpers below. This captive labor force worked feverishly inside a primitive machine-driven line. A series of chutes churned out ground scabs from the lower level and endlessly fed this line. The chutes belched up plumes of powder as they continuously pumped out more scabs. Many of the workers coughed violently and frequently stopped to rub their eyes, most likely from the gritty substance they were inhaling. With no safety equipment provided, this was considered a lengthy and miserable death sentence.

One of the Marck guards stepped over to a worker and slammed the butt of his rifle into his back for stopping too long to cough. "Don't stop working," it commanded.

The workers were scooping up the ground scabs and tightly packing small tubes, and then using a pistol-like device to seal the tops. Kerriah and Crix instantly wheezed and coughed at the first few breaths of the dust-filled air. Four large, bulb-shaped machines hung from the ceiling with no apparent purpose, though they looked ominous to those below them.

High above were a series of long overcrossings lined with armed Marck guards, which stood by motionless like a meticulously set up toy army, poised with their rifles pointed downward. Their light armor was tinted dark grey and layered with dust and grime. On a separate platform slightly above the guards stood a solitary Marck tinted red with large black tines rising from either side of his head. In the center of his head was the faded mark of the Knactor Legion, the most notorious of the Marck legions. This infamy derived from their technical and mechanical enhancements over the common battle Marck, coupled with their unique capability to store and refine their own experiences. They were the designated shock troopers of the UMO.

This well-seasoned warrior panned the area slowly as if looking for anything out of line. Like a predatory hawk watching mice below, it was obvious that nothing would go unnoticed by his watchful gaze. Upon their entry, his head slowly turned in their direction, placing them under his seamless observation. His name was Zeltak, and it was easy to see that he was the one in charge.

The Marck guards walked them onto an open elevator platform, and they descended below to the same level as the workers and then proceeded forward to a circular platform. A sudden scream shrieked out from a worker as one of the giant mechanical bulbs above extended down with four silvery, snake-like arms and pointed in his direction. The arms drew back like cobras preparing to strike. They speared into each limb of this hapless worker and towed its victim up like a string-controlled doll.

This unnerving killing device sucked the worker into its bulb and then spewed out a splash of blood-red jelly into a nearby basin of black slime. The pool of stagnating slime looked like the last stop for workers unable to maintain an acceptable pace. It was not clear to Crix if their Marck escorts stopped to simply observe or to ensure that the three of them observed this horrific scene, but stop they did until it was over. One thing was clear; the cesspool of gore was an ominous reminder for the prisoners to push themselves to their bitter limits.

A strong, commanding voice far above made an announcement to the prisoners below. "This is another reminder that insubordination will always be dealt with, and liquidation is the penalty for failure to comply." The tine-bearing Marck, Zeltak, gave a slow nod, and the escorting guards resumed shoving them onto the platform.

Several nearby workers snuck a dismal look over to them with blood-red eyes. In spite of all their apparent suffering, there was still a sense of pity in their expressions toward the group that was boarding the platform. A guard on a control tower that overlooked the area below activated the platform, and it rotated slightly, and then descended, leaving the processing level. A sharp pit crawled in the deepest part of Crix's stomach. He felt beads of sweat forming around his cheeks and brow as his nerves began to rattle.

The group remained vigilant and quiet as they nervously looked around to see what emerged in the darkness below. The platform hummed and groaned as it descended deeper through the stone chute. Eventually, the walls turned from a smoke-stained black to a grey, packed-on dust. A pungent odor filled the air, similar to the smell on level one but much stronger. Finally, the platform plunged into an area known as the upper scab mines. The environment was cloudy with grey dust that made breathing strenuous from a burning sensation that filled their throat and lungs.

It was difficult to see past a few meters through the dust-filled air, and a hollowed hum echoed in the distance. The group followed close behind the shadowy silhouettes of Eetak Five and Six, who followed the Dispor Marck guards. They moved forward at a moderate pace. In the distance, a faint red glow became visible, as the haunting hum drew closer. Crix looked to the side and could barely see a dust-covered handrail nearby. His eyes burned, and he found himself blinking erratically. Crunching and popping rang out in every direction and was so loud that at times it was startling.

They found themselves surrounded by an eerie red glow that had a slow, flickering strobe. Two rings came into view that moved up and down in opposite directions from each other. A dome in the center of these rings gave off the red glow and was responsible for the monotonous humming that could be heard everywhere.

"What is that thing?" Crix leaned into Kerriah, careful not to let the guards hear him.

Crix found he was unable to focus; his mental state melted away, and he felt emptiness pour over his spirit. He felt alone. The constant humming throbbed through their minds, and only Kerriah appeared to be mostly unaffected. All around, machines pounded the walls and floors, and the shadowy silhouettes of workers could be seen sifting opaque disks from the debris. Some wore crude masks to shield their eyes and nose from the dust, but most stammered about without any protection.

They stopped upon a pitted metal sled that sat atop a shaft opening, which led down into a ninety-degree drop below. The guards fastened belts hooked to the sled around the passengers and themselves. One of the guards grasped a nearby lever and pulled, sending the sled blasting down to the lower scab mines. It was a short, intense ride; the group could barely hold on. Their restraining belts pulled tight from the force of the downward momentum and cut off their breath. The sled screamed to a halt, placing them into a pitch-black area with the exception of some random strobe lights.

"Level three reached. Proceed to prisoner assignment handling," one of the guards commanded. The guards dismounted the sled and led them to a dimly lit corridor in the distance. The lit area was repugnant and filled with grime. The four Marck guards that kept watch over access to the area were beat-up and laden with dirt around every joint and cavity within their armor. The Marcks that guided them down from the first level stopped, motionless.

Crix looked over at Kerriah. The time passed by. Minutes became an hour; their feet and backs wrenched from the pain of standing still.

Krath started to lose his patience and blurted aloud. "What the heck? Are we goin' to just stand around here all—" Before he could finish his complaint, one of the Marcks that guided them from level one drove the butt of its rifle into his gut, sending him down to one knee. Krath looked up slowly at the Marck. His eyes were on fire with the urge to unleash his fury, but he held himself back and got back up to his feet in silence.

Clank . . . clank . . . .clank . . . .metal against stone echoed from deep within the guarded corridor and became louder with each subsequent clank. A tall, slender shadow stretched through the corridor and slowly crept into view, keeping pace with the approaching noise. From the shadow emerged a black, skeletal figure of a Marck at least a meter taller than most and with a lumbering gait. The surrounding Marcks all cautiously took a step back to give this superior Marck its space.

The lofty Marck stopped and turned its head toward the group; its eyes were radiating red with a dusty glow as they illuminated the particles floating in the air around them. Its appearance was nothing short of menacing: equipped with longer arms and legs fused together from various parts of other Marcks. Its darker shaded metal showed signs of damage and scarring all over from its feet to its head.

An echoing laugh bellowed from this darker Marck as it approached the new prisoners. "Fresh meat, gooood."

It brushed a long, razor-sharp fingertip gently across Crix's cheek. The raspy, mechanical voice broke in and out. Its soulless shell coupled with the ghoul-like voice sent a quiver down his spine.

"I am Sintor, your new master and the commandant of the lower mining and hive levels of Dispor. Work hard, and I may allow you to stay in the mines, where you can serve me for years, and maybe I will choose to endure your pathetic existence." It raised its hand as if to strike them. "If I get the sense that anyone's not providing sufficient work efforts, the horrors of the hive awaits you. I tell you that we need hive workers more than miners, so do not test me! The neuro suppressors placed throughout the mines will aid in subduing your rebellious will, but the strong of will individuals are now warned."

It turned to the Marck guards. "Take them to get changed and properly outfitted for work. I wish for them to start immediately."

Two of the Marcks grabbed Kerriah and Crix, shoving them further into the darkness as Krath followed. Eetak Five and Six followed as well, but Sintor stepped in front of them.

"I do not know what you are, but you are not of Dispor." He looked them up and down sharply as if sizing them up for parts. "However . . . I do have need of you both more than you'll know." He stood erect, and his multi-jointed arms and legs extended, giving off a distinct creak from each joint.

Eatek Five's threat detection systems activated and he raised his rifle, but before he could take a shot, slender rods impaled through the backsides of their heads, destroying the CPUs of both Eetaks. Two lower mine guards behind them withdrew their ballistic rods and re-sheathed them to their belts as both Eateks dropped to their knees then crumbled to the floor.

Crix looked back at the loss of their escorts with sudden doubts fluttering around in his mind. He tried to keep his thoughts on his keeper, his father, and the words of Suros to regain his mental fortitude to press forward. Kerriah always seemed so confident in everything she did, and Krath feared nothing. It gave him a somewhat lonely and isolated feeling, being the only one that was struggling with fear and uncertainty.

Through the darkness, they passed dimly lit pockets of workers wearing makeshift masks and holding tools that crunch into the walls exposing fossilized scabs. All around them, heavy machines ground through rock as the floor shook. There was an occasional scream in the distance, keeping the anxiety level of the group elevated and second-guessing their plan. However, they kept silent and followed the guards to a rusty bridge, which extended over a deep, black crack in the floor.

Overlapping hisses swirled up from the depths below like voices whispering over the top of one another. A warm breeze brushed against them as they mounted the bridge. The air from the breeze smelled of vinegar over feces. The bridge creaked and rattled with every step as they made their way to a large, circular enclosure at the end. Orange floodlights illuminated the outer perimeter of the building.

"These are your barracks," a guard announced as they entered a rough opening outlined by brown stains and green veins weaved throughout the rock. They entered the barracks, and an older Solaran stammered up from a steel plank secured to the wall by chains. He had a short but square build, typical of Solarans due to the stronger gravitational pull of their world. His right leg was missing from the hip down, and he leaned heavily on a metal rod with both arms. He pulled his scraggly grey beard away from his lips and brushed his hand back across his heavily scarred bald head as if to nervously gain composure.

"How may I be of service, my gracious masters?" His voice was shaken and feeble. One of the guards replied in a stern but still mechanical tone.

"Prepare them for immediate scab excavation. We will return in thirty minutes to take them to their mining stations."

"Ye—yes, my masters, right away," he answered, fidgeting his fingers through the tangles in his beard. The guards unshackled them and then turned to exit the barracks, leaving them alone with the old Solaran.

"Follow me, and I will get you some mining jumpers and show you your quarters." The Solaran wobbled down to the far end of the barracks. The inside of the living quarters was mostly a bare room lined with dirty mats and some rusty bins. He opened up one of the bins and started to sift around.

Kerriah stepped right next to him to gain his attention. "Solaran. What's your name?"

"What is this you're asking of me?" he replied, and then mumbled to himself incoherently while sifting faster and tossing out dirty garments.

"Your name, what is it?" she restated.

"Icad," he answered as he continued his sifting. He stopped, and then pulled out a rather large, faded, blue jumper stained with sweat and blood. "This looks like it should fit onto your build." He held it up with one arm in front of Krath.

"Icad," Kerriah said, still trying to get his attention. "We are looking for someone, an Andor."

"A who . . . or what . . . an . . . an . . . Andor, w—what is an Andor?" He turned away, wanting strongly to avoid any more questions.

Crix interrupted, somewhat annoyed in his delivery. "An Andor, from the great equine tribes on Soorak: you know, strong, noble, and steadfast."

"Yes . . . yes, the Andor. We don't get many of those here. In fact, only one," Icad answered. Kerriah's eyes lit up. She took a step toward Icad, and he skittishly slid back.

"Then you know where he is?"

Icad timidly shook his head. "Oh no . . . well, yes . . . I mean, no." He stood up a little straighter. "You must put those garments on! If the masters' return and you're not ready to work, they will put me in the castigation vault. I . . . I . . . I can't go back there, ever again."

"Okay! We'll put these on, while you tell us the location of the Andor. How does that sound?" Kerriah spoke slowly as if speaking to a small child.

"Fine. Just please get changed quickly." He closed the garment container lid and turned around. "Now, over here are your resting mats. You get four hours a day . . ."

"Icad!" Kerriah stomped her foot out of frustration. "The Andor, where is he?"

"He's gone." Icad looked down and refused to make eye contact.

"Gone where?" Kerriah persisted.

"He's just gone, okay! Just leave me alone, he was a hero down here, and now, he's gone." Icad buried his hand against his face and began to weep.

"Aw, what the heck. The Solarans I remember were a hard bunch. What the heck is wrong with tya?" Krath recalled a time during the war that Solaran soldiers would remain resolute during even the bloodiest of battles. It was difficult to witness one this broken.

"Krath! Please." Kerriah positioned herself between Krath and Icad. "Please, we need to know where he is located. I know you're hurting, but we are his friends and are here to help." Icad lowered his head. The thick skin on his neck folded over like old leather left out to dry in the blistering heat over many years. He felt the pressure of the three staring at him across the room.

"Some time ago, I don't recall as we don't know time down here, he saved me. I was operating a torso drill, and I was one of the most productive workers, still youthful and strong in that day. The masters, they gained favor for me because of what I produced from mining scabs. The ones they favor get extra rations, masks, additional rest time, and a hope that someday, maybe there could be a parole of some sort. The Andor called Creedith. He also held favor with the masters and was the only one that could outwork me. One day, a deep rumble was felt under our feet, and the lower mine shook until we could no longer stand afoot. It was a burrower. Terrible monsters they are!

"Zeltak, the Master Warden of Dispor, slew the only other one that was ever encountered. That particular burrower chewed through most of Dispor's guards with ease, and as the story goes, Zeltak managed to trap it inside of scab silo eight and skewered its central nervous system with a thermal breacher. He then fused the beast's tines to his helmet in a haughty display of his superiority."

"I think we've seen him up on the first level," Crix said.

Icad turned to him with a slow draw in his voice. "Yes, and even Sintor, the sub-warden, fears him, though his ambition is to continue to enhance himself with parts of whatever Marck he chooses in a secretive scheme to take over as master warden.

"Anyway, we encountered the second burrower the day Creedith saved my life. We had hit a practically rich spot of scabs, you see. Burrowers feed on scabs. The burrower blasted through the floor. Its spine-filled tendrils flailed all around, grabbing everything near it and ripping them into shreds.

"I had turned to run just before a tendril wrapped around my leg and tightened, grinding the flesh and bone away. It burned like nothing I have ever felt before. I tried to drag myself to safety, clawing the coarse ground with my fingers until they were raw and bloodied until my leg finally severed completely away. I was able to drag myself toward a nearby crevice low in the wall. I struggled to pull myself into it as I could hear howls of pain from others in the mine that were consumed by the beast and plasma blasts from the Marck guards, their metal crunching from its wild wrath.

"Just as I slid myself deep within the low crevice, another tendril wrapped around my torso, yanking me back out and into the air. As I looked back, I saw a horrifying sight in the face of the burrower. It had hundreds of tiny black eyes and teeth that were clear like glass but dripping with flesh and stained in blood. As it swung me around to drop me into its grisly jaws, Creedith came out of nowhere wielding a scab fork and pinned down the tendril holding me to the floor.

"The burrower dropped me in an effort to break free. Creedith grabbed me up over his shoulder and tossed me into a maintenance shoot to sub-level four, a terrifying place in its own right but, at least for the moment, better than with the burrower.

"From there, the story goes that Creedith grabbed hold of one of its two low-hanging tines, which the burrower used for movement. He climbed up the tine to its top near the beast's chin, pulled out a pulse saw he had tucked into his tool belt, and pierced clean through the tine, sending the burrower turning violently over until it pinned itself against the wall. Creedith took the beast's newly liberated tine and drove it through its jaw and the top of its head, slaying it.

"He was a hero, at that moment, to all the workers in the lower mine, but that is not how Sintor saw it. In fact, when he discovered the burrower was slain by one of the prisoners, he went mad, having wanted to kill it himself to draw closer in stature with that of Zeltak and—"

"Stop," Kerriah interrupted, "am I understanding this correctly? Did you say a Marck was furious and envious? Earlier, you mentioned Zeltak taking a position of arrogance over slaying a burrower. I have heard reports of Marcks displaying characteristics of emotion, but I thought it just a rumor at best. Are you certain of this?"

"Unfortunately, I am. So much so that he banished Creedith to sub-level four because of his fury. That's a place that is considered a near term death sentence as life expectancy is days or weeks at most." Icad looked nervously toward the doorway.

Crix's heart sunk. "So he's dead, I presume."

Icad now realizing that the guards would be back at any minute, seized up for a second, and then responded. "No . . . no, I don't believe so. There is still someone down there sending up scab quotas, and if anyone were to survive there, I believe it would be him."

Seconds later, the guards returned and pinned Icad against the wall with a forked rod. "Why are these prisoners not awaiting their work requisition outside?" one of the guards demanded. Icad struggled with both hands grasping the fork in a feeble attempt to loosen it from his neck.

"I—I—aghh—was, masters. Please—aghh . . . we were ha—having difficulty finding a jumper that would fit the big one," he said gasping. The guard's head slowly turned to look at Krath then turned back to Icad, dropping him from his fork. Icad dropped to the floor, holding his neck with one hand.

"A few days in the castigation vault may break that willful spirit of yours." The Marck guard stared down at Icad.

"Please, no! I am at your service and have no will of my own." Icad felt fear strike the back of his neck and roll down his spine.

The second Marck guard leaned over, picked him up by the arm, and held him dangling and squirming to get a foothold on the ground. "Very well, only two days in the castigation vault for being a faithful servant." The Marck turned and exited, dragging Icad along. His agonizing screams for mercy faded away into the distance. Crix felt highly agitated by the injustice.

Krath took a half step forward.

"Mind your own, or else find yourself in a similar fate or worse," the Marck guard warned, raising his weapon on Krath.

Kerriah looked over at Krath and nodded. A wide grin crawled across Krath's face as he looked sharply at the Marck. Kerriah sidestepped toward the doorway. Foolishly, the Marck turned to look. Krath took advantage of the Marck's unwise but predictable move and grabbed its rifle. He promptly swung it, smacking against its metal head and leaving it dangling from a few bent rods and shorting power threads. He forward kicked the mangled Marck in the torso and sent it smashing into the wall.

"Okay, I guess it's on." Crix looked pumped. He felt a tingle of energy travel through both arms.

"That's my boy," Krath was pleased. "Now, let's get ourselves thrown into level four and have a little fun in the process." He charged out of the barracks like a wild animal going on the hunt.

Crix and Kerriah followed shouting and screaming as they embarked on their rampage of intentionally destroying equipment and disrupting workflow. They pushed the limits of their chaos just to the edge of not drawing Marck fire but instead had the guards clanking after them in an attempt to subdue the new troublemakers. For a short while, the three actually had a little fun for the first time in many days as they executed their plan at the expense of the Marck guards and sent them running in circles. The other prisoners stopped and watched as well as they could in the darkness, listening to the three have fun tormenting their jailors. A smile cracked across the faces of many; most prisoners of Dispor had not had a reason to smile for years, but that day, the strange threesome was their unlikely heroes.

Then at once, they converged together and stopped, crouching down, hands on their knees, to catch their breath. The guards swarmed in, knocking them to the ground and placing proton shackles on their legs and wrists. A commanding officer strode in and ordered them immediately to level four. He stopped in front of Krath and looked into his eyes, the red glow reflecting off Krath's black eyes.

"Not this one, take him to Sintor," the Marck captain ordered.

"Wait . . . Krath, nooo!" Crix shouted as they dragged Krath away. In the distance, he could hear Krath yelling.

"Hang in there, buddy; hang in there for your—" His voice went quiet; their uplifted spirits suddenly soured by the unexpected detour in their plans.

***

Dragged away, Kerriah and Crix found themselves in a rusted and stained elevator marked with a sign, which dangled from a broken chain that read "Caution! Scab Hive!" Six guards surrounded them with weapons drawn as one unshackled and tossed them each a small pack and a long spear, which had an energy charge at the tip.

"You will kill no less than four scabs per day to receive your rations. You will load them on the delivery crate with your number. When we receive your quota, we will send back your rations. Fail to meet your quota, and you will starve," the Marck captain explained as he shoved them on the elevator and activated a lever sending them below to the hive level.

The elevator screamed as corroded metal ripped against itself, sending them further into the depths of Dispor.

"If we work together, we will survive this. We will find Creedith; just stay close," Kerriah shouted above the noise as they put their backs against each other. Crix's heart raced, and he started to come to terms with his mortality and the odds of their survival.

CHAPTER 19

K erriah?" Crix turned to look at her in the faintly illumined box.

The elevator's screams quieted to a churn, and moisture filled the dry air. She turned around, and he lightly placed his hand behind her neck and into her soft hair, pulling her into him. His mind was a blur. He pressed his lips on hers. It was an awkward moment at first, but she did not pull back. She placed her small hand on his lower back and wrapped her leg around his. He lifted her from the ground, fully partaking in this intimate moment. She felt safe and empowered; her heart beat faster. They both understood it would take their complete trust and love for each other if they were to find a way out of Dispor alive.

The elevator slammed to the ground, and they quickly moved with their backs against each other in a defensive posture, unsure of what to expect in the darkness before them. The air was thick with humidity, and an underlying stench crawled like scurrying rodents into their lungs, weighing heavy with each breath. The pungent stench was a mix of acetone and rotted garlic. The smell was almost dizzying from its hazardous toxicity. In the distance, there were numerous hissing and squeaks, along with wings pattering in the air as if a flock of birds was suddenly disturbed.

"I can't see anything down here. It's nearly pitch black. How the heck do they expect us to kill these things?" Kerriah complained.

Crix dug around in his pack and found what felt like a light emitter. He activated it, and an intense beam blasted out and illuminated the area. Kerriah looked at him with a half-smile from the corner of her cheek.

"Oh, that's how."

The large, domed cavern moved from wall to ceiling as if water was rippling across it in every direction. "What the heck?" Crix strained to get a better look at the walls. Flat, scaly creatures with long, forked tails swarmed the walls and ceiling crawling atop each other, in some cases, three layers deep.

"Well, look on the bright side; looks like our quota should be easily achievable." Kerriah meant for her statement to be sarcastic, but her voice carried with it a noticeably worried undertone.

The cavern took a steep dip off to their right side and disappeared in the darkness. The floor was smooth with a layer of slime, which made it difficult to walk. They remained frozen, motionless, for a little while, trying to get a sense for the scabs, whose activity had begun to settle since the elevator had dropped them off and disrupted the area.

"I think we should move deeper in and start looking for Creedith," Kerriah whispered, pointing her spear in the direction of the right side slope.

"I'll go ahead while you watch my back. Let's move slowly, and maybe we can avoid getting these things too excited," Crix hastily volunteered, not wanting her to take the dangerous point position.

They stepped lightly as they moved into the open area. The scabs hissed and squirmed around anxiously as they walked through the cavern. Crix and Kerriah occasionally paused to allow the scabs to settle back down and then moved ahead slowly once again. The slow stop-and-go pace made the time drag on, and they were unable to gain any significant distance. Something fluttered by, brushing across the top of Kerriah's head, and then across the back of her legs. "Crix, did you feel anything brush against you?"

"I did feel something across my back, but I thought that was you."

She swept her hand past the back of her leg. "It's not me."

Another flutter whizzed by their heads. She shined her light up toward the ceiling. A scab flapped by overhead. The underside of the critter had a circular opening that bulged down with dark, bristly teeth gnashing in the air. Kerriah let out a small squeal. Startled, she pushed her back snug against Crix.

"These things can fly! I didn't realize they could fly."

"Youch!" Crix yelled as he jumped away from Kerriah.

"What are you doing?" she asked, concerned that he had moved away from her side.

"One of them just bit a chunk out of my leg." He shined the light down at his leg, revealing a patch missing from his pant leg, along with a small chunk of skin about the size of a large coin. "Took a good piece of me . . . nasty little suckers." Crix tried to shake off the pain while holding pressure on the wound.

Kerriah tore a couple of pieces of cloth from the bottom of her pant leg and wrapped Crix's wound. "We need to move quicker and get ourselves somewhere a little less hostile if there is such a place down here." She remained steadfast in her focus.

They stuck close and moved into the depths of the virtually pitch-black hive. In an effort to avoid stirring up the scabs, Crix gave out just enough light to keep track of where they were going as they kept their distance from the scab-infested walls. There were no other signs of life aside from the thousands of unrelenting scabs that lined the walls and ceilings.

Crix shook his head, trying to clear his mind from the tipping point of his thoughts. The overlapping hiss of the scabs threatened to drive him to a hasty madness. He struggled to keep focus.

I must keep myself together for her. That was all that mattered to him at that moment, so he pushed forward, guiding the way. As they moved down the slope, the path split: one side narrowed to a low ceiling, and the other had long tendrils cascading down from a higher ceiling. The shiny black tendrils slowly dripped water from their tips.

Crix carefully shined his light up and down both paths. "Neither of these routes look inviting."

He focused the light up high in an attempt to see where the tendrils ended before a voice called out in a loud whisper from the low ceiling path.

"Hey . . . over this way," the voice called. Crix whipped his light in the direction of the voice, picking up a shine against a pair of eyes. "Get that light off me and get over here!" The voice said in the same loud whisper, but now with a slight hint of agitation.

Crix and Kerriah carefully made their way over to where the voice originated from, crouching low as they entered the cramped area. There was a small hollow further within the wall where a short, square individual stood, who had sparse, wiry hair atop a muscular, square head.

"You almost made the last mistake you would have ever made a minute ago." His voice was a bit low and crackly. "Had you shined your light up in the face of that burrower, it would have most likely been the end for all of us."

"You mean tha—" Crix started then was interrupted by the strange individual that almost looked like a wooden block with legs.

"Yes! That was a burrower, and if you were told about them, you now realize the mistake you almost made. That one has been hanging around there for a while, I suspect, just snapping up stray scabs as they pass by. It appears to be getting enough of them down here to keep it pacified, for now, or maybe it's just in some sort of dormant state. It's like we have an understanding: I leave it alone, and it leaves me alone. They don't like lights, though. A shined light directly toward its face will almost certainly cause the beastie to go into one of its legendary killing rages."

"My name is Kerriah, and this is Crix." He strangely looked over a Crix as though he had just seen a ghost. "Who else is down here?" Kerriah asked, shrugging off the strange look and the mention of the burrower.

"You're looking at it. I have the whole hive to myself, and of course, that burrower if you aren't counting the hundreds of thousands of scabs down here. Ohh . . . I've seen others come and go, but prior to your arrival, it was just me. Let's get away from this area. The burrower makes me a little uneasy. I know this hive pretty well, and there is a quiet spot down this way." He started to walk further into the low tunnel.

"Wait!" Kerriah demanded. "You say you're the only one down here?"

He stopped and turned around. "That's right, just me and the scabs."

"We are looking for a friend of ours that's supposed to be down here. He's an Andor named Creedith." Kerriah continued to push him for more detail.

The rugged, almost square-shaped individual looked at her with a scrunched brow. "I'm not sure what an Andor is, but I don't think there have ever been any down here. I don't think so."

Kerriah let out a frustrated exhale. "Creedith! His name is Creedith, and he's a big, strong individual with a long mane going down his head and neck."

He rubbed his head as he looked to be in deep thought. "Oh . . . that fella. Yep, I do recall him now. Please, follow me before we get that burrower's attention. If you'd like, we can speak of it more in a safer spot."

He waddled away and they followed. Sometimes he crawled on his knuckles as his arms were just slightly on the larger side and longer than his legs. He grasped a heavily worn spear and wore nothing more than a well-weathered loincloth with a rag wrapped around his torso. An occasional scab flapped or scurried by, but they did not appear too interested in the three of them at that moment. As they passed by several clusters of scabs, the square-shaped stranger advised them to crawl as low to the floor as possible to avoid disturbing the scabs on the walls and ceilings. Eventually, the low path opened to an immense area filled with a chilly breeze and icy sleet raining down throughout. The ceiling was high above and not visible through the constant precipitation and the scant light of their emitters.

"The scabs don't care for the extreme cold and ice, so this area is safe from them," he hollered above the noise of sleet peppering the floor. He then waved them in his direction as he charged into the icy cold.

They followed and the breeze cut through their clothes like a thin sheet on a cold winter's night. They made their way to a narrow cutout in the wall and barely squeezed their way through, and yet, somehow, the stout character was able to manipulate his body through the spot easily, like a square peg made of soft clay. Inside the wall was a deeply set opening, circular in shape, that appeared to be well lived in. The area seemed to be illuminated by glowing rock pieces that were carefully placed along the walls. All around them were scattered relics of minerals, tools, and the meager possessions of other inmates. The muffled tapping of sleet from the outside helped to mask some of the uneasy clamor from the creatures that lived down there.

"Welcome to my home," he spoke loudly while standing as erect as his incongruous body allowed. "I know it's not much, but for a Solaran condemned to the scab hives of Dispor, it's about as good as one could expect. Besides, down here, I have no metal things pushing me around."

Crix squinted, taking a closer look at him in the low light. "Wow . . . another Solaran! You're the second Solaran I've met today, and the other was the first I've ever seen."

"Well, I've never had someone so intrigued by me before, but here you go . . . name's Bletto, in case you were curious." The Solaran spread his massive arms out and twirled around to give him a better look.

His squatted mass was a result of a thousand years of evolution due to the oppressive gravity of the one-time penal moon of Solara. The moon's higher gravity was considered an additional punishment to those sent there as prisoners so many generations ago. The people of Nathasia wanted no criminals breathing their air, so they created an artificial atmosphere on Solara and cheered as Solara's newly located inhabitants suffered under almost one and a half times their own weight.

Kerriah crossed her arms and rolled her eyes, feeling a little annoyed. "Don't be too flattered; less than five days ago, Crix hadn't seen any other non-Soorakian species."

"Well, it's nice to get some guests, once again. The last fella I had down here didn't last long before becoming skeletonized by a brooding mass of scabs," Bletto cordially remarked.

"How long have you been here, Bletto?" Crix asked but really wanted to engage in a discussion of what it was like to live on a world that had almost 50 percent more gravitational pull than Soorak. Crix found himself sidetracked by the Solaran. Bletto was noticeably excited to tell his story again. He loved to talk but rarely had company, as most did not survive longer than a day or two on the level.

"Thirteen years now . . . I think." He rubbed the back of his head, trying to think the time through. "You know, I'm not really sure. You see, you lose all sense of time down here, and the only concern you have is your own basic survival. That means hunting scabs before you get too hungry and sending the quota up the crate to get your day's rations. And let me tell you, there is nothing to eat down here. Scabs are toxic to us, and you'd be better off to leave that burrower alone."

"What can you tell us about Creedith? He was supposedly transferred down here some time ago." Kerriah eagerly steered the conversation back to the reason they were there.

"There's no one down here. I can tell you that for sure. All the others have been killed, or in a rare instance, transferred to level five."

"Now wait a minute, you told us you did remember him." Kerriah was becoming irritated.

"Well, my memory isn't so good these days, but I'm really not sure. I just needed to get you guys away from that burrower."

Kerriah threw up her hands in frustration. Crix gestured for her to calm down as he approached Bletto. "Level five? I've never heard of a level five on Dispor. What's level five?"

Bletto stared up at Crix before he settled back on a shabby blanket that he shoved under his backside, giving scant comfort from the hard surface.

"That's because it's not supposed to exist. The only reason I know of it is that I have seen it firsthand. It's an unsettling place and an area I would not want to go back to ever again."

"But you said, on a rare instance, there have been prisoners transferred there. Could Creedith have been transferred to level five?" Kerriah disputed.

"Listen, child, even if he was there, he's no use to you now. Besides, what would you do if you found him? Escape?" He chuckled at the thought.

Crix stepped forward, pointing at Bletto with anger. "If you thought our plan was to stay down here with you until the end of our days, you're highly mistaken."

Bletto gave a deep and loud exhale. Having seen numerous hive prisoners become broken and die over the years, he gave little concern to his newfound companion's bold statements. "Settle down. Let's take things in baby steps. Get some rest. In a little while, I will show you how to kill enough scabs to make your ration quota without getting de-fleshed. No matter what you decide to do, you're going to need your strength to do it."

"How do we know when to send up our quota? We can't even tell what time or day it is in this hole," Crix asked.

"Use your stomach as your guide." Bletto laughed. "It always lets you know when you need to work on your quota and just how hard you should be working for it."

Bletto threw each of them a musty old blanket caked with dirt, obviously remnants of former inmates. They laid down and attempted to get some sleep, or at least as much as their minds would let them rest. In the distance, the underground ice storm tapped away at the rocks, and sporadic screeching made for restless sleep. Crix mostly laid awake, staring into the darkness, watching as shapes formed in his imagination and thinking back to Troika and lessons of wisdom from Haflinger.

The hard floor was cold and unforgiving to his body. He thought of things that once were points of worry and concern and now seemed muted in comparison to what laid ahead. He clenched his arms tight together, longing to have those worries back again, to have his youth back again.

He looked over at Kerriah, who appeared to be sleeping, and he found some inner solace. She made him feel calm, encouraged, and strong. She was everything to him, and he felt that surprisingly, looking at her, there was some good at this moment.

"Get up . . . come on . . . get up." Bletto's tone was stern as he jabbed Crix's side with the blunt end of his spear. "Now is the time to go hunt some scabs. They have stopped their mineral grazing and will be docile for a little while. We must go now!" He stammered around like a spastic toddler.

There was no longer any screeching, only the persistent pelting of the storm outside. Crix and Kerriah pulled themselves up from their bedding and grabbed their spears. The stone floor had left their muscles sore and their joints frozen.

Bletto darted out into the storm and across to the other side of the vast opening. He reached the far side and started climbing up a rock wall to an opening a little ways up. It was hard to accept that such a square, hunkered figure could scale the walls like a spider, yet that was exactly what he did, and they both watched in amazement, wondering if he sprouted extra limbs that they were unable to see. They followed closely behind him, though not as efficiently. He hunched down low as they came into an area that had numerous long, skeletal-like formations webbed throughout the space. The formations were dense and emanated a haunting glow which made one want to turn away in fear. However, the celestial formations held them visually captive; their gazes were entranced as they tried to dissect in their minds what these structures must be.

Bletto squirmed through the formations, bending and contorting himself to fit around each structure.

"What the heck are these? They almost look like bones from something," Crix asked while struggling to keep up with the nimble Solaran.

"These strange formations together with the mineral base have mixed with a substance that is creating a chemical reaction giving off the radiance you see. To put it plainly, this is what is left when a burrower dies." Both Crix and Kerriah slowed their stride for just a brief moment on that disconcerting information. Bletto stopped and looked back at them with a sneaky grin.

"The important thing is that the scabs hate the light these things give off," Bletto said.

Crix and Kerriah continued to follow his lead until they reached the end of the maze of radiated bones. Before them was a substantial area with a funnel-shaped ceiling that extended upward into darkness. Lined on every inch of the walls layered upon one another were scabs, quiet, and motionless. Littering the floor were hollowed shells of deceased scabs, as well as the bones of their victims.

Bletto motioned to be silent with his shorty, stubby index finger over his mouth. He lightly stepped over to the wall of scabs nearest to them, moving so smooth and quiet that anyone would have thought he was a ghost. Lifting his spear, he pointed at the widest part of one of the scabs, which was just below the head, and then he signaled for Crix and Kerriah to do the same. They quietly assumed the same position on their chosen scabs. Bletto gestured with his finger for Crix to raise his tip a little higher on the scab. Crix could hear himself breathe; it was so quiet.

Bletto nodded, satisfied with their position, then plunged the spear into one and then another and another, skewering four upon his spear without hardly making a sound, aside from a slight flinch from each scab as the spear ended their miserable existence. He moved closer to them and lightly whispered, "If you hit them in that exact spot, they won't make a sound when you stick them. It severs their vocal cords."

Kerriah aptly speared her four in the same way Bletto did, and then looked over at Crix with a haughty smile while swinging her hips in a taunting gesture with a flirtatious undertone. Crix looked intensely at his scab and wrinkled his brow in anticipation of his attack. He could not let her show him up. He drew back and thrust the spear deep into the scab. The impaled scab let out a shriek so loud that any glass on the hive level would surely be broken as a result. Its alarm awoke the rest of the hive, and the whole room began moving and rumbling.

"You went too deep! Quickly! Get back!" Bletto yelled while galloping as fast as his stout body could back into the area with the glowing bones. Crix pulled his spear back with one dead scab and another flailing about at the bottom. He tried to stick another before taking flight, but Kerriah pulled him by his collar.

"Forget it! Let go!" she shouted. The scabs flooded the room, pouring down from the funnel above and swarming off the walls and ceiling.

They made it to the skeletal wall and squeezed into its glowing protection. The mob of scabs stopped short of the radiating glow and formed a high, black-red barrier that rapidly increased in mass as more scabs arrived.

Bletto looked at the two and strongly exhaled with relief. "No worries now. They won't follow us in here."

"We are supposed to get four each for our ration quota. I only have two," Crix pointed out.

Bletto looked sharply at Crix. "That's right. Your hunting is not finished yet." The scabs continued to swarm the area before them, pouring out from the funnel and filling every part of the cavern's empty space but keeping their distance from the natural illumination. Their hissing and screeching became deafening.

"Follow me back out there again, but keep your back against the webbing."

"Are you nuts? I'm not going back out there. We'll get ripped to pieces," Crix protested, looking over at Kerriah for support.

Bletto became annoyed by his reluctance. "Look, you want to eat today, don't you?"

Crix rolled his eyes. "From the look of this, we are going to be the meal here." He was still waiting for Kerriah to chime in joint opposition to Bletto's plan. The response she gave was not at all what he expected.

"We can do this. They appear to be amply repelled by the radiance given by these formations. Bletto's right; we can easily pick a few more off here and duck back inside this webbing before they get brazen enough to overcome their instinctive fears."

Crix dragged his hand down his forehead and nose before stopping on his chin. His eyes were wide with dread over the thought of it. "Just great!"

Bletto and Kerriah daringly stepped back into the scab-flooded area, and Crix reluctantly followed. The scabs swarmed, each one had their blackish-red eyes trained intently on the three, and the focus of these predators gave some pause to the approaching trio. The perimeter was only about an arm's length, barely enough to get their spears into position. The noise coming from the scabs was so intense that they scattered one's thoughts, and the thick, acidic smell they emitted forced one's breath to become short and labored. Crix's sinuses burned with the vaporous fumes filling the room.

"Pick off what you need quickly from the swarm and duck back into the glow," Bletto shouted over the commotion. "Don't hesitate; they don't like the glow, but they will endure it as they get more frenzied." He noticed the worried looks in Kerriah and Crix's expressions. "Don't worry. Just follow my lead . . . Now!" With that, Bletto started pumping his spear in and out of the swarm of scabs, and they followed his lead, doing the same.

The scabs became louder and scurried in a complete panic, and that panic turned into aggression. Bletto and Kerriah's spears were now full; they ducked back into the formations as the swarm slowly converged inward. Crix, still short one scab, had run out of space to spear any more.

"Above you!" Bletto shouted to Crix. His back was against a column. He was trapped.

The scabs stirred into a maddened frenzy, taking wild chomps at him as they tried to build the courage to brave the detestable glow. Crix noticed a large stalactite above him that had a cracked base. He thought a solid push could send it plummeting to the surface, causing enough chaos to create a temporary clearing in the scabs' swarm.

269

"Forget it, Crix! We have plenty now!" Kerriah shouted for him to return to the safety of the illuminated webbing. Crix would not retreat, though. He would not allow them to carry him. He had to get his own quota.

The scampering wall of scabs was close enough to Crix he felt a few scraping bites that ripped through his clothes. He forcibly snapped off a narrow column, which was loose from the floor. Having noticed a large stalactite, which had a noticeable crack in its base, hanging at the inside edge of the scab swarm, Crix had a plan. He thrust the broken off column into the swarm and pushing against the stalactite until his muscles burned and veins bulged from his neck and forehead. The rock formation wiggled and let out an echoing pop that startled the scabs for just a brief moment before it broke loose from the ceiling and crashed to the ground below.

The broken chunk of stone toppled onto its side, sending scabs scurrying and screeching away from the impact. Bletto and Kerriah covered their faces from the spray of rock shrapnel that blasted in every direction. After the impact, Kerriah frantically looked around for Crix and found him poised with his spear atop the fallen stalactite, with the look of determination on his face.

"Yes! That's how you do it!" Bletto shouted in excitement over what he had just witnessed.

Crix darted around, spearing two scabs with renewed fury. He flipped back and dashed into the safety of the webbing. The scab swarm slammed against the formations trying to get to him. Their jaws broke through into the light, and their hesitation began to wane.

"They're too frenzied. I don't think they're going to hold back any longer. Run!" Bletto shouted as he squirmed through the radiant maze for the other side. Crix and Kerriah tailed closely. Behind them, rocks snapped, and scabs screamed out as they approached with a manic frenzy. The three could feel an air pressure change, and a gust of warm air pushed against their backs as they ran.

They reached the other side and looked back, observing the scabs' haste as they threaded themselves through the maze of tightly woven bones. Bletto reached the edge of the maze.

"Into the storm!" He hopped down upon the smooth wet stone, backsliding into the icy storms of the lower level.

Crix and Kerriah followed close, making their way into the center of the storm cavern. They stopped to see if the scabs followed. They did not; instead, they retracted at the sight of the falling bits of ice.

"You see, scabs are fickle, and it's the key to their weakness. They don't like the cold and will not come in here, which is how I have stayed alive thus far. This sleet blows around like a natural ice guardian. Now, follow me to the depot, and we can send up our quota and remove the growl from our stomachs."

The depot was an area past Bletto's homestead where there was a simple rusted and battered crate just large enough to fit four hefty-sized scabs. A primitive pulley system and a cable attached to the dilapidated crate. Bletto placed his scabs in the crate, and then pulled a nearby lever, which sent it upward into a shadowy hole in the low ceiling. The crate creaked and clattered as it swayed into the wall until it faded into the distance. There was an echoing clank from the crate stopping, and the cable remained motionless for a while until it finally started moving back down.

Several minutes passed. The cage returned with a small metal bowl filled with a brownish mush, several withered leaves, and a canteen of water. Bletto snatched up the canteen and bowl. He tore into it with the same ferocity of a dog over a plate of table scraps. The smell from the bowl was similar to a two-day-old corpse lying in the sun.

Kerriah repelled back in pure disgust. "Awww . . . You can't be serious. This is what we nearly got ourselves de-fleshed over? A bowl of rotted mush? I'm not sure I want to send my scabs up at this point."

Bletto stopped for a minute and looked up over his bowl. "It's really not bad, a taste you learn to appreciate after a while. Besides, going hungry is far worse than this is." He resumed smashing his face into the bowl.

"I'm hungry, but just not that hungry—yet. Still, I'm going to send mine up if nothing less than to give it to Bletto," Crix said. Both Crix and Kerriah sent their scabs up, and in return, the same bowls of brown, odorous mush came back. "Here, you can have ours as well." Crix handed the bowls of mush to Bletto but hung onto the water. Bletto looked up at him puzzled.

He snatched the bowls from Crix. "You won't last long without eating. You'll need your strength to hunt again soon."

Kerriah crossed her arms tightly. "We are not here to hunt. Besides, that's playing right into what the Marcks want from us. To use us up for their purpose and then cast us aside. We need to know how to get to level five and for you to show us the way."

"Well, I could show you, maybe if you help me hunt just one more time. I like the idea of getting three times the rations— haven't ate like this in years." He buried his face into the extra bowls like a ravenous dog. Kerriah walked over to him and smacked the bowl away from his face, sending its contents splattering against the wall.

Bletto's demeanor quickly changed. He stood up and clenched his fist, but Crix stepped in between them. "You're going to have to go through me if you mean to strike her." His eyes stared down the Solaran with blackness. Bletto scrunched his face and turned away in a loud huff.

"Years ago, I might have taken you up on that offer. All I really want to do is make the best of what I have now. That's all, and it's the little things that get me through the endless time here." He turned back. "Fine, you want to get to level five? I will take you there, but I'm not going with you. I will only show you the way."

"Good. Where is it, and when can we get going?" Crix probed.

Bletto chuckled almost spitefully. "You're not going to like it, young one, not going to like it at all."

Crix, now irritated with Bletto's mocking tone, spoke with a bitter sharpness. "What do you mean by that? It doesn't matter if we like it or not, our friend is there, and we have to get him out, so us liking it is not relevant. So where is it?"

Bletto snorted and snickered, "Okay . . . in that hive nest we just got back from, up that dark funnel hole that the scabs were pouring down from, there is a small opening. In that opening, a natural passage leads down to level five." Crix assumed that Bletto was making up the most outrageous story to discourage their quest.

"You must be mistaking us for complete fools if you think that we're going to believe you ever climbed up there. Where's the real location?"

Bletto subtly smirked. "Oh yes, I and two others made that journey once. It was a time when I was younger and still full of hope about getting out of this place. The other two had learned to survive down here. In fact, one of them, an Ando . . . ahhhemm." He made an awful gurgle and cleared his throat in a fake manner as if he almost let something slip. "Anyway, he was the one who taught me how to hunt. That one told me of the spot in the deep cavity and that he had felt prevailing winds coming from the other side. He thought that it must have led to a larger area. So together, we decided to take the risk and enter that place at all costs. It costed us plenty. Both of my companions were killed, one impaled many times by thousands of sharp needles that shot out from around the queen, and the other vanished in level five itself."

"A queen!" Crix was shocked by the thought.

"That's right, and you may have better odds against a burrower than her."

Kerriah shrugged off the risks. "So . . . it leads to level five, right? What's there?" She was singly focused on the mission. Bletto was not going to dissuade her from rescuing anyone. Crix, inspired by her tenacity, listened more intently to Bletto's story.

"It did lead there, but it's not a place you want to be any more than here in the scab hives. In fact, I will take the hives. At least the hives are not infested with Marcks and their sinister works." Bletto was becoming angry at having to remember the abysmal place. He shook his head and paced the floor.

"Is there a way out?" Crix asked.

Bletto became visibly disturbed over the question. "There is, but you'll never get to it without a small army. There are some strange experiments being conducted on the poor souls who end up there, using the most sinister of Marck technology. No place for the likes of us."

"We're going, and it's not up for debate. So tell us what we need to do to get in there." Kerriah was not giving an inch for Bletto to disagree.

Reluctantly, Bletto explained how he was able to carry a chunk of the glowing rock to keep the scabs at a safe distance as he entered the secret opening. The biggest difficulty, he described, was in the stealth aspect of scaling the scab-covered walls in order to reach the entrance high above. To alarm even one scab would awaken the entire hive and be certain death to anything in the area. Bletto started rubbing his head and chewing his bottom lip.

Crix sat atop a small, round hump formation on the floor looking peculiarly at Bletto. "What's your story, Bletto? What did you do to get destined to this miserable place to begin with, and yet appear so content with your fate?"

Bletto looked down and stared at the floor for a few moments then slowly lifted his head, looking upward at the ceiling. Sorrow poured from the roundness of his eyes. He felt the agony and sting of thoughts that he had learned to suppress over the years, thoughts that were too painful to recall. Yet, he felt the need to tell his story. He wanted to tell the story.

"I used to live a normal life with my spouse—well, as normal as life can be on Solara. She was my childhood dream, and I always pursued her and, ultimately, had finally won her affections. We lived together for several years in a small place with simple jobs, just basking in the joy of each other's company. I am sure you learned in your schools about how regional gangs and warlords ran Solara through fear and intimidation of its local citizens. Well, when I fell upon hard times and was unable to pay my monthly tribute to Gorag, the lord of the Semptor Region, he sent his cronies and took my spouse as his payment.

"I was destroyed. I couldn't even eat. I felt sick and empty as I laid awake each night thinking of what's become of her. Until one day, I could no longer stand it. I had to get her back, and I set out to beg Gorag for her return.

"When I arrived at his castle, he sat upon his throne with his harem surrounding him, and there she was and lovely looking as I could ever recall. Gorag agreed to let her go if she still wished it, but something had changed in her. She no longer wanted to be with me. Then Gorag laughed at me . . . taunting me, gaining enjoyment from my suffering. I was so enraged that he turned her against me that I grabbed a nearby lamppost and ripped it from the floor, and then charged at Gorag with every intention in my thoughts to kill him.

"However, his guards seized me before I could land my blow. I was mercilessly beaten and charged with attempting to kill a regional lord and sentenced to the remainder of my natural life in Dispor. So you can see, I have little desire to leave anymore. There is nothing out there for the likes of me." He looked down again, pressing his hands across the back of his head. Crix watched him intently. He felt his pain and sadness.

"Your story is very sad. You've submitted to your misfortune and have nothing, just a miserable life down here by yourself," Crix said as he got up, walked over to Kerriah, and placed his arm around her shoulder. She looked at him and returned a warm smile. "You see, we haven't given up yet, and we will find our friend and leave this place intact, even if it takes every drop of my strength and determination. Perhaps this is an opportunity for your life to have meaning again, to stand for something, to stand up against your persecutors. Help us . . . help us get through that passage." Kerriah was impressed and treasured Crix even more.

Bletto squatted down and buried his face in his legs for a couple of minutes as he gave out a muffled groan, thinking of his lost love. "Okay . . ." He stood up slowly and rubbed his face. He valued the way Kerriah looked at Crix. "Okay, I will help you, but you'll have to listen to me and do as I say. If I say we back out, we back out and wait until a better time, no matter how long that takes."

"What exactly will we see there?" Kerriah asked.

"All I can tell you is what is there is not supposed to be there, and we don't stand a chance getting out if we're sighted. You will have to see for yourselves for I'm not good with explanations." He gurgled up a little indigestion, pulled up some loose flesh around his belly, and then found a comfortable spot in the corner. He had a look of someone who had no intention of moving for a little while or answering any more questions. They settled in for a short rest and gave the disturbed scabs time to resume their dormancy.

Crix cuddled close to Kerriah, and she gently placed her head to his shoulder. He caressed her perfect black hair. He noticed that it still shined even after all they have been through. It was flawless, and her green eyes glistened like gemstones.

"It's amazing . . ." He took a short breath and paused for a few seconds. "It's amazing, in an awful place such as this, where everything seems so dreadful, such beauty can exist. You bring an amazing brightness when you're present, one that I have never felt until the day I found you crashed in Drisal. I hope we are never apart from each other." Kerriah's eyes slowly rose up, meeting his, and she gave a soft smile, and then snuggled into his chest. The time went by too quickly for both.

Not yet asleep, Bletto listened, and his heart felt warmth for the first time in many years. There was something he needed to get off his mind, information he was privy to that could further their resolve.

"Hey, there's something I have been keeping from you about the Andor you're looking for. I did not want to tell you that was him before because I didn't want you to leave." Crix and Kerriah both popped up from their bedding.

"I knew it!" Crix cried out.

"He told me his story. It was a story about a baby he'd saved many years ago. I still remember all the details, and I believe you would be interested." Bletto propped himself up with a serious look. "I have to tell you about Creedith and baby Crix."

Crix and Kerriah both looked over at each other wide-eyed. Creedith and Crix?

Bletto began to tell the story with detail and amazing accuracy. It was apparent that he had heard this story many times and memorized it. He somehow understood the epic importance of Creedith's tale. He started by taking them back twenty years ago during the tragic war . . .

CHAPTER 20

Having utilized the speed of Plexo's specially modified ship, they arrived hours ahead of the pursuing Marck fleet. Creedith made his way to Lator, Corin's hometown on Soorak. He had a promise to keep. Corin took a mortal wound saving the remains of the Vico Legion from Zearic, and his dying wish was to ensure the safety of his family. Creedith was going to do more than that. He was going to take Corin there to see them before he passed. Plexo had stabilized the wounds for the trip, but Corin's time was expiring.

Just before daybreak, Creedith arrived in the rural community of Lator with Corin, who was half-conscious from his wounds. His plan was to move fast and get Corin's family to safety under cover of night. He was aware that there was a high probability the Marcks had already arrived ahead of him and already seized Sarie and Crix or set a trap to capture Corin as he arrived.

Creedith began carrying Corin slung over his shoulder. The effects of Plexo's wound-mending inducer were beginning to decline, and he noticed a warm, wet feeling against his chest where Corin's body rested against his.

As he entered the seacra forest that surrounded Corin's home, the sweet, organic fragrance that filled the warm air engulfed his lungs. Each step spooked up plumes of glow beetles that when startled, radiated red sparks for a couple of seconds, and then dimmed out again. The sight of the forest and the scent of the seacra brought out a rush of emotions from his youth of growing up in the native Andor wildlands of Troika. His hair stood straight up, and his heart fluttered for just a moment. He felt at peace for the first time in a long while.

Creedith set Corin down next to a tree and started to climb. He ascended high into the branches, and gracefully jumped from tree to tree. He needed to keep off the ground and prevent lighting up the glow beetles below that would give away his approach. Luckily, the trees were old and the branches thick, so they did not make a large commotion as he traversed them.

When Creedith reached the outer rim of trees that led up to Corin's homestead, he stopped and pulled out an infrared image enhancer. Viewing the home, he located two humanoid heat signatures and several cooler signatures from inside.

There must be Marcks on the premises already. He knew this was most likely a trap. *I should not have left Corin by himself in his condition. Maybe I should go back to get him.*

Upon hearing a gurgling noise in the tree above him, he looked up slowly and observed a pair of blue, flashing lights. At the same time, a blunt object smashed down on his face. The shock from the blow felt like the bridge of his nose was shattered, and all he could hear was a loud ringing in his ears. He plummeted to the ground below, his back cracking as he smacked flat onto the grassy surface. While staring up and trying to maintain consciousness, little red, glowing specks flew up and out in every direction before going dark again. As he laid there in throbbing pain, there was a loud thump behind him and a faint mechanical buzz.

Creedith squinted, having to clear the blur from his vision, and noticed the outline of a dark-shaded Marck standing there with his rifle pointing down toward him. The Marck paused for a moment, as though he was either relaying information or receiving information regarding his mission.

The Marck placed his rifle up to his shoulder. "Where is the current location of the renegade Commander Emberook and the blue orb?" The Marck squelched out as if his voice was coming from inside a can.

Creedith rubbed his eyes to get some focus from his still-dazed thoughts. "Let me up, and I will take you to him," he responded.

"Get up slowly," the Marck replied, keeping the rifle trained on Creedith as he backed up a few steps.

Creedith slowly pulled himself up from the ground. He grabbed the only object near him, a core seed from a rotted seacra. Having cupped the seed in his hand without the Marck noticing, he just needed to distract the Marck for just a second. Tossing the small but dense seacra seed to turn the Marck's focus away from him should buy him the chance he needed.

"So you guys must be the Marck Special Operations Force, huh? I'll bet you wouldn't last ten minutes in a skirmish against an equal number of UMO troopers."

The Marck gave no reply, and Creedith shook his head. *Of course he's not getting mad. It's a senseless robot, and he could care less about his ego.* Creedith walked forward in the direction away from Corin's location.

"Haahaahaa . . . You substandard carbon life forms would be eradicated like the vermin that you are!"

Creedith was startled and stopped . . . confused. He turned to look at the Marck. Did he hear the Marck's words correctly? Did it just respond to an attack on its ego?

"Gret ebb brahh han kebbo getir blotk bor mi." Creedith spouted off the ancient form of his native tongue, which translated to, "The ebb tree tiger behind you could easily dismember your metal frame."

The Marck turned his head slowly to look behind him. Creedith was surprised again that the Marck knew this form of Andor dialect. He quickly tossed the seed out to his side. It landed, making a rattle in the leaves, stirring up glow beetles. The Marck whipped its rifle toward the commotion as Creedith pulled his tectonic blade, and in one blinding swish, he removed the Marck's head from its shoulders.

The Marck discharged a flashing pop and gurgle as it dropped to its knees then fell facedown to the forest floor. The leaves crunching from both sides of him made him aware that the other Marcks were drawing closer. He picked up the Marck's rifle and scaled up the tree nearest to him. He climbed as high as he could go before the branches sagged.

The approaching commotion was directly below him, and he hugged the trunk of the tree tightly as he looked down the rifle's sights. It was too difficult to see anything in the waning darkness, but the morning light briskly cracked over the horizon, and the shadowy silhouettes of two Marcks emerged from the void below. At that moment, the Marcks noticed him and opened fire.

Creedith took a shot in the left arm and another grazed his face, causing an intense burn. He staggered back, almost falling from the branch before dropping the rifle. The pain enraged him. He pulled his blade while leaping down upon the two Marcks, and they crashed to the ground under his falling weight. With his tectonic blade, he dispatched one Marck before it could get back to its feet. The other Marck managed to get back up to a kneeling position with its rifle pressed against its shoulder. Creedith was fast, and he rapidly swung his blade down, smashing its metal head. The blow caused his blade to shatter from the impact. The Marck fell with its head compressed into its neck like an empty can.

He looked toward Corin's home in the distance and noticed three Marcks just outside the front entrance. Sarie was there as well with baby Crix cradled in her arms. Relief filled Creedith upon seeing them. Two of the Marcks were standing with rifles pointed out toward Creedith, and the third was holding a pistol at Sarie's head. The skirmish with the last two Marcks must have alerted them.

"Drop your weapons and step out into the yard with your hands atop your head," one of the Marcks ordered.

Creedith could hear Sarie pleading for the life of her child. She stood there weeping and holding her arms over his small, swaddled body. Her auburn, long hair blowing in the wind tussled over the baby's face.

"We will terminate these prisoners if you do not comply!" the Marck threatened.

Not willing to take the chance with their lives, Creedith slowly stepped out of the forest and into the courtyard with his arms up. Just as he appeared out in the open, one of the Marcks fired a shot at him. He dropped to his knees. The shot was to stun the Andor, not kill. Two Marcks ran over to him, and one smacked the back of Creedith's neck with the butt of his rifle, causing him to collapse. It then placed its foot against his neck, pinning him helplessly to the ground. The Marck's heavy metal body leaned into his neck and gave a sharp stabbing pain that ran down Creedith's spine as he struggled to breathe.

"Where are Commander Emberook and the blue orb? Tell us, or we will terminate both you and the hostages."

Even Creedith's thick neck was failing to take the extreme pressure of the Marck's weight. He started losing consciousness, and his vision dimmed into darkness.

"Noooo!" he could hear Sarie scream.

The weight suddenly lifted from his neck, and he drew in a swift breath of air. He rolled over to his back and could see the shadows of the trees strobe blue, and rifle blasts screamed out all around him. He felt small pieces of heated metal shower upon him and burn through his uniform before sizzling into his skin.

Sarie let out a blood-curdling scream. Creedith pushed himself up to his hands and knees to look in the direction of the scream. Corin was kneeling down with her in his arms and fragments of Special Ops Marcks littered around them. Creedith stumbled to his feet and hobbled his way over to Corin. Sarie's face was charred black. Her hair and flesh burned down almost to the bare skull. She was motionless but still clenching the baby, who appeared to be unharmed and crying anxiously. She had clearly protected her child until her last breath.

Corin brushed his hand tenderly across her face. This woman of his youth, the one he had pledged his life to, was gone, taken from the world. The pain he felt seared deep like a hot knife into his gut.

"My love, no . . . no . . . you can't leave. Crix needs you. He needs you, now more than ever!" He shouted with the last of his strength.

Creedith had known Corin and fought alongside him for years and had always recalled him being stoic and calm until then. Corin pulled her close and wrapped his arms around her. Giving his last bit of life to embrace her one final time, he crumpled backward. Her body slid from his arms.

Creedith squatted down and pulled the baby up into his arms. He knelt next to Corin and gently laid the child down at his friend's side. The dying Tolagon turned his head slowly and moved his arm to caress his child's soft brown hair. His eyes welled up, and tears poured down his cheeks. He looked up at Creedith.

"Take the orb and hide it with the child. Someday, Crix will grow into a man, and when the time is right, the Tolagon will rise again! You must see to his safety."

"I will," Creedith sorrowfully replied. His large eyes dropped, saddened. He watched Corin until daylight was in full bloom and the life had completely left the Tolagon's eyes.

As his friend took in his last shallow breath, a startling shriek came from Corin's chest as the orb raised outward, abandoning its now lifeless host. The blue orb hovered like a spirit over Corin. Creedith grabbed it and hastily wrapped it with what remained of his cloak. He also unclasped a bracer from Corin's wrist, knowing that it was an important piece that all Tolagons wore.

Corin had let the secret of its purpose slip out to his old friend when Creedith had asked about it years ago. It was then that he told him that it was required to access Phantos Gate—the place where all Tolagon knowledge was kept. He could not allow this to fall into Marck possession, and it would need to be hidden along with Corin's child. Knowing the Marcks would be upon him again, he departed en route for the land of Troika.

CHAPTER 21

After Bletto told them the story, Crix and Kerriah looked at each other in astonishment over such a tale. The details provided many answers regarding Creedith and helped only to further their resolve to find him. Crix slept lightly, recounting the story repeatedly in his head. Kerriah processed the information in an effort to find something useful to their task. Neither of them slept well, and their minds stirred until the time Bletto announced it was time to go.

Returning to the *queen's* lair, after their last incident, felt like willfully aiding in their own destruction. It just felt wrong, and Crix's stomach appeared to be the only thing that understood just how wrong as it tightened itself into a giant knot of anxiety. They already spent the first part of the morning slicing the Dispor tracking tags out from the backs of their necks, which ended up being immensely painful due to the dull blades and lack of nerve-blocking medication.

"The scabs have receded back into their lair," Bletto observed.

Many of the glowing formations had been broken down from the force of the earlier frenzied swarm, and they all knew that there was no guarantee that the light would repel the scabs again. Still, this was a one-way trip, and they had to hope for the best.

Crix and Kerriah both picked up chunks of glowing rocks and fastened the fragments to their bodies with strips cut from blankets.

"They should be sleeping again around this time. I just hope they haven't permanently overcome their fear of light after our last encounter," Bletto stated, stroking his hands across the surface of the rocks.

They reached the bottom of the queen's lair and found the scabs silent and still. Bletto pointed to the small opening. It was near the highest point where the cavern turned to darkness, upward into an area of pure terror. Crix looked up, worry poured over him. He could not see the entrance, which was completely hidden by the layers of sleeping scabs.

"So how do we get up there?" Crix whispered. Bletto smirked.

"What do you think? You climb the scabs." He grabbed hold of a scab attached to the wall and pulled himself up, and then grabbed another doing the same again. "You see, it's easy. Remember, in a dormant state; they are mostly docile unless they sense being attacked or are feeding. Right now, the only thing you need to be concerned about is the queen. If she sees us, she will think we are a threat to her hive and most definitely will attack, alarming all the other scabs. Be careful when we get higher up, and move only as she turns away. Even better is to just watch me and move when I do." Kerriah and Crix grabbed onto low-clinging scabs and started to climb, following Bletto upward into the living darkness.

The scabs gripped tightly to the wall as they climbed upon them and would shift slightly at times but remained dormant. As they got higher up, a strong, pungent odor filled the air, and the humidity was so thick that breathing felt labored. Bletto reached the opening and waved the others to hurry up. A frothing hiss emerged from the darkness above, and the many scabs stirred for just a moment in response.

Kerriah struggled to get a footing on one of the scabs as it wiggled loosely against the wall. She pulled herself up, finding a different spot for her foot, but as she did, the scab fell away to the floor and slapped against the hard surface below. The three of them froze, and their hearts skipped a few beats as they waited for the hive to come alive around them. After a few minutes, their arms, hands, and legs were throbbing in pain from holding themselves up against the wall.

Bletto started to wiggle the scabs from the opening, but the inexorable hissing above them returned, this time louder and longer than before. He stopped and stared upward. There was a frothy growl, but he could not see anything through the darkness. Crix reached the opening and began helping Bletto move the scabs out of the way until a sudden snarl, and lively hiss from above stopped them from their careful task. They stared into the oblivion, unable to detect anything, only shadowy movements. A large, murky, grey object the shape of a giant teardrop oozed down slowly from the blackness. The surface of this entity was shiny and glistened faintly from the distant light below.

"Don't move," Bletto whispered from the corner of his mouth.

They remained motionless. A large eye with a milky appearance revealed itself at the tip of the oozing bulb, and it curled out sideways to face Crix and Bletto. There was a lengthy pause. It predatorily panned around the walls, stopping at Kerriah before moving closer as she remained frozen. The eye opened wider revealing a mouth with rows of various-sized teeth that had a sticky substance seeping from the top and bottom rows.

The mouth snapped toward Kerriah but stopped just short of her after hearing a surprising shout from close by. "Over here!" Bletto yelled.

His life had only been about his own survival; others would come and go, and it didn't matter to him. However, observing Kerriah and Crix, sharing personal stories with them, had brought things back into clarity. He understood; he remembered what was important. He felt empathetic and merciful for the first time in many years. He felt alive and important.

Bletto climbed away from the opening and then stopped to wave an arm out while yelling, then again moved further away. "Get going! I got this!"

The giant mouth full of teeth closed back into the eye and tried to get a position on Bletto. Kerriah swiftly moved up to the opening and helped Crix peel away the last scab that was obstructing their passage. Then Bletto, their unlikely hero, screamed out a torturous shriek. Dangling by his legs, he flailed helplessly in the grasp of the one-eyed monstrosity. Hundreds of needle-like arms moved down from blackness above. The grey, bulbous queen, shot her arms in and out of his body as if he were nothing more than a hunk of brown lard.

"Get going now!" Crix cried out while pushing Kerriah into the secretive opening.

Bletto's screams turned silent, and his movement ceased. The mouth dropped his limp body and morphed back into the eye, scanning the area again. The scabs began to waken and move about like fluid covering the walls. Observing the eye swooshing over in their direction, Crix frantically continued to shove Kerriah further into the threshold, but she was not budging. The eye spotted Crix.

"Hurry up!" Crix shouted.

"I'm trying, but I have an issue with a scab up here."

The eye formed into the mouth again, and Crix looked around for an escape plan. Its gaping jaws gave out a pungent smell of rot and mold, as it reared back for a strike. Just as it darted toward Crix, a whirling scab plunged into its jaws. It chomped down on the scaly shell and started flinging around violently. The scab gave out an eardrum-piercing squeal.

All the scabs in that tight space became wildly animated, and Crix found it difficult to hang onto the wall. Kerriah stuck her arm out and grasped Crix's arm. He felt her fingernails dig deep into his skin. She was not going to let go. She pulled him into the crawlspace. Inside the space were two scabs, half-smashed and motionless, their outer shells freshly beaten.

"We need to get going," she said, stating the obvious while crawling with extreme urgency through the tight, bumpy tunnel.

They went a short distance before hearing violent flapping close behind. A venomous hiss assured there was no turning back. They squirmed their way through the jagged rock tunnel, which at times forced them into uneasy, tight spaces. They crawled over the remains of dead scabs that littered the narrow passage.

Deep within Crix, a calm whisper chanted into his head with a voice that sounded neither male nor female . . .

"The child of the cherished race will emerge." He paused and squeezed his eyelids shut to clear his mind. *"Unsuppress . . . the power within . . . your spirit is the container."* The whisper became so vivid that he felt like someone was booming in his ear. A chill ran down his neck and all the way through his lower legs. He felt a renewed assuredness as if something within him had awoken.

The tunnel vibrated slightly around them as they progressed further into the passageway, moving down a dangerously steep pitch, descending . . . deeper and deeper. They gripped the walls until their fingers and palms burned raw to prevent sliding uncontrollably into the blackness ahead.

The tunnel leveled out. At that moment, a buzzing filled the air, becoming louder, and even louder ahead. Kerriah turned out her light emitter.

"I see a light glowing up ahead," she said.

She carefully slowed her forward movement, taking care of what peril might lay ahead. A rough opening emerged ahead, enhanced by a gloomy red glow. Kerriah approached the opening and stopped. She waved her hand back for Crix to be still. It felt like an hour passed, and his mind started going crazy.

What is she looking at?

She slowly backed up into Crix, forcing him to retreat further to give her space. She warily turned herself around inside the narrow tunnel and leaned back against the side of the rocky wall.

She whispered, "Sentries . . . there are automated sentries guarding the tunnel opening. I think the Marcks have put a defensive perimeter to keep wandering scabs and prisoners out of Level Five. If we move too close to the opening, we'll be vaporized." Trapped between frenzied scabs and near-certain disintegration, they both laid there motionless contemplating their options, which appeared to be limited.

"We can just lay here and die, or I can take those sentries out," Crix said. He sounded surprisingly enthusiastic considering their dire situation.

Kerriah squinted at him and equally confidently remarked, "If you use the orb, we could have Marck legions crawling down on us here to acquire it. That's out of the question at this point. We can wait for the scabs to calm down, and then back our way out. We'll try again once we devise a way to get past this."

Crix placed his hand on her leg. "Kerriah, trust me. I can do this. For a reason that I cannot explain right now, I can do this without giving us away." She stared at him, exhaled a deeply held breath, and did not ask any further questions. She nodded, placing her trust in him.

Lying on his back with his arms at his sides, he closed his eyes. The whisper spoke once again. *Merging . . . within the son of the cherished race . . . you will find deliverance.* Crix spilled his thoughts into the deepest portion of his mind and found a veiled path into his soul. He took captive every thought.

The path was a place within him that he had never visited in the realm of his own consciousness. His thoughts weaved back and forth uniformly. He found the orb inside. He grasped it, drawing it into this hidden place. He felt as though his mind and body were trying to escape each other as he tightened his grip. His mind swirled at the very edge of awareness and the tipping point of insanity. To go too far would mean there would be no going back; he would be forever lost to those that knew him.

A flash of blue filled his vision and entered like a scream in darkness. The void was no longer black but now filled like a deep blue ocean. Clarity . . . he opened his eyes, and a cloud of blue emerged above him, shimmering and alive. It darted out of the tunnel and into the guarding sentries. Crackling metal echoed out as the ceiling-mounted sentries crumpled like wads of paper. The living blue light breezed back to Crix and merged within him. He raised his head and looked at Kerriah. She witnessed a subtle cerulean glow from his skin now, a glow that was only noticeable in dim light.

"Your skin, what happened?" Kerriah asked, even though she already suspected the answer but still needed to hear it.

He felt focused and energized. "I know this is going to sound a little odd, but I have been able to fully merge with the orb. It's part of me now. The strangest part is that the orb explained to me how to do it, as well as how to use its power without releasing a major detectable energy signature. Also, I believe now I can better control the amount of power I dispense when I use it and make it less likely to be detected, especially in these depths."

"It? You mean the orb?"

"That's correct. It has whispered things to me for a while now. I used to think it was just my mind playing games with me, but now, I realize it was the orb the whole time," Crix observed. His eyes looked wiser now as if he had grown decades in a few minutes. His hair was now all white.

"Well, I like the iridescent blue look you're sporting now and the white hair. You pull the look off well." She winked at him, and he smiled back. His heart melted. She turned back around to refocus on the task. "I just hope it doesn't stand out in the daylight as much as it does in the dark." Now would not be the time to announce to everyone that he had the blue orb.

Kerriah edged forward, and then popped her head out of the passageway. It opened out on the ceiling of Level Five. The buzzing was now clearer.

"Ohhhh boy. I sure hope you have more surprises in you because I think we're going to need them." She looked down from the ceiling to the massive area below. Far below them many stories tall were racks filled with powered down Marcks, row after endless row going almost to the top of the twenty-story-high ceiling. In the distance, she saw an opening with radiant green light spilling out, mixing with the dim glow of the recessed lights that illuminated the Marck storage area. The buzzing was steady and soft, coming from tall, rectangular units evenly spanned throughout the racks. Each large unit had ribbed tubes that fed into each rack.

Kerriah looked over with a smirk. "You wouldn't happen to have a ladder back there, would you?" She asked.

Crix crawled forward and grabbed her waist. She felt a strange tingling sensation from his touch. They slid out from the tunnel opening and into the open air. Hovering high above, he pulled her in close, and then steadily lowered them both to the floor below. "I guess you did have a ladder after all." She turned and gave him a soft kiss on his cheek and a playful half-smile as she turned away.

"These Marcks look to be outdated. My guess is they are the same model that relieved the old UMO forces a generation ago," she said, brushing her hand against one. The Marcks were polished and clean with little to no dust on their armor—strange for outdated units to be in long-term storage in a place like Dispor.

Crix had an uneasy feeling in the midst of a Marck army, even powered down, and as such, he scanned the area for an escape route. "Let's just hope they aren't easily awakened." There was no apparent way out aside from the way they came in or the lighted green opening in the distance.

"Yeah . . . good point, let's get a closer look in that chamber ahead. Try not to touch anything, just in case." Kerriah carefully and quietly moved forward, staying clear of the Marck storage racks. As they neared the opening, the light flickered as if something passed in front of it.

"Someone's in there," Crix whispered. Kerriah did not respond and continued to walk slowly ahead, but now more to the side, staying out of the direct sight.

There was a faint purr in the area beyond the opening. The purring intensified, and the light dimmed. Kerriah dashed back between two Marcks and motioned for Crix to do the same. The purring now echoed loudly into the Marck storage area. Kerriah peeked around the Marck she was hiding by to get a look.

A small platform hovered a few meters above the floor. Mounted atop the platform was a strange, mutated figure that had a mix of both tendrils and arms, some mechanical and some flesh. The arms squirmed about from a blob-like body that appeared to be fused to the floating platform. She ducked back out of sight as it continued down the rack aisle. It moved past her without pause. Its limbs flailed around, grasping at unseen things floating in the air. A faint, incoherent grumble came from the creature as though it was speaking to something.

It stopped near Crix for a second then started to ascend to the Marcks in the higher racks and halted three rows up. There was a flickering, bright flash as sparks showered down for several minutes. Slowly, it lowered back down, grasping a Marck arm and head.

It started to move ahead toward the lighted chamber but stopped just as it approached Kerriah's hidden position. Both Crix and Kerriah remained deathly still and flat against the metal rack, hidden between two Marcks. A wet spattering noise came from the creature as a black globe peeled out from the topside of its torso. A thin linkage held the globe up, and it bent around in Kerriah's direction. The creature dropped the Marck parts on the floor and mumbled loudly. A hollow voice echoed out from loudspeakers scattered throughout the storage area.

"It's okay, Guttel; they are our guests. Bring them to me."

Guttel picked up the previously discarded Marck parts and began to leave the storage area. Crix and Kerriah slowly emerged from their hiding places but did not follow. The hollow voice rang back out again.

"Please follow Guttel, and the answers to your questions will be revealed. Don't be afraid, come." The hollowed voice in some strange way, was inviting. Crix followed a safe distance behind Guttel.

"Let's go, Kerriah. At this point, hiding is pointless. Let's get what we came for." She followed close to Crix, however a little less enthusiastic about tailing the strange creature.

As they entered the illuminated area, the radiant green lighting was so intense that it filled every crevice. It was so immersive that it brought on a faint, nauseous feeling that started in the mind and crawled into the gut. All around them were parts, both mechanical and organic. Limbs hung from boney wires of various lengths. Some of the parts looked to be animated, twitching and flinching without rhythm. There were so many different parts that the area around them looked textured in some sort of horrific, yet artistic scene. Piles of rifles and assorted weaponry littered the floor. Most likely the former armaments of the Marcks in the containment area.

They both trekked ahead boldly in spite of the revulsions around them, weaving around a maze-like path and through the dangling parts. The maze of parts ended at a tunnel lined with glass conduits that contained a bizarre array of cyborg warriors, each one menacing in their own unique form. Some were Solaran, others Hybor or Mendac, and there were even some morbidly weaponized Thraxons in this display hall of sorts. A hall of what appeared to be someone's apparent science experiments and trophies of war and weaponry.

The unfortunate beings in the glass showcases had found themselves outfitted with various blades, rifles, disruptors, and projecting explosive apparatuses, and each one was bulky with mechanical reinforcements of their limbs that looked to aid their movements and augment their strength. A dusty mist swirled within each tube as if some sort of suppressant or preservative kept these organic fixtures of warfare asleep.

Crix tried to keep his eyes on Guttel, even as he passed a particular Thraxon that had shiny blades fused into the ends of each of its six arms and a thin spike protruding from its mouth. He was sure that its head turned, but it must have just been an illusion from the swirling mist within its enclosure.

Kerriah and Crix could not help to be alarmed by these sights, but they tried not to make an obvious observation of them and, instead, looked at each other, verifying through their eyes that they were of the same mindset. They were likely walking into the jaws of death.

The long hall opened to a ghostly vastness where seemingly endless rows of clear cubes gradually disappeared into the darkness beyond. Each cube contained a body. The faces and frozen stance of these bodies bore a look of shock as if a reaction to their last sight or a brief moment of immeasurable pain.

Nearby, a small contingent of Marcks stood nearby armed and at attention but took little notice to the approaching trio. To one side, a snaking stairway rose to a mezzanine above them. All around, vapor spewed from massive machines with wide bases and heads that coiled around, poking and dipping into vats of liquid metal and fluids. Other machines were slender with segmented attachments working tirelessly to stitch optics and cable through strange skeletal bodies.

"Well, well, well . . . what a surprise we have here today," a nearby voice announced as a slender figure emerged from the shadows. "We haven't had unexpected visitors in quite some time. However, these are particularly special guests, to say the least." He stepped further into the scattered light that provided a glimpse of his eyes, which consisted of thick, perfectly rounded metal rims embedded into his face, each with a backlight illumination that changed subtly from blue to red with the tone in his voice. His left arm was fully mechanical and outfitted with numerous gadgets used for medical and scientific precision. He approached with an aristocratic swagger in his stride, filled with arrogance. A metal dome capped his head, topped with a raised plug that blinked red occasionally. He was garbed in a form-fitted grey coat less the left sleeve that draped to his knees.

He neared Crix and started to circle him. His head tilted as he observed the subtle blue radiance from his skin. Then, he snapped his head over toward Kerriah and gave a sideways smirk and stared intently at her; his eyes filled bright with blue.

Crix rolled his eyes while shaking his head. "Whatever you have on your mind, get it out now," Crix said, feeling uncomfortable with the way he was feasting his eyes on her. He snapped his head back around to Crix again, his eyes now glowing slightly red.

"My apologies, you're correct. That was quite rude of me, particularly since we lack a formal introduction. I am Merik of the ancient order of house Spancer, and my voiceless assistant there, whom you've already met, is Guttel. This is our development laboratory, and its singular purpose is designing a perfect harmony between organic and mechanized technology. Now please, if you will, enlighten us as to who you are," Merik requested, his eyes pulsing slightly between blue and red.

"Isn't it obvious from our attire? I mean, can't you just look up the prison manifest?" Kerriah snapped back sharply, appalled by the view of the captives in the surrounding cubes. Merik noticed her discontent over them and slowly turned back, acknowledging the containers.

"Ahhh . . . you have an issue with my subject containment area. It's to be expected since most will not appreciate the cost associated with our work here; however, I can assure you it is truly for the greater good of all who trace their lineage to the Oro System." He placed his right hand on his hip and took a relaxed posture. "Why, of course, this seclusion has turned me into a terrible host. My instrumentation indicates that you're both famished, and yet, I have rudely accosted you for coherent replies.

Let me offer you a bit of rest, and we can discuss all this over dinner. I will have my culinary servant put together something special for the occasion."

A strangely petite Marck servant led them to a small room that contained several black reclining seats and tapestries that lined the walls, which depicted images of black-winged beasts with protruding fangs. A dark circle in the background overshadowed the beasts. The room was toasty warm, and the ambient lighting cast a soft glow from the rim of the floor and ceiling. They both sat back exhausted, even though they knew they were in danger in this strange place. Yet, it was difficult not to take ease in the room.

"We can't get too comfortable here," Kerriah whispered. "This Merik character is crazy. Gossip has it that he was once the greatest biogenetic engineer in the Oro System but was expelled from his noble house for supposed horrific experiments on live subjects. When his patriarchs discovered his work, they were so disgusted they banished him from their lands and stripped him of his titles. His was the only remaining noble house of the ancient world. He disappeared shortly after, and no one has heard from him since."

"At least until now." Crix shook his head then grabbed a tall fluted glass and took a sip of what the servant had poured for him. The taste was sweet, followed by warm. He instantly felt mellow and at ease.

"He's been down here all this time working for the Marcks and worse . . . Zearic." Kerriah looked over and noticed Crix was asleep, strange he could fall asleep after what she had just revealed to him. "Crix . . . Crix . . . wake up," she whispered in as loud of a whisper as one could before it became a low shout. Crix did not react. Just then, there was a step at the door, and a tall, dark figure zapped her. She crumpled to the floor.

***

She awakened in a long, formal dining hall. Fiery thermal lamps pulsed gently above a shiny black table, which filled the length of the room. Banners with images of winged creatures adorned the walls. Nearby were several biomechanically engineered beings that were setting fine cuisines down in front of them, along with goblets that they filled with spirits. At one end of the table sat Merik. From his mechanized arm jutted a thin metal rod that curled downward and swirled the burgundy tinted drink in front of him. With fully prepared plates placed in front of them, Crix and Kerriah sat at the other side of the table from Merik.

"It's a pleasure to finally have you join us. I was worried we would have to commence our meal without you." Merik's voice carried a conceited drawl. He stabbed a small piece of meat from his plate with a tiny blade from his left arm. With an unpleasant look on his face, he withdrew, scowling, and then snapped his fingers, gesturing at his plate.

A nearby servant that looked like nothing more than a tall, narrow cylinder with dark organic flesh corkscrewed around it, moved in, and extended a coiled limb, which shot a torch-like flame over the meat, sizzling it to perfection. A small, dark head with two black eyes peeked from atop the cylinder to inspect it and then moved back away. These bizarre and almost grisly servants made Merik's guests uneasy, and it was apparent that he relished in it.

"Go ahead and enjoy. If anything is less than perfection, please speak up, and it will be corrected," Merik chimed as he resumed his meal. Crix was reluctant to partake but was weary from hunger and decided that whatever harm tampered food could present was worth the risk of restoring his strength, and he began to take in his fill. The food was the best he had ever tasted, and he tried a bit of everything.

Kerriah watched Crix eat and slowly picked at her plate. Merik grinned and pushed his chair back slightly to observe his guests.

"Very tasty, is it not?" he asked but received no reply. "Now, you can start to understand what the basis of my work here is. To be clear, I take the strengths of one's talents and immaculate them in their profession. Medics, scientists, engineers, laborers, soldiers, and even chefs are all enhanced to the pinnacle of their capabilities."

"They appear to be more like tortured slaves for the elite to me," Kerriah lashed out as she slammed her utensils down. Merik's eyes turned to a bright red glow as his smile morphed into a flinching scowl.

"I find it impossible to believe that someone of your creation would fail to comprehend the manner of this work." Kerriah looked confused by his statement and stood.

"What?" she pointedly remarked before Crix interrupted.

"I've some bad news for your little plan to create this perverse world of yours. There are many out there that will fight you, and I'll stand by my upbringing that good will always prevail over the wicked such as you."

Merik's brow crinkled around his metal eye inserts. "Why would you stand against me? Do you wish to see your kind consumed? I'm working on perfecting our species so we can develop beyond that of our enemies."

Kerriah laughed. "What, the Thraxons? Please spare me that rhetoric. The Marcks are the threat I see, and you're obviously their crony, sick and twisted."

"Little girl, you're so naive. The Thraxons are stronger than ever, yet you think they have been defeated. You are gravely mistaken. They are, in fact, evolving at this very moment. If we are to survive, we must evolve as well." Merik finished his plate and then grasped a nearby flexible pipe that hung from a bulb-shaped canister by his chair. Appearing relaxed, he took several puffs from it, while a light pulsed and mist fed out with each successive inhale. "Care for a little after dinner radiance?" Offering the pipe to his guests. Crix shoved his plate away, toppling his goblet.

"Hardly! We certainly have no interest in your stimulants. We want to know where our friends are. Where have you taken Krath and Creedith?"

"Yes, you are an interesting one I'll have to admit, and I look forward to finding out what gives you that magnificent blue luster. I can also clearly see the emotional fixation you have with your companion here." Merik gave a long grin as he looked slowly over at Kerriah. "Such a pity you appear to know so little of one another, else I might imagine that emotional childishness would be quickly extinguished." Merik settled back in his chair and rubbed his chin with regal smugness.

"I once had a foolish love during my youth and lordship over at house Spancer." Kerriah rolled her eyes. *Lordship? Yeah, right.* Merik left her response with only a brief pause before continuing. "It was the young and beaming Lady Coraye Britte. Ahhh . . . a beauty she certainly was with her blazing red hair and face as smooth and flawless as purest cream." His story already annoyed Kerriah. However, always interested in people's backstories, Crix calmed down slightly to listen.

"I was not necessarily the most handsome, but being a Spancer certainly helped to win over this lady from Yorly. I met her at a Cruxx dueling soiree thrown by the great Himilan Buric." Kerriah let loose an extra loud exhale in protest of the drab tale.

"We're really not interested in whatever former love life you may have had before you were kicked from your inheritance for being a mental case."

Merik's eyes glowed a fiery red and his cold lips pursed together tightly. "How dare you insult your host?" he snapped, furious over the interruption of the story he had not told since his stint began on Dispor years ago. A tale that still represented the failing bits of his humanity. His ego flamed up, telling him that there must now be a reckoning of their insolence.

"You lout! I shall see you pieced out like an obsolete grunt for your blatant show of disrespect." Merik raised his mechanical arm and pointed it at Kerriah. A thin rod slid out from the end and flickered. Her eyes glossed over as if caught in a trance.

Crix kicked his chair back. Pulses and cracking filled the air around him, while a blue glow shot out and became a blinding glare. For Crix, the last vestige of his patience with Merik had been depleted, and he was ready to reveal the power of the orb to his *host*. He would not allow anything to harm Kerriah, nothing. Merik took notice of the imminent threat and backed off Kerriah. She snapped back instantly from the trance.

"Crix, no! You mustn't," Kerriah shouted but quickly realized that if they had any charade to this point, it was now over. There was a brief look of rare shock on Merik's face just before a hollowed snarl moved in behind him. A tall, well-armored Marck stormed in, unexpected to even Merik. The once-controlled scene was instant chaos.

"Sintor!" Merik shouted as he turned to see his unwelcomed guest. Sintor was radically modified from the last time they saw him on level four. His arms, legs, and body were now bulkier and more refined. It became evident to both Kerriah and Crix that Eetak Five and Six had been parted out to make Sintor's armored shell impervious.

Sintor grabbed Merik up by his arm like a child's toy doll. "You fool! He has the orb, the one the Knactor Legion has been scouring the system for! You idiot! We must kill him now!" Sintor tossed Merik across the room as he broke for Crix like a lion that had zeroed in on its prey.

Crix braced his arms together, creating a shield, just before Sintor unleashed a crushing blow with both arms slamming into his torso. Crix slid across the room and smashed up against the wall. Shaken briefly, he slowly raised his head, and his eyes appeared to spark blue with fierce determination. He sprung forward, taking to the air and wrapping himself around Sintor's head. He pulled Sintor off balance and sent the raging Marck commander staggering back. Sintor twisted and reached backward in a flailing effort to pull Crix off. Crix plunged his thumbs into Sintor's eyes and sent an orb power surge through Sintor's circuitry. Like a zip foil screaming to the brink, Sintor overloaded and collapsed to the ground. Kerriah and Crix looked around but found that Merik was no longer in the room and must have slipped out during the scuffle with Sintor.

"Great, we let that slimy jerk get away," Crix said as he swung around, noticing Kerriah had dashed out of the doorway. She chased Merik down a narrow hall that led to a control room.

Kerriah spotted Merik. His robotic arm was plugged into a nearby panel. "Back away!" she ordered.

He let out a sinister chuckle. "I'm afraid you do not have the upper hand here."

At that moment, the clanking of Marck footsteps rang out from the hallway as Merik's personal guards surrounded Kerriah with weapons drawn. Two Marcks restrained her arms behind her back and pushed her head down. Merik slowly approached her with a thin rod protruding from his arm. A tiny ball at the end started to enter Kerriah's ear.

"Now I'm going to find out what you . . ." Merik paused as the echoes of Marcks in the hall firing their weapons and blue flashes strobed back and forth. The two Marcks holding Kerriah fell to the ground as two blue beams flashed from their faces.

Behind her stood Crix with the look of a seasoned warrior blazing from his eyes.

Kerriah gave a warm smile to Crix and then turned sharply back toward Merik. Crix handed her a confiscated rifle, which she swiftly pointed at Merik's head.

"Now you're going tell us where our friends are, or we are going to start de-Marckanizing you the hard way." Her tone gave no indication that reasoning was an option.

"Even if I give you your friends, what will you do then . . . hmmm? It's not as if you're getting off Dispor. No one ever leaves here, not even me." Merik slowly backed up to the control panel.

Kerriah placed her rifle muzzle at the back of his head. "If you touch anything aside from what will free our friends, it will be the last thing you ever touch." Merik slid his hand away and walked over to a panel on the other side of the room.

"Fine, as you wish." He placed his thumb into a lit indentation, triggering a metal panel that slid away in front of them to reveal a window. The now-open window provided a clear view of the cubes that contained the captive life forms they had observed earlier.

"I imagine the Hybor that I received yesterday is one of them you're looking for. He was a feisty one for sure, much like the two of you, but a tad bit more on the temperamental side. Which was his undoing as well." He plugged his arm into the panel again, and the cubes vibrated and shuddered. The movement was so faint that it was almost hard to detect. The cubes started to spin, and several flew by their view in a flash as if standing near high-speed zipfoils blurring through the skyway pipes of Soorak. The chain of cubes instantly stopped. One of the cubes hovered in front of them; a hunkered Hybor with rage in his expression stood frozen in time.

"Krath!" Crix cried out with excitement, yet anxiety was in his voice with his concern over the state of his friend. Krath appeared to be yelling hostilely in his expression but was motionless like all the others. The cube moved to a platform close by and dropped down, landing squarely on the surface below. A large drill bit spun down from high above, cutting into the cube's top. Blinding light poured into the cube. As the light dissipated, a familiar voice barked out in anger.

"Tya crummy Marck turncoat—what the—" Krath's appearance went from looking like he was about to smack something to befuddled.

"Guttel, please remove the subject from the diffusion platform and take him to holding silo nine," Merik called out over the console. Guttel hovered out and shot a single proton charged manacle around the neck of Krath and started to tow him off the platform.

Krath fought and struggled, but the proton charge proved too strong to fight. Guttel drug him over to a circular opening in the floor and pulled him over the top of it; the proton shackle released, and Krath tumbled into a cone-shaped holding cell that was lined with alloy walls that were so smooth that one could see their perfect reflection. Krath took several futile leaps, grasping at the sides, before accepting that escape was improbable without assistance.

"Now that was a really dumb move. Get him out of there right now!" Kerriah commanded, putting the nose of her rifle firmly against Merik's temple. Merik stiffened his stance and relaxed his arms.

"Fear not, youthful one, I am merely taking necessary measures to protect all of us. Please understand that your brutish friend has no presence of mind over what has transpired here. Had he gone into one of his barbaric rages, I might be unable to retrieve your Andor comrade. It is just a precaution." He cautiously raised his arms again in a gesture to resume his efforts. "Now, if I may, I will awaken the equine." Kerriah nodded and lowered her rifle.

"Okay, quickly."

Cubes zipped by the display rapidly once again, and after several moments, they stopped with a cube in front of their window. Inside was a hefty and ragged Andor. His mane was dark with silver swirled in, and his skin was a glossy brown, rippled in muscles. The scars of war and torture layered across his body. His profound eyes reflected a labored soul and a wildness that was still evident, much like a caged predator.

CHAPTER 22

S
o that's Creedith," Crix said to himself, having heard so many tales of his heroics but never seeing an actual picture of him since images of oneself was forbade by Andor culture.

"Yes, I do remember this one," Merik replied to Crix. "He was a handful for us to restrain at that time. Interestingly, he is the reason for the added turrets in the Marck storage area, not that those prevented your entrance, but prior to those, there was merely a crude grid to hold back the possible stray scab. Who would have ever guessed that an inmate would rip it from the rock from which it was embedded? He was strong indeed and is—err—was going to be a masterful specimen for my weaponizing developments.

"Pity, he could have been an unstoppable Marck hybrid soldier and was the only of his species I have ever had in my possession. Alas, there were political delays in his processing, though." Merik gave a long, mechanical sigh. "He wasn't supposed to be here actually. Something regarding his knowledge had Zearic's interest, but I wasn't about to give my prized specimen back freely. He was going to have to come down here to get him . . . and never did. My mistake was that I never finished my efforts; I did, however, start them."

The cube pivoted to the right exposing scales of black plating on the left side of the Andor's face, and it could now be seen that his left arm was synthetic black and slightly larger than the right. "Yes, he is better than before. He is integrated with the advanced alloy Bracix, which has virtually indestructible properties and is as lightweight as a piece of cloth. It will absorb energy blasts and allow that energy to be refocused to any intended targets. He is a beauty, indeed."

Crix slammed his fist against the hardened doorframe. "You butcher! You lowlife filth! Just get on with his release before we do everyone a favor and bury you here . . . right now!" He was outraged at the sight of Creedith's face.

"Very well," Merik replied, cross, as he moved the cube to the diffusion platform.

Crix let out a fleeting groan, and Kerriah looked back at him. To her dismay, she observed Sintor standing atop him with a large metal bar pressing against Crix's head. Crix, taken off guard, struggled to maintain consciousness as the immense pressure increased from the giant Marck's wrath. She whipped her rifle around at Sintor only to have it smacked from her grasp before she could get her sights on him. He laughed, the echoing chuckle gloated over them.

"You see, now I will kill this one and remove the orb from his lifeless corpse. Then I may have Merik make a few modifications to you so that you may be my personal entertainment." Kerriah's heart sank as he laughed again and put more pressure on Crix's skull. Crix started to bellow in pain and frustration. Unable to move or think, he could feel his consciousness slipping from him.

Looking for anything she could use to level the odds, Kerriah took notice of a section of fusion tubing sitting on a glass shelf near the door. When contacted with metal, it would instantly create heat for makeshift welds. If she whipped it around the narrow section of Sintor's knee . . . maybe . . . but no, it was just out of reach.

However, all was not lost. Realizing she still had a move left to make, Kerriah remembered Plexo's transmitter. Feeling behind her left ear for the tiny speck implanted there, she gave it a hard pinch. Her heart was pounding, hoping this would work. Within several seconds, an unusual vibration shook the walls and ceiling.

Sintor took notice and let up slightly on Crix in an attempt to ascertain what they just felt. Within a minute, an alarm chirped from the panel in front of Merik, and a green image swirled into view, an image of a Marck guard alerting to something. The console flickered in and out. Merik tapped the console's sensing controls, bringing its clarity back. The ceiling rumbled repeatedly.

"Alert all personnel . . . we are under attack . . . we are under attack . . ." the guard announced as he continuously looked over his shoulder. Plasma bolts zinged back and forth in the background, and the image shuddered.

Merik was bewildered and annoyed by this announcement. "What's that you're saying? Attack . . . by whom? Thraxons?" He asked.

The image went dark, and the lights flickered around them as another rumble shook the walls even more violently than before, toppling any loose objects in the room.

"How can Dispor be under attack?" Merik said, turning to Sintor for an explanation.

"It is of minor concern to us. Besides, whoever it is will dispose of Zeltak for us." Sintor's obsession with power and vengeance blinded him of any danger, and he viewed this unexpected peril as an opportunity for him to take his self-proclaimed place as Master of Dispor. Ever since his relegation from that title due to his unsanctioned acts of cruelty, he had made it his primary focus to see Zeltak meet a toxic fate.

"Energize and release the racks if they make it down here. I doubt they will get far against such numbers," Sintor said.

"As you wish, but realize this, my lord, most are unregulated, and we cannot predict their behavior. Marck control graciously provided them to us as parts for a reason," Merik advised.

"Their standard protocol is still to neutralize threats . . . so they will serve our purpose here. Activate your arch battle hybrids as well, if required. We will use them to quell the rabble once we are in the clear," Sintor ordered. Just then, Kerriah reached for the fusion tubing she had seen on the shelf and whipped it around Sintor's knee. On impact, it glowed with intense, blinding heat, causing the separation of the lower part of his leg. Sintor fell back and braced himself against the doorway. He struggled to pull himself to an upright position.

Crix struggled up to his knees, and his mental cognizance slowly started to return. Kerriah helped him to his feet. "Keep an eye on Sintor." She hurried over to deal with Merik. Crix gave Sintor a shocking jolt from his orb, which sent him flat down on his face.

"Free Creedith, now!" she demanded. Merik gave her an edgy smirk and then triggered the holographic controls energizing the Marck retention racks. He let out a sardonic chuckle.

"Here's your beloved Andor," Merik said, pointing to the containment cube still sitting on the platform. "And . . . here are seventeen hundred Marcks with no central control and no orders . . . only their primary directive, which is threat neutralization to drive their actions. I would say your chances of leaving here with your lives have just dwindled to something less than naught!"

"Crix," her voice was cool and calm, as she looked sharply back at him, "please explain it to him." Crix's eyes flashed blue as he pulled his fists tight against his chest. His skin started glowing brighter, and Merik felt his insides twist and retch. Merik buckled over gasping in excruciating pain. He placed his hand up to signal for Crix to stop. Crix looked over at Kerriah.

"Give him a few more seconds for assurance, and then let's see if he sees things our way."

Merik grasped his chest, turned to the control panel, and completed the sequence to free Creedith from the cube. An alert system sounded off with a female voice. "Warning . . . mechanized retention system jump process has been finalized. Warning . . . unsupported Marck systems now activated."

Merik regained his composure. "You're still not leaving here alive . . ." The area shook, and the lights powered off then on again. A massive explosion sent all of them off their feet.

Crix was feeling unsettled over the turmoil. "Let's get Creedith and Krath and get out of here." He grabbed Kerriah up and pulled her to the doorway. Before they could make their way out, a vice-like object seized Kerriah's heel, sending her smashing down into the metal floor. An echoing laugh filled the room. Sintor crawled back onto one leg, and he drew Kerriah closer, and then followed with a grasp around her neck. The pressure from his clamp would have killed most, yet Kerriah found a way to endure the cracking in her neck even though it was paralyzing her movements. Blasts continued to rock the area around them, causing metal support beams to buckle, and whistling bursts of energy rang out in the distance.

Crix swung around, hoping to send a debilitating orb blast at his tenacious foe's head, and then paused in fear of burning Kerriah in the process. Instead, he pointed his index finger straight at Sintor. Every emotion bottled up within him pulsed, and he was able to bring to bear all his anger at that single point.

Sintor stared into his eyes. "Pathetic Tolagon, strike me with your power, and this pitiful being you care for will certainly die. Do it! I am going to kill her regardless." With that, a thin blue needle shot from Crix's finger and passed through Sintor's head, severing his central processing core. Sintor's body instantly crumpled to the floor.

"Are you okay?" Crix asked, running over to her and sliding down onto the floor next to her small frame. They clasped hands, and he helped her stand up. Kerriah winced in pain as she rubbed her neck, trying to get it to move. She knew that time was their biggest opponent and that she could not let it gain a minute on them due to her pain.

"Yes . . . we have to get going quickly. Remember, that Eatek is going to detonate once his power core finally overloads. We have to be off Dispor before that happens!"

They raced out into the area lined with the containment cubes. Marcks scurried in every direction, firing frantically at any object out of place. They located the diffusion platform, but there was no one there.

"Okay, I saw Merik complete the release sequence for Creedith, so where is he?" Kerriah said panning the area for a glimpse of the Andor.

"Looks like something was here." Crix stood over the scattered remains of Guttel.

A heavy thump came from behind both of them. As they spun around to see what it was, a muscular, well-weathered Andor grabbed Crix and pulled him down into a chokehold with both hands firmly around his neck. Creedith's eyes were crazed, and veins bulged from his neck. He let out a rasping snort and tightened his grip.

Crix clenched the old warrior's arms with both hands turning white, trying to free his breath. "Who are you? Why am I here? Speak!" Creedith shouted, his voice gravelly but imposing.

Kerriah carefully approached with her hand extended in a calming gesture.

"We came here to free you of this place, and the one you hold there is the Tolagon of Soorak, Crix. Please . . . I don't have time to explain, but we need to leave here quickly." Upon hearing the name Crix, Creedith immediately loosened his grasp and looked into Crix's face. He took a deep gaze, almost peering into his soul.

"Crix? The child of Corin Emberook?" Creedith gently placed Crix down and fell to his backside. Sitting heavily on the ground, he pulled his tattered mane back from his eyes. He noticed his synthetic appendage when it brushed up against his side, and he stroked the side of his face with horror over what he had become.

"I . . . I remember now. I would have never dreamed of seeing you again, much less here. A young Tolagon you truly are." Creedith's voice carried with it a gentle assertion.

Kerriah stepped between the two warriors. "Look, I realize this is quite a bit to take in at the moment, but we really have to go now, or we are going to be buried in this place." The ground trembled and fragments of metal and stone showered down. From the distant tunnel, the blasting had suddenly ceased.

Crix snapped a look toward the tunnel. "Agreed. Eatek may be down. We don't have much time. Let's get Krath." He rushed over to the holding cell containing Krath and looked down. Krath leaned casually against the wall and stared up at Crix. He cracked a brief smile as he noticed his all-white hair and how it made it look more like Corin.

"Well . . . are tya going to get me out of this rodent trap or what?" His tone was annoyed, but at the same time, there was an underlying hint of pride for his young pupil as he cracked a smile from the corner of his mouth.

Crix dropped to his knees and placed his palms face out to Krath. The young Tolagon started to glow a bright blue, and the air swooshed around Krath as he slowly rose up to the top of the cell. Krath buckled over and chuckled as he reached the top.

"What could possibly be so amusing?" Creedith said with some friendly scorn in his tone.

"Well, it started to tickle somewhat. Anyway, who's askin'?"

"Try giving a good rub on those old black circles that reside in that big plump head of yours and take a look," Creedith replied.

Krath's mouth widened up with a rare smile. "Well, well, well, finally! There tya are, a whole bunch uglier, but hey, everyone pretty much thought tya were dead already anyway."

"Not quite yet, but when time permits, I would sure be interested in what you're doing here," Creedith said just as he felt the heat from a plasma shot zipping over his shoulder. A large group of Marcks, having gained sight of the prison escapees, were storming down the tunnel.

"Where do we go from here? I mean we can't exactly go back the way we came in." Crix was praying that someone would have a clever reply.

"There was a lift that stopped between levels. At least, that's what they sent me down here in. Of course, they bash'd me in the head to get me on there and again to get me off of it, so I'm a bit fuzzy on where it was." Krath rubbed his head, recalling the sharp blows he took.

Several more blasts hit near them as the Marcks opened up into the main containment area. Krath looked over calmly at the incoming Marcks and then tilted his head as if he just had some sort of recollection.

"That's it," he stormed out, leaping into the air and crashing down upon several Marcks in a reckless display of boldness. With a focused rage, he started ripping and tearing Marck limbs off and swinging wildly, taking down double digits of the incoming horde.

Crix noticed that Creedith stood with a posture of casual spectating. "Shouldn't we assist him?"

"Not to worry, young Emberook, hand-to-hand melee is Krath's passion. He would take offense to the notion that he required assistance."

CHAPTER 23

B ehind a billowing heap of smoke and popping power
discharges emerged a lumbering silhouette dragging Marck
heads attached by their ripped optical lines. Without saying a word,
Krath passed the group and started down a nearby stairway.
Creedith shrugged and gave Crix a wink before following down the
stairs. A blinding light slowly filled the area in the distance as Eetak
Two overloaded its power core for detonation. Kerriah was
growing frustrated by the casualness of her companions.

"Am I the only one here that cares at all about the gravity
of this situation?" She and Crix followed them down into a
hexagon area. This recessed area had two levels with the lower
filled to the knee with scrap metal and discarded electronic
components, much like a small landfill.

Krath was busy pressing his confiscated Marck heads into a
pole that lowered from the ceiling and then chucking the head to
the side before trying another. This pole had a clear panel of
swirling red lights, which followed a repeating pattern that pulsed
side to side at its base.

Krath started grumbling to himself, and he tried one after
another. "I know this is what they did. One of these garbage cans

stuck their ugly mug in this and activated this thing." Then a familiar laugh bellowed out from behind them.

There was Merik, flanked by three heavily weaponized arch battle hybrids, the apex of his military work, with their armor stamped with the Kreillic, the mark of the house of Spancer. The Kreillic was a menacing, four-winged creature of the ancient lore that had a long pitchforked tongue and drove fear into its prey. It was difficult to tell what the original species of these weapons of terror were due to the heavy assimilation of Marck technology into their forms.

"Step back, mongrel!" he ordered Krath as one of the archs raised a rotating missile launcher. "By the way, I did get the privilege to see your customized Marck that was the cause of all this panic. Impressive as it was, it did fall to my own arch soldiers. What a shame that its ingenious power core is building up for eventual and inevitable detonation. That will turn this facility and all my precious work into a molten slab. We even tried to move it to see if there was a way to re-stabilize it, but alas, its core has permanently fused itself to the floor." He stepped up to the panel and stared into it.

The red lights went from a back and forth to a circular pattern, and then hexagonal tubes lit up and made a steady hum, letting its operator know it was ready. Merik and his arch troops stepped upon the elevator. "I fear our parting is bittersweet as I would have enjoyed better understanding you. These caverns are now to be hollowed with your corpses, and I bid you farewell." He stared at Kerriah with a slight touch of admiration.

"Do you think we are going to let you just leave us down here and you escape?" Krath said, lurching forward. Merik's arch troopers aimed their weapons on him right as the cavernous facility gave out a slow and continuous vibration.

"I don't see that you have any options at this point. I will leave you with this, however. I was able to get a rough estimate on the time remaining before your rogue Marck obliterates this place. Since I would like you to feel every second before your demise, I will tell you. You have roughly two minutes and thirty seconds." He sent the elevator upward just before one of his arch troopers blasted the control panel, rendering it inoperative.

Krath kicked a piece of the exploded control panel across the room. "Well, that's it then."

They felt deflated, stranded in a place that they had just come to realize was to be their inevitable tomb. It was enough to throw even the most positive individual into a fit of despair. Yet a voice filled with confidence cut through the thickness of inevitability and provided a twinkle of hope that was to regain their strength once more.

"No, that's not it." Creedith stepped forward, pointing to the scrap pile below them. "The refuse propulsor. It shoots all this out from the sub-levels into orbit. That's how all the garbage is removed from the scab mines, and I would think the same holds true here."

Krath leaned in, peeked up the shaft, and gave his chin a curious rub. "So tya are saying that we have less than two minutes to decide if we want to get incinerated and buried down here or

325

suffocate in orbit. That is if the G's don't turn us into piles of goo on the way up." He jumped atop the scrap and debris. "What tya waitin' for? My buddy Crix has us covered on this one." He gave Crix an assured nod as if he knew what to do without explanation.

They all jumped on the refuse platform as a slow rumble intensified to a panicked quake, giving the sensation that the world around them was about to end. "Didn't they just shoot the control panel? How are we going to activate this thing?" Kerriah shouted above the noise.

"That was for the elevator; this is for garbage." Creedith slammed his fist into a nearby recessed switch, sending them firing up with an intensity that turned everything around them into a blur.

Crix fought to keep focused as he created a protective sphere. Within seconds, they launched deep into orbit with the ghostly surface of Dispor below them. Fire spewed from the same opening they just launched out of seconds ago. The flames curled upward at them like a finger coaxing them back. Floating helplessly in a lifeboat bubble of pressure and a rapidly depleting air supply, the four of them stared back at the surface of Dispor with the vastness of space behind them, looking for any hope of cheating death once more. Again, with rapidly depleting air, time was not on their side. His palms pressed against the side of the orb's sphere, Creedith, the steadfast warrior, panned the lifeless skin of Dispor for a shard of something that could steal away this short fate they now faced.

"Fear not, my friends, our faith will spare us," Creedith said, trying to calm the frenzied nerves of his doomed companions.

As he settled back to pray and make his inner peace, the stillness was shattered.

"There!" Kerriah shouted with the fervor of a person that had spotted a long lost love. A ship veered from around the horizon and turned directly in their direction. The bulky vessel dipped forward with a pointed nose. Around its sides were large, wing-like sections that drew upward as it accelerated toward the doomed escapees.

Creedith squinted; this ship was familiar to him. "I recognize this ship. This is an old UMO corvette class. It was one of ours during the war. We should be cautious."

Kerriah stared carefully at the ship, looking for a marking. "The insurgents took over some of those old ships. It could still be ours." Then a smile crept across her face. "It's ours! I see the old UMO and Tolagon emblems."

A blinding light broke open from the ship's belly as it passed over them. They felt a sharp tug upward that caused them to pile atop each other.

"You're crushing me, get off!" Kerriah complained as she attempted to push Krath's backside off her torso. He lifted himself away, giving her a chance to draw a breath from the thinning air.

The blinding light from the ship glared down upon them, masking their surroundings. As they moved upward into the ship, they dropped upon a solid surface, and the light dimmed. Crix dropped the bubble, allowing them to breathe freely again. The cool, clean air was sweet as they took it into their lungs.

"This can't be." Creedith noticed a large cobalt V painted across the bay doors, the crest of the Vico Legion. His mind raced with possibilities.

Kerriah cupped Crix's face in her hands, eagerly kissing him, and embraced him with all her strength. He held her tight.

Krath gave Creedith a friendly elbow to his side and chuckled. Could it be some remnant of the Vico Legion? As far as they knew, the last two members of Corin Emberook's Vico Legion were sitting amongst them. Still, it was easy to become elated, given that just moments ago, their deaths were almost certain.

An orange beacon lit up as a large door groaned open at the far end of the hangar area. The lighting was softer beyond the doorway. "Congratulations on completing your quest and liberating the Andor. I have engaged the atmospheric support systems for you so that you may breathe," a voice echoed out over the ship's loudspeakers.

Plexo? Kerriah relaxed her embrace of Crix.

"Do not be alarmed. Please exit the hangar for your debriefing," the voice continued.

Krath's brow furrowed and he firmly placed his firsts upon his hips. "Plexo? How 'bout tya get out here and give us a proper greeting?"

Kerriah recalled the story Plexo told them about his failing health. "Well, he can't actually be here. Remember what he said about the green orb and that he couldn't leave his ship?"

Creedith rubbed his chin. "We should be cautious, of course. However, if their intention was to harm us, they simply could have allowed us to die in orbit. They could also release the air dock retention system and blow us back out into orbit and kill us now. I'm not yet convinced that this reception is nefarious."

"One way to find out." Krath started through the doorway, in his normal bold swagger.

Crix looked over at Kerriah and then Creedith, who both appeared somewhat concerned and less than eager to just traipse through the doorway. He shook his head, exhausted, and then hurried behind Krath. "Wait up!"

The corridor was warm and inviting, with the perfect temperature and lower lighting. "Please proceed to the forward briefing lounge; I will be with you shortly." A small door slid open, and light peeked out. Krath slowly stepped into what appeared to be a well-weathered briefing room, with worn high-back seats, and encircled a center podium.

He felt at ease and let down his guard. "Tya can come on in. Nothin' to worry over." He announced to the others that followed in behind him, their curiosities peaked.

"You're right. We are going to be all right," Crix agreed.

They all entered and took a seat. It was nice to finally relax. The chairs were cozy and they all felt at ease. Collectively, they all somehow knew that everything was going to be fine except for Kerriah, who still had doubts.

Crix took notice of her unease. He smiled at Kerriah and gripped her hand. She was safe, and they were together. His touch helped to calm her nerves. The last of the noble Andors, Creedith, was rescued, and they were all together again.

Outside, the tattered war ship's engines spun up, and bright blue cones jutted from its rear thrusters. It slowly pushed away from Dispor's orbit, leaving behind it creeping debris and dissipating smoke, which floated out from the charred remains of the prison. The old corvette's next mission was still not known to its new passengers, but one thing was certain, their journey was far from over . . .

The journey continues in THE QUEEN PROTOCOL—
Book Two of the Tolagon series.

ABOUT THE AUTHOR

Gregory Benson grew up in the Midwest and married his high school sweetheart, Dawn. He graduated from the University of Missouri-Saint Louis and works in the technology field.

As far back as he could remember, he would spend much of his childhood daydreaming about alien worlds and immersing himself into science fiction and fantasy. As an adult, he's enjoyed adventures traveling with wife Dawn and his son Luke, as well as sword fighting, pinball, and of course, writing sci-fi/fantasy.